THE GAFFER

P.J. LAVERTY

THE GAFFER

P.J. LAVERTY

P PCORN

P R E S S

First published in 2022 by Popcorn Press, an imprint of Fair Play Publishing
PO Box 4101, Balgowlah Heights, NSW 2093, Australia
www.popcornpress.com.au

ISBN: 978-1-925914-46-7
ISBN: 978-1-925914-54-2 (ePub)
© P.J. Laverty 2022

Cover illustration by Anastasiia Osypova
Cover design and typsetting by Ana Sečivanović

All inquiries should be made to the Publisher via sales@fairplaypublishing.com.au

NATIONAL
LIBRARY
OF AUSTRALIA

A catalogue record of this book is available from the National Library of Australia.

DEDICATION

To my father for instilling in me a love of football and laughter.

To my mother for instilling a love of story.

To my wife and children for offering their love and support.

And to my publisher Bonita Mersiades for taking a chance on
The Gaffer, *and her relentless championing of* The Beautiful Game.

1

Transcript from BBC Radio Cornwall
Saturday, January 7, 1989
2.53 p.m.

EDDIE REAGAN: And now we're heading off the mainland, where rookie reporter Marcus Briars is at Faery Meadow to take in the clash between Guff Rovers and Burnley. And Marcus, the season of good tidings is over for the home side, we hear?

(silence)

Marcus, you there?

(more silence)

Marcus?

MARCUS BRIARS: *(muttering to someone off-mic)* I wanted to do law. But *no*. Do journalism, they said. I thought, yeah, all right. Maybe I'll get to flee this shit-stain of an island and cover politics. Get involved in some murder trial or Swiss bank heist or something. But then sport cropped up. I thought, yeah, okay. Tour de France, the Masters, maybe an Olympics. Can't beat that. But no, here I am, confined to the hairy armpit of the universe, covering a shower of duffers posing as professional footballers in subarctic weather.

EDDIE REAGAN: Um, we seem to be having a few technical difficulties, so we'll leave Marcus for now.

MARCUS BRIARS: Eddie, you're there? Sorry, I was getting an update on the team sheet from the ref. *(clears his throat)*

EDDIE REAGAN: I was just saying, we hear there's some strife for Guff Rovers.

MARCUS BRIARS: Indeed, Eddie. Winless in seven and hovering two points above bottom place and Division Four's relegation zone. Rumours are rife of players not getting paid with the threat of administration hanging over the club. Yes, it's fair to say things have been better for the Faeries. It's a wild afternoon too, with a vicious gale whipping in from the Celtic Sea which would decapitate a South Devon cow. Yet for some ungodly reason, the officials have given the game the go-ahead, despite both keepers being knee-deep in sludge. Guff have a mountain to climb against a plucky Burnley outfit who've won three on the bounce, though they are buoyed by the return of captain Jamie Pullman after a four-match ban.

EDDIE REAGAN: And Marcus, could you tell us—

MARCUS BRIARS: *(screaming)* Aaargh! I'm sorry Eddie but c'mon.

EDDIE REAGAN: Excuse me?

MARCUS BRIARS: *(rustling, pause)* I'm sorry, Eddie, but … fucking c'mon! That donkey of a centre-forward has sliced a ball into the stand and sent my Bovril flying over my nutsack. Oh my God! I'm fucking scalded here!

(click—Marcus is cut off)
(pause)

EDDIE REAGAN: Sorry about that, listeners. We'll let Marcus get some medical attention and check back in with him after kick-off, on what is sure to be an eventful afternoon. And, um, yes, on behalf of all at BBC Radio Cornwall, we apologise once again for the industrial language. Let's hear what's happening at Anfield.

2

While Kylie and Jason's 'Especially for You' faded out on the tannoy, and the match restarted, it wasn't just the BBC reporter that Guff Rovers' striker Darren Dangerfield was mis-hitting with the ball. He also caught a rusted Lada Riva in the carpark behind the away end, taking out its wing mirror with an effort from the edge of the six-yard box when it looked easier to score. Two minutes later, he struck a two-year-old in a stroller (fortunately strapped in) from a header via a corner.

Then he hit the corner flag with a penalty kick, awarded when he slipped in the box with no defender within touching distance. A tumble so inexplicable that the referee didn't think twice about blowing for it, and the minibus-load of hardened Lancastrians behind the goal didn't even bother complaining about it. Everyone thought there must have been contact somewhere, somehow.

Meanwhile, Guff right-back Zak Bates was passing like he had two left feet, which he literally did. He'd unknowingly put his two left boots on after losing his contact lenses in The Wizard's Sleeve— the local nightclub and the *only* nightclub on the island—the night before. He was too embarrassed to tell the dugout about the error.

Then there was Lance Posobiec, backpacking Canadian keeper and part-time concreter, who was saving up for a ticket back to Nova Scotia. He'd been working earlier in the morning, laying new tarmac at the Texaco. He hadn't informed Rovers manager Gary Pullman that six months of moonlighting in all weathers had taken its toll. Struggling to lift his arms above his head, he'd failed to claim a single one of the avalanche of crosses coming from the sprightly Burnley flanks.

He'd also gotten nowhere near the two efforts from the opposition's playmaker, one of which hit the back of the net while the other luckily careened off the crossbar. More embarrassingly, he'd missed a simple back-pass which saw his left knee seize up as he swung at it, allowing the ball to trickle under him and over the line for the visitors' second.

With wayward passing, mistimed tackles and slack marking which they couldn't put down to the inclement weather, the fact that Guff had leased their training ground out to the island's paintballing firm for Christmas party season was becoming apparent.

The club's plight was underlined when midfielder Ross Coyne caught a stray elbow to the nose. All that physio Jimmy Dolan (who also doubled as kit man, groundsman and chief scout) could administer was a spray of cold water followed by a child's Mickey Mouse plaster, which he'd found helping his great-niece clean out her school bag the afternoon prior.

And even Dolan, as committed to the cause as he was, couldn't fail to spot that Mickey Mouse was becoming a familiar motif bleeding throughout the fabric of his beloved club.

3

What was affecting the home side more than anything, though, were their fans. Or, more specifically, one fan. Thomas Bamford.

Known to all on the Isle of Guff as 'Tam Bam'.

When manager Gary Pullman emerged from the tunnel for the second half, the first thing he saw was all twenty-five stone of the man hanging over the 'Visit Cornwall' hoarding surrounding the disabled section, penning in—as it always did—Tam, and only Tam. Pullman couldn't help but hear as, red-faced, currant-eyed and wearing his trademark garish lime-green mac, Tam Bam told the team exactly what he thought of them.

"You're an embarrassment to the shirt, to the island, to the beautiful game itself, the lot of youse," Tam raved, half a pasty in his hand. The other half was on or around his lips and tongue, tiny bits shooting through the air in the side's direction.

Pullman's head throbbed. In the heat of making two subs, throwing a right boot at the head of his full-back who wasn't wearing one (yet again), and then slipping on an orange slice and falling hard on his arse when he'd dashed to get in the face of his centre-forward (who had the audacity to argue that he was more concerned about winning throw-ins and using his impressively gangly arms to show off his thirty-yard throws than how many goals he scored), Pullman had forgotten to take his customary four half-time aspirins.

"I've left stuff dripping down the side of the toilet pan that's been harder than you lot," Tam called. "And easier on the eye."

Pullman ushered his players onto the pitch. He thought of his beloved Millwall. He wondered how they were going in the cup against Luton. If he hadn't been so hasty to take any managerial job going, he'd be sitting in that home dugout right now as assistant to boss John Docherty. That was a man who knew more about football than all these hicks combined.

As the last of his players made it out, Pullman pumped his knuckles. He popped a Juicy Fruit into his mouth. He massaged both his temples. It was hard enough thinking of ways to turn this fixture around with the squad of kids, drunks and geriatrics he'd inherited without having Tam bloody Bam drone in his ear for another forty-five minutes.

"And as for you, gaffer, I've had stiffies that have lasted longer than you'll be in this job."

Whoever had decided to put the disabled section behind the home dugout needed shooting.

Pullman bit the bait. "I've had enough of your shit for one season."

"And I've had enough of this 'We Are the Wombles' balls you've brought over here with you," Tam hit back.

Pullman picked a shard of mince from his earlobe. "Away and get another pie." He flicked the offending matter at Tam, hitting him square in the eye.

"I'll pie you, you Chas & Dave bastard!" Tam shouted after him.

As he made his way to the dugout, Pullman spotted something in the reflection of his new Hugo Boss frames, which his wife had mentioned made him look like a balding Paul Newman in *The Color of Money*. It was Tam's crutch swinging hard and fast in his direction. Pullman's old centre-half instincts (honed from playing in front of The Den for a decade) kicked in, and he swivelled around in time to grab the offending object. He yanked it with such force that Tam tumbled over the advertising board, landing on top of him with a thump.

Try as they might, Tam couldn't get up, and Gary Pullman couldn't move.

It was at that moment the referee walked out. And from his vantage, the picture didn't look good.

"Get to the stands," he ordered, brandishing a red card as his linesman waded through the mud to pry the manager from under the larger man.

Guff Rovers' captain Jamie—who also happened to be Pullman's son—sprinted over from the centre circle. He latched his thick dumbbell arms round Tam's bigger neck, dragging him off. "C'mon, ref. It's not our fault we can't afford stewards. This fat bastard shouldn't be anywhere near the general public, never mind a professional football match."

"Some ambassador for the club you are," Tam spat, wildly swinging the crutch in an effort to break his hold.

Jamie screamed, collapsing in the mud and clutching his leg in agony. "Aargh, my knee! You've done my knee again!"

With no match stewards, it took nine whole minutes to get the game restarted once Jamie was stretchered off following the recurrence of the old knee injury that kept him out for the majority of the previous season.

Pullman Sr., meanwhile, had his new specs crushed in the melee. Unable to see, he'd had to be led away by the kit man/groundsman/ chief scout. He felt that familiar pain sear through his upper torso and knew from experience that he'd cracked a rib or three.

On his way up the stairs, he heard a fan mention that Millwall were 3–2 up. That would be some game and some atmosphere. He should be there. He'd rather be anywhere than here. The Millwall chairman had told him to wait it out, that a good gig would crop up in London, maybe even the Lions' top job itself. Pullman didn't listen. He never listened.

But of all the places to go in the world of football, how in the name of shittuckery did he end up here?

4

"Stay." Gus Pinkle blocked the exit to his office after he'd watched Guff's Canadian keeper collapse on the Burnley forward and concede a penalty. "Please."

He took the young Atlantic Gas advertising executive's arm, guiding him towards his prized collection of rum, both local and international. He kept these under lock and key in the pine-panelled boardroom, which also doubled as his office. It was the most luxurious room in the stadium. Probably on the island. Not that that would be hard.

"We can stop watching this tripe now," he said as the resulting penalty went in, the keeper not even moving. "Get a few of the local lovelies up here to party. Get Genesis on the record player. I've holidayed with Phil before, you know. Barbados, it was. During the *No Jacket Required* years, as well."

"Honestly, Mr Twinkle—"

"Pinkle."

"I need to be on my way." The younger man grimaced as he looked out at the crumbling stadium below. The advertising hoarding was still down, the fat man now having a heated altercation with a pensioner in a pink bunnet. The fat man snatched the item from his head, throwing it. The bunnet caught a gust of wind, whisking it towards the Guff goal where it evaded the grasp of the goalie, landing in the net to ironic cheers from the Burnley faithful.

Gus gobbled another strip of Nicorette from the packet his grandkids had given him for Christmas. Apparently, they helped you live longer. He didn't think his nerves would last the distance without a real hit of tobacco.

"With investment from Billy Big Bananas such as yourself, we'll clear these players out," Gus told him. "We can be a force in this league. Might even get a cup run going. Imagine Arsenal or Liverpool here. Imagine that atmosphere."

"I can't for the life of me." The other man sighed. "I'm sorry. I can't. And I don't think that renaming the place Atlantic Gas Pty Ltd Stadium is quite the branding we're looking for."

"How about a shirt deal then? No? Your name on the team bus? A half-page ad in the program with a picture of your good self?"

"The idea of Guff and Gas together doesn't work. I really must be on my way."

He lifted his leather briefcase and edged as close to the door as Gus's weedy frame allowed. Gus could tell that the young man with the soft Yorkshire lilt was regretting not taking in the Pirates' game instead. He was thinking the exact same thing. He'd never admitted it to his father, but he'd always preferred rugger.

"This room is a treat, but as for everything surrounding it …"

"How about something to eat? It doesn't have to be another pasty. I'll order in." Pinkle buzzed his secretary. "Hello, Felicity, you there?"

She wasn't. Gus remembered he only paid her until four o'clock. In her job interview, she'd gushed about how big a football fan she was, how she never missed a Guff game. But every second Saturday, as soon as half-time arrived, she was out the door. He should have paid her until five.

Money, however, was too tight to mention, as his pal Phil Collins used to say. Or was it that ginger Jessie in the red velvet suit he shared an elevator with that time in Magaluf?

He heard the executive run down the stairs. The door slammed and sent swaying the ornate crystal chandeliers that he'd purchased back in the 1970s in Nice. They used to rock when Guff scored a goal. It had been a long time since that'd happened.

Gus hoped for better luck with the House of Fraser director, pencilled in for next week. He was the brother of his old university pal, Eoin, and a fellow Mason. That would go better. It had to.

He looked down at the stadium. The rust-eaten roof on the main stand. The cracked steps. All those broken seats and peeling paint. Venezuelan prisons had better facilities than this. It would cost millions to do it up. Probably cheaper to torch the lot and begin again.

But not his office. No. It looked like a replica of Corbin Bernsen's suite in *LA Law*, and that's because it was. If the fans knew he'd spent £25K on making it so—no, wait, *invested*—they wouldn't understand. They'd lynch him. Well, one in particular would.

Tam Bam.

The likes of him wouldn't understand that he needed a place to entertain sponsors, investors and the occasional minor celebrity. These people couldn't be expected to sail across here to the Isle of Guff and slum it out there with the plebs in ice age temperatures, the threat of peeling asbestos literally hanging over their heads. No one in their right minds would want to do that on a Saturday.

Not that many buggers came anymore. The young Atlantic Gas chap was the first from the lodge he'd been able to entice. And he had to fly him over in a charter. No six quid ferry for him. He'd even offered him a lady escort, not that he'd obliged. *Might've got the wrong gender*, Gus berated himself. He always made that mistake. It was all so different these days. Though getting one of that persuasion would've been a stretch in these parts.

The rain was lashing down now. Perhaps the game would be abandoned. No, that would be worse. They'd have to come back and do this all again. Why didn't he move to Spain and be done with it?

Sabrina wanted to. Or buy that big yacht and sail the oceans like he wanted to? The kids had left uni and were abroad now. Paris, New York, Tokyo. They hated football. They hated this island even more. But Gus had made that promise on the deathbed of his father, Royston, that he would care for this club, care for this island. The fool that he was. He'd regretted it ever since.

Gus saw that some of the crowd—the ones with some semblance of life in them—were leaving. There were barely twelve hundred of the browbeaten bunch here. The gate receipts would be lucky if they'd cover the fuel for his helicopter to take him over the waves and home to St Ives. He should have shared the young cad's ride when he dashed.

Old Royston Pinkle may have cared about the club, but did the people of the island care anymore? Most of the young ones knocked around in England or Liverpool tracksuits. The only man on the ground who really seemed to give a shit was that reprobate Bamford down there, swinging his crutches. Great irony it was that this club would go nowhere with him acting like that. You didn't see people like him in the great stadiums of the world.

You didn't see people like him anywhere.

Gus threw back the rum and dry he'd been nursing in order to appear restrained. If it weren't for the executive, he'd have sunk a half dozen of the bastards. There was more at home. There was more on the helicopter too. A whole cabinet more.

He lifted his mohair coat. He'd head out the back way and beat the rush. Ha-ha-ho-ho-hum-hum, some rush. At least he'd been savvy enough to stick a grand on Burnley to win. That would be something. If Guff had scraped a draw he'd have been in trouble, but that was never going to happen.

He pocketed the bottle of Pampero. As he locked the cabinet, he saw the police enter the ground, no doubt ready to give the club another severe bollocking followed by a fine for providing no stewards.

Unsurprisingly, they were heading in the direction of the fat man. Gus knew that before anything got better around here, before anyone would even think of putting money into this shipwreck, he'd have to do something about Tam Bam once and for all.

5

Five minutes from full time, Guff's Darren Dangerfield outmuscled his marker like Gullit. He chested the ball down like Rush, turned like Butragueño and then struck. But the effort didn't go straight in the net.

It went left, far left, going out for a Burnley throw.

"You're not a danger to opposition defences, you're a danger to the human race!" Tam shouted loud enough so the already low-in-confidence striker would hear. "You couldn't kick my arse."

"He couldn't miss that," the old man half a dozen rows back replied, now minus his pink bunnet, which was still nestled in the home side's net. "Stevie Wonder couldn't miss that."

"You should've seen me when I was out there," Tam blustered on. "Target man, so I was. They could always find me."

"They could have been firing balls from outer space and they wouldn't have missed you," the old man said to laughter.

"I invented the bicycle kick, y'know."

"This coming from someone who's never been on one."

"What do you lot know about football?" Tam continued, ignoring the taunts. "How many of you were childhood pen-pals with Alex Ferguson?"

"If any of your Fergie stories have a solitary percent of truth, then I'm a bigger womaniser than James Bond."

It seemed like the entire stand laughed at the comment. They were used to Tam's surreal tales about being best mates with the Manchester United manager. And how Tam was an even better player than him until his "hip started playing up".

Tam edged his filthy moon boot around, craning his neck to find Gary Pullman, who was stationed in the back corner. "Aren't you going to at least try and do something about this funny farm out there?"

"I fucking well can't, can I?" Pullman shouted down, fingers still clasped to his skull, the headache not abating despite taking six aspirin. "I'm fucking well up here because my own fucking fans are trying to fucking assault me when I'm trying to do my fucking job."

"You're ruining this club, so you are. Ninety-nine years we've stood proud."

"Aye, and you've whinged for every single one of them," the old man quipped again.

Tam ignored them all. "And now we've got an imposter at the helm intent on dragging us to the fiery gates of hell."

"It's your fault our captain's out," said another voice.

"Deep down you know I'm right," Tam roared, pointing. "Deeper down you're probably all emmets. Grockles. I bet you have Devon blood. You're nothing but a bunch of blow-ins."

"Who in their right mind would blow in to watch this rubbish?" the old man said. "I've lived here all my life."

"Aye, well, you'd all rather be watching rugger, or playing golf, or poking your log fires at the country club and sipping your sherry. Or whatever it is that twats drink nowadays."

"I'm on the bloody brew, you maniac," said the old man's grandson.

Jamie Pullman was sat next to his father. He clutched his strapped-up knee, readying to jump down the twenty-odd rows and stick that crutch up Tam's arse. He had resisted the temptation all year. "You're lucky, tubs," he mumbled. "You're fucking lucky."

Tam, having made his umpteenth point of the match, returned to the game. "You're a joke, Bates. I've arthritis in both my ankles, and I can pass better. Bloody hell, I could pass wind better."

"No arguments there," the old man said, and the crowd laughed again.

Tam had been unaware of the two police officers who had entered the ground, making a beeline for him.

The policewoman cleared her throat. "Mr Bam."

"It's Mr Bamford to you, young lady, and you know it."

"Mr *Bamford*—"

He wagged his big sausage finger at the pitch. "I hope you're here to arrest this lot. Impersonating footballers, so they are. It's criminal how they're robbing the last pennies off a poor and vulnerable man and serving up this tripe."

"We're actually here for you," she told him, clasping his arm.

"What are you going to do me for now? Supporting my team? Having pride in my island? Is that a crime? Because no one else seems to be imbued by that spirit."

"We're here to take you to the hospital."

"My ticker's just fine after that quadruple bypass, thank you very much."

His bravado was cut short when she quietly replied, "Yes, but your mother's isn't."

A few moments later, Tam trundled to the exit, much to the home crowd's delight. Even the Burnley fans gave up their biggest cheer of the day. They hadn't been entertained like this since Cannon and Ball did a residency in the Empire Theatre last summer.

"Put him in with the window lickers," shouted Gary Pullman.

"Put him in with the nonces," screamed his son.

"String the fat bastard up by his ballsack," cried the old man without his pink bunnet.

The group of younger Guff casuals who congregated behind the goal, sneakily drinking cider and occasionally waving a king-sized brown-and-pink bed sheet onto which they'd crudely spray-painted the Guff crest shipwreck, began a chant pertaining to the particular squalid area of the Isle of Guff which Tam lived:

"Tam the Bam from Struther Hill,
Never worked and never will."

Tam was upset. Not by the abuse, or the news of his mother. But by how he'd never missed a single minute of a home game since Boxing Day 1973 against Workington when he'd eaten a dodgy turkey sandwich instead of a trusted pasty for his elevenses and had to spend the entire second half in the stalls.

If ten-men Guff staged an epic 4–3 comeback, he'd be mightily annoyed at the old witch. And if she hadn't taken his Saturday night staple of microwave beef burger out of the freezer—the only night he didn't consume a pasty—before her little episode, he'd be ropeable.

It was the only thing that made the wait for *Match of the Day* bearable.

6

"Would you look at the state of that?" Jill Donahue blew smoke out the staffroom window as they watched Tam being led into the hospital on a stretcher. "Bugger all wrong with him, and the tubby git still insists on getting the works."

Doctor Saaj coughed, putting her Silk Cut out in the sink. They made half-packs of cigarettes. She wondered why they didn't make half cigarettes. She didn't mind a puff or two, but a whole one, at least when she wasn't drinking, was too much.

"People think it's ragheads like yourself ruining Britain," the matron rasped to the young doctor, who wasn't actually wearing any headwear. "No offence."

"None taken."

"Others say it's them bloodsuckers in Westminster. But deep down everyone knows that it's lazy white bastards like Tam Bam."

She tossed her fag end out the open window into the garden bed below, just missing the hedge. Doctor Saaj had heard the story many times about how, following her promotion to her post of head nurse three years back, the first thing Jill did was declare it acceptable to smoke in the staffroom. And despite local council regulations, no doctor was brave enough to turn anything other than a blind eye to this.

That was because, rules or no rules, Jill Donahue was one tough bitch.

The nurse lifted her backpack. "I'm away to drain Mrs Buchanan's lungs, then you'll find me in The Wick. Make sure you drop in for a wine and fill us in on what's going on with that windbag."

"I will," the doctor replied.

Doctor Saaj's husband was a home loan specialist at the Guff branch of the TSB. But with three children under six, their own home near the docks to pay off, and a biting recession, she returned to work eighteen months ago, taking the weekend shift at the hospital.

At first, the nurses in the staffroom seemed cold towards the new doctor. She couldn't work out if this was because of rudeness or racism. She eventually surmised it was because she didn't smoke or drink in the pub across the road before, during and after working hours like all the others. Nor did she gossip about co-workers and patients. She was seen as dull. Aloof. Vanilla. She knew this because Jill told her so during one particular tea break when she stood at the window smoking, while Doctor Saaj sipped a chai tea and read a hardback copy of Salman Rushdie's *The Satanic Verses* she'd borrowed from the library, minding her own business.

So she started to have the odd cigarette, the first she'd had since her student days back in Chandigarh. Soon she was invited across the road for a sauv blanc (just one or two, but for someone like her it felt like a bottle or two). She became immersed in idle chit-chat about the patients and the island. And, being a doctor, she had a lot of it. Sure, it was against her code, but it was better than being an outcast. She couldn't go through all that again like she had in Surrey when they first arrived in the country. All that bullying and intimidation.

Black lung and liver cirrhosis were better than that.

Doctor Saaj saw Mr Bamford most weekends. Aches, pains, slipped discs, a hip replacement, knee reconstruction, hernia, ingrown toenails, you name it. Some of this was because of his latent hypochondria. But all his visits were connected to his weight. There was no denying this was the main cause of last year's open-heart surgery. She'd warned him on a weekly basis to diet and exercise, though she might as well have been trying to get Enoch Powell to volunteer with Amnesty International.

She went to meet him, and they walked at snail's pace—known here as Tam Bam pace—down the busy corridor. She'd rejected his demand to be stretchered to his mother's room. He scuffed his grey moon boot annoyingly along the vinyl floor. The one he'd had for over a year and still refused to remove despite the foot he'd broken having long ago healed. Surely, he took it off to wash? She didn't want to think about the state of it if he didn't. She didn't want to be here to deal with the fallout of that. Hopefully, that would fall on a weekday.

"Your mother has had a fall. She's ruptured her bowel."

Tam said nothing, something Doctor Saaj found odd for him. She saw white chalk powdered around the man's chunky lips. He was forever chewing Rennie by the handful. She'd warned him to cut out the Lucozade and endless Cornish pasties. That it would lead to another ulcer, and yet another ailment. But like everything, he knew best.

He was usually so hostile towards the doctor, who'd arguably been the one keeping him alive since she started in the hospital. But she realised this must be so hard for him, a middle-aged man who'd never known life without his mum. Her heart softened in sympathy.

"I'm really sorry, but I'd give her twenty-four hours at best. In my experience, in these situations it's better to have no regrets. If you have anything you need to talk to her about, to tell her, or t—"

"Why is that pretender even out there?" Tam suddenly yelled.

Doctor Saaj stopped. "I beg your pardon?"

"Three–nil at home? Bugger my backside numb!"

The doctor noticed the single headphone hanging out of the man's brown-and-pink checkered scarf tied around his neck.

"Three–nil to that lot? I can't remember things ever being this bad."

She stared, aghast. "Mr Bamford, I hope you realise how serious this is."

"Aye, aye, you've said it all before." He removed the bud and turned off the transistor radio in his pocket. "You don't know her. See that old battle-axe in there, she's the bloody Terminator."

"Maybe she was, but that is no longer the case."

He didn't even answer.

They entered the room. Doctor Saaj remained by the door as Tam approached the bed.

"Where've you been, ya big useless nugget?" the old woman croaked, not opening her eyes.

"Where do you think I've been between the hours of three and a quarter to five on a Saturday afternoon? Panning for gold?"

"Thought as much. I'm on my deathbed, and football still comes first."

"You're the Terminator. The Predator. Bloody RoboCop," he said, unwrapping a Cadbury's Eclair from her bed stand.

"Even those pictures had to end sometime."

Tam sat, the wooden chair creaking under his weight. He flicked through the sports pages from yesterday's *Daily Mirror* he found on the floor.

His mother opened her dying eyes, reaching for his grubby paw. "I need you to promise me something." Tam was too busy pouring himself a tall glass of Lucozade to take her hand. "Look after our Janine."

"Aye, I'll look after Janine, so I will. Straight into Struther Hill Care Centre." He grinned as he scanned an article about Neil Warnock taking over at Notts County.

"Not there. I mean properly. Give her the home care she needs."

"How am I going to do that? An invalid myself of limited means. Increasingly limited means."

His mother reached for his other hand. She withdrew it when she realised he was cradling another Eclair. "I found your father."

Doctor Saaj watched Tam tense up at the words. She was sure it was the only thing the old woman could have said to stop her son from downing that sweet.

"You what? And how long have you kept this crucial vignette to yourself?"

"That's not important. What is important is that now you know."

"And where is he?"

"He was away. On the rigs, like I always told you. Only not on the north shore. Down in that bloody Arabia." She looked over at Doctor Saaj, realising she was still there. "Excuse my French, Doctor."

Doctor Saaj pretended not to hear. She made herself look busy, scribbling faux medical notes in her pad when she was in fact scribbling down word-for-word what was happening so she could tell Jill and the girls.

"Just you wait till I get hold of him," Tam vowed. "The things he's done to me, running away like that. Ruining my budding football career."

"That will be hard."

"How come? There're flights that way from Bristol."

"He's dead."

Tam dropped the Eclair. His voice was raised. "How bloody long have you known this, woman? How long have you kept the truth from me?"

"I didn't want to hurt you, son. Not like he hurt me."

Tam stood. "You old bag. I should leave you to rot, so I should. And now you want me to care for your daughter, a near stranger who hasn't spoken to me in all my puff?"

"She's your sister. She has cerebral palsy."

"Balls." Tam reached for another Eclair and forced it into his mouth, wrapper and all. "Why are you telling me all this now?"

The old woman's eyelids became heavy. "Doctor. Please. You've been very good to me, but I need a moment with my boy."

"Yes, of course," the doctor replied, quickly pocketing the notebook.

"And top up the morphine when you return, love. No sense in prolonging all this. Not now."

"Indeed, Mrs Bamford."

Doctor Saaj exited, though she continued eavesdropping behind the closed door. She couldn't wait to tell the girls in The Wick just what she was hearing. It would take her at least two and a half glasses to divulge it all.

Her husband wouldn't be happy when she came home smelling of wine and cigarettes. He'd worry what the other Punjabi family who ran the off-licence would say. However, the wife had early-onset dementia, and the man worked fifteen-hour days and was too tired and broken to take in the majority of what was happening around him, so it was doubtful the news would reach their village back home.

Doctor Saaj's husband knew this was preferable to her being discovered in East Surrey Hospital toilets, having to be resuscitated after overdosing on Oxycodone. He'd be glad he didn't have to tell the village about that one.

He'd be glad that wasn't happening again.

7

Father Gonzalez shivered as he placed the cassock over his head. He had on the thermal vest and long johns his aunty had insisted she buy him last summer when she holidayed here. This was under his Colombian away jersey (the real thing), an army jumper he purchased from a surplus store last time he visited London's Camden Markets and a quilted red-and-black lumberjack shirt. Yet, he was still cold.

He cursed the bishop's directive that heating was no longer allowed in the vestibule in order to reduce the power bills. He remembered when he was a deacon about to graduate. He'd hoped to be placed in Rome, or California, or Australia. He'd even have settled for something around his hometown of Cartagena, one of its leafier villages. Yet here he was, nipples erect, in deepest south-west Britain. Not even on the mainland. He must have been a right *cabrón* in his past life to have earned this.

What he wouldn't give to be snuggled up between the sheets with Nora, his housekeeper. Slim. Supple. Experienced. Seventy-three years of age. Father Gonzalez could never understand the predilection of some within the priesthood to pursue younger types. They'd obviously never met anyone as charming and seductive as his Romanian Queen.

Or anyone with gums quite like hers.

The priest opened the Bible to the loose Ecclesiastes pages and blushed as he thought of the previous night. It had started innocently enough with vodka shots and chocolate body paint. Then escalated to jiggle balls, vibrating butterfly clamps, and ended with him climaxing to a studded spanking paddle. Sitting down today would be a problem.

Father Gonzalez peered out to the altar to remind himself who it was they were burying. He'd been here almost a year and still knew very few people. That was the thing about arriving in a place where you were seen as an oddball if you didn't consume cigarettes and alcohol and fried everything by the lorry load. And that rubbish was so bad for business. Lately, he was burying three times as many as he was christening.

He heard the church door creak open. In it stomped: the Bamford boy in that lime-green mac that made him look like an out-of-shape Incredible Hulk. And with that Guff Rovers scarf that was seemingly glued to his neck. No black suit for him today. Not that the priest ever saw him in church. He only saw him at the football.

You couldn't help but see him and hear him at the football.

His mother had been a different kettle altogether. She was never away from the church, taking up every confession, endlessly griping about her two errant kids. The youngest she couldn't do much about with her condition, awful luck that. But the boy was a different sack of manure.

Nancy Bamford was always requesting items from the foodbank. Seeing the size of this sweaty beast up close, he now knew where all those day-old Cornish pasties went. Boxes upon boxes of the putrid things.

If it wasn't food or counselling, it was help with their bills. Donations of clothing, furniture, electrical items. TVs in particular. He didn't know what the Bamfords did to them.

Father Gonzalez stepped out onto the altar. He felt a peculiar shiver go through him, which didn't come from the cold. Things could get much worse now the old woman was out the way. These two *haraganes* might never be away from the church, demanding and taking. And in this, one of the poorest parishes in Britain with its ever-dwindling congregation, there wasn't a whole lot left to take. And yet, he'd still be expected to help them. To guide them. To go and check in on them and make sure they were okay.

He stood at the pulpit. He noted that the children looked older, older even than his Nora, yet he knew they were in their forties. Their mother had told him this. They could go on for years.

"Here we are today to celebrate the life of Nancy Bamford." Yes, celebrate, Father Gonzalez thought. With four people in attendance. The son, the daughter, the old woman's home help—Zulula or something— who always brought her to church. And old Pat Flanagan at the back, mouthing the rosary. A man who never missed any service, rain, hail or nuclear fallout, despite having no idea what year it was.

"It is always sad when a bright light extinguishes, and God calls one of his angels home," Gonzales went on.

The daughter at the front—Joanne, was it?—wailed out, the sounds reverberating through the eaves of the tired structure. But Father Gonzalez couldn't tell whether this was because of her grief or her condition. Not that the son was much good sitting three rows behind and to the right. Arms crossed, body hunched, he looked asleep.

"But go on we must, each and every one of us, when our loved ones hear that call." He hoped that Mr Flanagan was immersed in his Hail Marys and wasn't having one of his more lucid days where he'd realise that Father Gonzalez was pedalling the same old *mierda* he did at every requiem mass.

"She was a good woman, taken too soon. A woman who'd do anything for anybody, who always had a smile on her face." Even he couldn't believe this bit. The woman had been seventy-four but looked one hundred and four. Haggard, tired, too busy looking after her adult children to have any time to tend even to herself. The church had been her only respite.

"She will be missed by all." *Hmm, all four of them*, the priest thought. He looked to the daughter. She was quiet now, contemplative. She may have been sobbing.

But the son, the son was smiling.

Out in the carpark, it was far colder. The dull ache between the priest's exposed ears told him snow was on its way. Nora had offered him her deceased husband's sheepskin coat that they'd brought over with them from Pitesti, but the garment swallowed his lithe frame whole. By this point in proceedings, a member of the deceased's family would've normally pushed a padded envelope into his hand for the parish by way of thanks. If this had happened, he would have been right over to Debenhams on the mainland first thing to buy a winter coat. He chuckled a little at having gotten his hopes up about this. These people looked like they'd struggle to rustle up the pennies for a pint of milk. Tam might have looked ridiculous in that oversized coat as he spoke to the carer, but at least he looked warm.

The African lady with the bright orange braids mopped her tears with a hankie as she spoke with Tam. "What about Janine?" the priest heard her ask.

"I'll take care of that," Tam replied. "I promised I'd get her the greatest care affordable. You mark my words, I will."

She nodded. "I'll see you at the graveyard."

"Don't be silly." Tam pointed at the waiting cab. "After all you've done for my mother? Get in. I'd be glad of someone covering half the fare."

Father Gonzalez sighed. That winter coat would definitely be staying on the Debenhams' racks this winter.

Why, oh why, was this big *tonto* so happy? It must be the medication that the hospital he was never out of was feeding him. The man would surely be dead before the end of winter without his poor mother to wipe his backside. And that, Father Gonzalez conceded, would be another thing resting uneasily upon his conscience. It never ended.

This job never ended.

"How will you cope, my son?" He put a consoling arm on Tam's back as he prepared to get in the vehicle. He felt odd calling Tam "son" when the priest was around half the man's age and half his size.

Tam grinned wider, showing those dull yellow canines poking down either side from his top lip. "See me, Padre. I'll be fine as a dime."

"But you've just lost your mother. And your father."

"I was an abandoned child long before that. My mother spent so long kneeling before your altar, worshipping you and your false idols."

Father Gonzalez wasn't surprised by this response. The little communication he'd had with Tam at the football had only ever been hostile. "But what about money?"

Tam laughed. "Money? Oh Father, I'll never have to worry about money ever again."

Tam joined his sister and the home help. The doors closed, and the vehicle gave chase to the hearse which wasn't hanging around. Tam didn't even ask if the priest wanted a lift to the graveyard when he was the one supposedly running the show.

Father Gonzalez made it across the frosty gravel to his battered yellow Skoda, counting the hours until both he and Nora could creep beneath the sheets and try out that cock sling they hadn't got round to using last night.

His bum cheeks flexed tightly at the prospect.

He got in and tried the ignition. Nothing. Oh, how he wished he'd followed his heart and studied theatre arts and moved to Bogota after all. Was it too late now? His mother wouldn't care, she died last autumn. She wouldn't know. She wasn't looking down on him. She was in a hole in the ground being feasted on by worms. Nothing more, nothing less.

Wasn't that how these things really worked?

8

"No, you're fucking not!" The giant blue-shirted figure of the psychiatric nurse sprinted down the cobbled streets. Roger Greenfield, in the waiting taxi, had never seen Tam move so fast. He bolted from the nurse towards the vehicle, his bulging sausage legs pumping like pistons.

Roger considered driving off and leaving Tam here. He knew the nurse, Sam Statham, from the football. Former hooligan, arrested in Spain at the '82 World Cup. He'd been a bouncer until he was done for GBH on a minor and put away. Roger daydreamed about the Lego-headed monster ripping the fat man's head off right there on the street and shitting in it. The image charmed him.

Roger believed himself to be a good man. A Christian man. A man bestowed with an OBE for services to the community. But Tam brought out the absolute worst in him.

He always had.

Then he remembered that Sam was a reformed citizen who'd earned a diploma in the big house, scoring a job in the hospital. Maybe Roger could stick the car in reverse and accidentally on purpose run Tam over? Do the island a real favour. No, that wouldn't be quick enough. Or painful enough. On the main street, there'd be too many witnesses. Plus, it would almost certainly do more damage to his brother's taxi than to Tam.

How about letting Tam get in the car, then take him back to the farm? Drug him. Rack him up. Give him the blood eagle. Torture the bastard. Then again, the man was so much larger than him, at least twelve stone larger. He'd need Rowena's help to sedate him, and his wife would never go for that, no matter how much she loathed Tam Bam.

The handle lifted. A heavy fist rattled the glass. "Let us in!"

How Roger hated Tam and the way he made him think these things.

Sam was drawing closer. If it was anyone else except an overweight, recovering steroid addict giving Tam chase, he'd be toast. Sam was almost as slow as him.

"Let. Us. In!"

Roger pushed the button. The door clicked. Tam forced his lumbering shape through the door frame, slamming the door so hard the taxi nearly flipped.

"Drive!"

"B-b-but he wants to talk."

"I'm not paying you for a kiss and cuddle. I'm paying you to drive. So bloody well drive!"

Roger reluctantly put the vehicle into first. He turned off Chris Rea's 'On the Beach' on the cassette player, checked all was clear and pulled away. The imposing form of Sam Statham got smaller and smaller, and angrier and angrier, as his legs slowed, his arms began waving and his fists started violently shaking.

Roger did not like having enemies. In fact, in all his forty-seven years on the island, he liked to think he'd never made one. Local councillor, head of the Rotary chapter, governor on the school board. Then there was the £50K he donated each year to various charities on the Isle of Guff, proceeds from 'Breakfast at Granny's', the line of muesli he created at the beginning of the decade which he'd licensed to Nestlé. The cereal still sold in every major supermarket in the country.

Roger was no cabbie. He was filling in for his older brother, Ralph, who was feeling under the weather from his latest round of chemotherapy due to leukaemia. Roger offered his mornings to help.

Many of the islanders didn't have cars, and local transport was almost non-existent. The Isle of Guff was an afterthought when it came to government funding.

"What's going on, Tam?" he asked, mostly to break up the heavy panting coming from the back. There was definitely something going on. Dropping your sister off at a psychiatric unit and then doing a runner was not normal for anyone. Especially for Tam Bam, who hadn't been seen running since he was in short pants. And even then, he'd sit it out on the sidelines during sports days with a pasty, a bottle of pop and The Tiger for company.

Tam didn't reply. To add to the mystery, he began dialling on a phone. An actual mobile phone. Roger was possibly a millionaire and even he'd never seen one of the things before, not even in London. Surely it wasn't real.

"Hello … What trips do you have going to Italy? … How about Brazil? … Do you have to fly there? … So, I'd have to sail instead? … What do you mean it's one or the other? … Well, thank you very much for being absolutely no help whatsoever."

How else would anyone get there? And why was he going there? This was not normal at all.

"Are you sure you're all right, Tam?" Roger asked.

"I'm not paying you for someone to confide in either," he was told.

Roger was relieved that Tam had considered paying at all. The meter was already up to twelve quid. His brother had told him many stories over the years about how Tam had done numerous runners on him. Or tried to. And when he wasn't running away, he was moaning about the price during his innumerable trips to the hospital and crying poor to get a discount. So much so that his brother had taken the bold step of barring him, and he'd never barred anyone. But Roger didn't have the heart to turn him down. Or the guts.

"Fair enough," Roger told him, his kinder side returning. "But you've had a trying week. If you need an ear to bend, don't be afraid."

Roger drove past the empty boatyards where his grandfather used to work, where he and his brother played as children. There were no kids playing there now. They were stuck indoors, computer controllers in one hand, bag of crisps in the other, thought Roger glumly.

He moved on by the dilapidated grain silos where smoke used to billow out, covering the island in a lush smell of barley. Now there was no smoke, no smell. There was nobody. The only people he saw were those hanging around the Jobcentre. Teenagers, mainly. Smoking, passing a bottle of cider. No money, no hope. This island used to have heart, soul, imagination. Maybe it was Roger's own imagination playing tricks on him but growing up, the sun always seemed to shine. Now everything was washed in grey.

Roger braked at the crosswalk. He remembered what his wife had told him on his way out the door. The FA had got back and were donating fifty strips for Malawi. That was some good news. They were visiting the charity in the summer and building a school out there in a township near Blantyre. They were bringing a container of goodies. Those old England kits would have the kids doing somersaults. He'd requested something similar from Guff Rovers but was told no chance. Gus Pinkle wanted a tenner for every shirt.

Those people in Africa had nothing. No factories, no boatyards, no Jobcentre. Nothing at all. The people on the Isle of Guff lived like kings compared to them. And yet there wasn't the same despondency as there was here.

It felt like he and his wife were the only ones rising above it all. Was it because he'd got lucky finding a major distributor for the cereal? If he hadn't, perhaps his farm would've failed, and he would've ended up washed up like the rest. Like his older brother struggling with some bullshit illness. Like those hanging around the Jobcentre, begging for crumbs.

Or would it be even worse? he thought, as he watched Tam punching numbers into his phone with one hand, picking his nose with the other and mumbling, "You're the last person I'd confide in, you bootlicking prick."

Roger was respected by all on the island. He was liked by all. Everyone, that is, except for Tam.

They'd been in the same year at school together. Roger was a good middle-distance runner, representing the county. Straight-A student. Revered by the lads. Fancied by the girls. Yet Roger always stuck up for Tam Bamford—the school loser—in front of them all. Later, he invited him to his wedding. Offered him a job at the processing plant when the muesli took off, an offer never responded to. He refused to berate and belittle him like everyone else did, the majority with good reason. Tam was, to every last one of them, a monumental pain in the arse, but Roger had tried. And yet this was what he got in return.

"Hello, is Alec there?" Tam said down the phone.

Alec? Alec Ferguson?

"Well, where is he? … You tell him Tommy Bamford called … Aye, maybe you can … How much to buy your club? … About twenty million? … You've won bugger all in years … Have I lost *my* mind? Cheeky cow. Aye, well enjoy another generation of mediocrity."

Alex Ferguson. The manager who broke the Old Firm monopoly with Aberdeen and now managed Manchester United?

Poor Tam.

The big guy had obviously lost his mind. Maybe Roger should do the right thing and drop him back at the psychiatric hospital. Explain everything that happened. Get him checked in. Sam was a reasonable guy. Roger had sorted him out with tickets to away games in the past. It would mean missing out on the fare. His brother wouldn't be pleased, and Roger would have to make up the difference and help Tam out once again.

"Everything all right there, mate? Are you really sure?"

Just when he expected another tirade, Tam's phone rang. The thing must be real.

"Aye, this is he ... Who's this? ... *The Post*? ... Good, there're a number of things I need to bring up with you. Your love affair with Gary Pullman for starters ... Right ... What do you mean, I can't? ... No, I'm not making any comment about the money ... How do you know about that? ... Can't a grieving orphan have some privacy?"

Tam hung up, stuffing the phone back into his inside pocket, its rigid aerial sticking out ready to poke him in the eye the next pothole they hit. Roger wanted to study Tam's expression in the rearview mirror but didn't dare.

A visit to the mental hospital?

The first mobile phone on the whole of the island?

Enquiries to the travel agent for an exotic getaway?

A call from the local paper?

An attempted takeover of a First Division giant?

Roger pulled over at the council house, which constituted Tam's home. With a boarded-up front window, overgrown lawn and crude graffiti covering the garden wall, it stood out even in Struther Hill.

"How much do I owe you?"

"That will be £16.84, please, Tam." Roger flinched, expecting a crutch in the back, or worse.

Instead, he got a crisp twenty-pound note slotted into his hand, followed by a gentle hand on his shoulder. "Keep the change."

"Um ... thanks."

Something was up.

"And tell nobody about anything that happened during the ride."

Roger swallowed and tried to laugh it off. "The passenger is king."

The gentle hand became a stern grip. "Nobody."

Something was definitely up, all right.

Tam got out of the car. He tapped the roof and hobbled into his home. He didn't need a key as the lock had been ripped out.

Roger hit play on the tape deck, and 'It's All Gone' by Chris Rea came on. He surveyed the pissing rain, the houses crumbling brick by brick. The town, the island, ripped at the seams. And then there was the football club. That bloody football club.

His wife was over it. If he was honest, so was he. His love for it all, his deep, abiding love, had turned to loathing. Loathing at what it had become. His island, the island seven generations of his family had called home, was on its last legs. He cursed the few who got away, called them for everything as they fled to the mainland. Cursed the luckier few who made it to London, Spain and Australia even more. The great brain drain. That was one of the reasons the island was in such a state. He didn't want to be one of them. What would the island become then? But swapping the rain for the sun, these crumbling housing schemes for a sparkling villa with a pool. Trading his team for Tottenham Hotspur, Real Madrid or Sydney Whatever, and getting to watch real footballers who gave a shit. It appealed. He was human, after all.

It would be okay if he could have a say on how Guff Rovers operated. Every year for the past decade, he and the other members of the fan-led consortium (made up of butchers, bakers and candlestick makers) submitted a bid for the club. They had a clear, realistic plan for a new stand, a training complex and to bolster the youth system. But there was never enough money to entice Gus Pinkle. He wanted an unreasonable amount or nothing at all.

Roger was tired of dealing with him. Tired of seeing him running the club he loved into the ground. Fleeing appealed, all right. And not having to deal with wastes of space such as Tam Bam … well, that was more than tempting. His wife wanted that new life. Why was he fighting it?

Roger drove in the direction of his brother's house to return the vehicle. Hopefully, Ralph would feel better tomorrow and wouldn't need Roger to fill in. Roger had calls to make and contacts to chase on behalf of the foundation.

He passed the old rec centre they used to play indoor football in as kids. Where all the young ones would hang out, roller skating on Friday nights. Its windows were now smashed, the roof burned down. That had happened around '73, and it was still the same. He paused at the roundabout. He thought of his wife. Thought of stopping at a phone box and telling her that in Tam Bam he might have found someone else with money who could help the Malawi foundation.

Because something was definitely up.

9

Transcript from BBC Radio Cornwall
Tuesday, January 17, 1989
8.33 p.m.

EDDIE REAGAN: And now we join Archie Madden at Faery Meadow. How are Guff's cup dreams going, Archie?

ARCHIE MADDEN: Oh, this is just … this is just something else. I've been given a free Bovril as well. On top of my ticket. And a complimentary program. Mam, if you can hear me, I hope you're proud.

EDDIE REAGAN: Yes, very good. And what about the game, Archie? Guff Rovers' coach Connor Whelan is in the dugout alone due to the suspension of Gary Pullman. And who's in place of injured captain Jamie Pullman?

ARCHIE MADDEN: I mean, I'm not even finished college and here I am on the radio. It's just, it's just …

EDDIE REAGAN: Yes, indeed, but what about the match, Archie?

ARCHIE MADDEN: Ah, right, yes, sorry. We're getting beat 2–1. I couldn't actually see the goals because I was chatting to Craig Cameron, who used to write for *The Observer*. He reckons they have cadetships going every September and says he'll put a word in for me. Haha, the maniac.

EDDIE REAGAN: Yes, Archie, but—

ARCHIE MADDEN: And to all you dicks behind the goal who used to nick my schoolbag, and bitch-slap me for doing my homework, and for having brains, and not running about with yez ... well G-I-R-F-U-Y! You hear me? You enjoy the dole, and I'll enjoy the BBC, fucktards.

EDDIE REAGAN: (mumbles) You enjoy it, pal. Just you wait till I tell your mother.

ARCHIE MADDEN: It's not much of a game, to be honest, Eddie. But the experience, oh, the experience is brand new.

10

It had been a poor season for Guff Rovers in the league, even by their own mediocre standards, but the Sherpa Van Trophy was another story. They'd scrambled through to the quarter-finals with two draws and penalty shoot-out win at Hereford.

It was the main reason Gary Pullman was still rated.

The Faeries made a dream start against Third Division Bristol Rovers in the Tuesday night clash at Faery Meadow. Ross Coyne, his nose taped up after his injury on Saturday, side-stepped his marker and cracked a twenty-five-yarder off the post. The rebound smacked Darren Dangerfield in the face, the ball ricocheting into the net. The roar from the crowd was the biggest there'd been in weeks. The roar when Dangerfield was stretchered off the pitch with concussion was almost as big.

From Tam Bam, at least.

Normal service was soon resumed, however. Zak Bates, who this evening had left his boots at home and had to borrow odd ones—the right one with moulded studs, the left one with screw-ins (the screw-in boot made his left side an inch taller)—was getting a roasting from the tricky Bristol Rovers wingman, and Lance Posobiec offered little protection. He'd failed to tell his doctor he was a professional footballer, and the codeine he'd been prescribed for his aching shoulders meant he was struggling to stay awake, never mind throw himself around the goalmouth. The winger set up a hatful of chances, two of which were dispatched by the visiting side's frontman, to give them the lead approaching the break.

The Guff fans in attendance weren't exactly enjoying the spectacle. The pitch may have been dry, but the temperature hovered around the freezing mark. And Tam Bam was more animated than usual, propped up in his regular spot, with black armbands on both arms and half-eaten pasties in both hands.

"You're running like you've got two legs down the one knicker, Bates … Posobiec, you daft wank-of-a-yank. I can move quicker than you, and I'm twenty-five stone … Dangerfield, your daddy left the best bits of you sliding down your mother's thigh!"

Everybody was getting their share. Everybody except young coach Connor Whelan. It seemed Tam was relieved that Gary Pullman was banished to the stands and would have been happy if Mister Ed had taken his place. Though that didn't mean that the manager escaped Tam's ire.

"You're pure shite, gaffer," he shouted up into the enclosure. "The minute we get you off the sidelines, we start playing with a bit of fizz."

Tam's barbs were ignored as Gary had his eyes on his paper reading the pre-match report about Millwall's clash with Southampton. But his son Jamie, injured because of the knock to his knee from Guff's supposed biggest fan, wasn't having it.

"We'd have a ton more fizz if half the squad wasn't banned or injured. Mostly due to you, ya fat fuck."

"Insulting the very people who pay your wages now as well, hey?" Tam tutted. "I should phone my old mate Graham Kelly at the League and have him keep you up there all season for the good of the game. I've been meaning to catch up with him."

"You don't know Kelly at the Football League. You don't know anyone."

"I know you're nothing but a stringy streak of Cockney piss and that we're better off without you."

Pullman grabbed his son's arm, stopping him from lifting his own crutches, launching himself down there and giving Tam a taste of his own medicine.

"I also know," Tam continued, "that you and your daddy should return to Sin City post-haste. And take the chairman with you if he's not going to spend some filthy lucre."

"This town's got nothing no more," said the man with the pink bunnet (the bunnet having been safely retrieved). "The man upstairs has nowt as well."

"That pencil-tached ponce has more than you and I know."

Roger, a row along from the man in the bunnet, intervened. "Can we please stop arguing? It's so counterproductive."

"You're as guilty as hell, too, Mr Porridge Oats. You could do something."

Roger arced up. "I do more than my fair share for this island."

"For the island maybe, but not for the club you pretend to love."

Roger scowled. "I believe Guff Rovers should be owned by the fans, not one man. Every year the consortium offers to invest."

"And you're always told no because you offer nothing more than the spare change stuffed down the backseat of that cab you run. A cab you operate, Moneybags, to fleece more exorbitant sums from us."

Even Roger was shocked that Tam had taken the discussion down this route. And after knowing Tam for so long, he didn't think he could be shocked by anything the man said or did.

"And we all know why that is," Tam went on, pointing his crutch at Roger's wife who was shielding her face so that she didn't have to look at him. "It's because her there won't let you spend a penny of your own money."

"I beg your pardon, you … you … ignoramus of a man." Rowena

clung to her husband's arm, almost imploring him to go down there and sort Tam out. "Our finances are of zero concern to you."

Roger sat there stewing. He'd never been much good with conflict. And he'd never known how to deal with Tam. How he wished to be one of those people who could sock someone in the jaw and be done with it.

A small part of him was thinking, though, that perhaps Tam had a point. It was Rowena who stopped him throwing every penny he'd made into football. Of course, he could buy out Pinkle himself and put some decent fare out there on the pitch. The island would really love him then. But what would the consortium say? What would his wife do?

She'd leave him—no question.

The man in the bunnet turned on Tam. "Why don't you put your hand in your pocket for something else apart from another pasty?"

"What are you talking about?" Tam asked suspiciously.

"You're rolling in it," the man's grandson clarified.

Tam pointed at the armbands. "How dare you attack a poor defenceless orphan with your lies?"

"The whole town knows about it," continued the old man. "Why don't you back this club instead of planning a round-the-world trip and trying to buy Man Spew?"

Tam zeroed in on the priest a few rows to the left who was sat next to his old friend, Nora, the couple clandestinely holding hands under the brown-and-pink knitted rug draped over their knees. "You'll burn in hell for revealing my secrets."

"I don't know what you're talking about," the priest said. And by his look of surprise, he really didn't.

Tam turned on Roger. "Or was it you? Is there not some cabbies' code you have to abide by?"

"Well, I didn't say anything."

"Very well then, I might have come into a coin or two." Tam waved the crutch high in the air. "But I wouldn't give twenty pence towards making you shower of ingrates happy." He brought the crutch down hard, denting the 'C' on the word 'Cornwall' on the reattached advertising hoarding.

The whistle sounded for half-time. Yazz's 'The Only Way Is Up' rang out from the tannoy, competing with a chorus of boos from the crowd. Not at the players who'd fought hard against their higher-calibre opponents, but at Tam, who was pointing and calling out each player as they made their way to the changerooms.

"Moron ... Queer ... Ladyboy ... Wife-beater ... Mong."

He was halfway through the squad when a newly appointed steward entered the disabled area. Face caked in ghost-like foundation, dyed black hair and eyeliner to match the black clothes under his hi-vis vest, he'd never watched a game of football in his life.

"Sir, you have to come with me."

"Why? Who's dead now? I'm already sans parent, you know."

"That's not why I'm here."

"Are you saying it's wrong to say the word mong now? You anaemic, fascist shithead. Don't even try to chuck me out for supporting my team."

"I've been sent by the chairman. He wants to see you in his office."

Tam gripped the 'Visit Cornwall' sign so hard it made another imprint on the tin. It was the only thing stopping him from keeling over in shock.

11

"I'm sorry, Mr Wrinkle—"

"Pinkle."

The London-based assistant of the House of Fraser's advertising executive didn't stumble—"but he had an appointment with the Penzance Pirates."

"Ruddy rugby," Gus boiled, gripping the phone tight. "He said he'd be here. I laid on catering."

Gus was so nervous that he hadn't eaten all day. He snatched one of the pasties, tearing into it. It was stone cold and as awful as he remembered from his childhood. He spat it out, the stodgy ingredients landing on the framed portrait of his father on the wall, sticking right on the old boy's nose.

"We did say it was very much a maybe that he could attend tonight's match," the lady said. She sounded young, possibly Welsh. Sounded without a doubt that she didn't give two shits about the exploits of a struggling fourth-tier English club.

"That's the last pair of Balenciaga loafers I ever buy from you lot of leader-oners."

Gus flung the cordless at the portrait, the device striking the mouth and bursting through the canvas. Wonderful. He cursed. Another thing he'd have to spend good money repairing.

The chairman was all out of ideas. The club was haemorrhaging twenty grand a week. Who knew how much more if they got relegated? He'd have to cut back on top-shelf rum. These pasties he'd brought in from the bakers (the good one), along with the hevva cake, had cost him the best part of fifty quid. More money down the shitter. If he could give the club away, he would. If only it were that easy.

With half-time upon them, he looked through the window. The self-harming and probably bedwetting steward the security firm had sent (obviously for a joke, a dare or both, he surmised) was leading Tam Bam up to his office. Gus didn't think the young man could shift a slice of toast. But here he was, holding his nerve while the big man was pelted with wrappers and cans from the Guff faithful.

Gus might have to pay the firm after all.

"I'm glad you decided to pay me a visit," he said as Tam entered, slapping on his brightest smile, and shaking Tam's hand with two of his own, which made it an even fit. Gus almost gagged from the stench he'd brought in with him. Stale pasties and misery. He knew of Tam's family. How could they suddenly acquire wealth? Must be the pools or bingo or whatever else it was that poor people did in 1989.

"I didn't decide shit. I didn't have a choice."

Beetlejuice was, indeed, a lot scarier than Gus gave him credit for. "It is much appreciated." He poured two rums.

"Not for me." Tam waved his away. "I don't drink. Don't like poisoning my body with that rubbish. Got to look after oneself."

"Yes, yes, of course," Gus replied, pouring the glass into his own. "Please, have a bite."

Tam dived in, shovelling half a pasty into his mouth, his jaws churning away like the back of a bin lorry. Gus's appetite left the building and wasn't returning tonight. He'd be cancelling his usual reservation at Rick Stein's restaurant on the mainland.

"Did you get the calls about my mother and father?" Tam mumbled, his mouth full. "About the black armbands?"

The fucking armbands! Gus noticed a pair of them around Tam's flabby biceps, ready to snap off and shoot off across the room, striking him in the face at any moment. Felicity had mentioned this. He'd meant to get her to nip across to Debenhams and acquire a box-load of the things.

"Of course, of course. It was just a bit soon to sort something out with this being a midweek game and all," Gus bullshitted. "But you're right, we should do something for such great pillars of the community. In fact, that's why I've called you up here. There should be a minute's applause before our next home game."

"Two minutes' silence."

"Um, yes, of course."

Content, Tam sat back in his chair, as much as he could. "Now you're talking."

Gus felt that his charm offensive might be working. "And how about a commemorative match at the end of the season in their honour? Perhaps against Saltash United?" He was still owed a favour or three from the amateur outfit's chairman after Gus had persuaded the police not to arrest him after an incident in the toilets at St Petroc's during a particularly lively Christmas week party.

"I was thinking Manchester United would be better."

Through a painted on smile, Gus said, "Well, it doesn't hurt to ask."

Tam Bam was flying high in the solar system tonight, thought Gus. But no matter, the bullshit was working. And then some.

"If you think that's the right thing to do, Mr Chairman. I reckon that would be just fine."

Mr Chairman? This was getting better.

"It was actually your parents' tragic and untimely passing I wanted to talk to you about, Tam." Tam was halfway through the box of pasties. Hadn't there been a baker's dozen in there? Gus waited until the other man looked up before continuing. "I'm a man of means myself as you know, and men of means can often spot other men who've joined the—"

"You want to know if the old girl's left me a wad?" Tam cut in, pastry crumbs flaking down onto the plush Stainmaster. Corbin Bernsen never had to deal with this barbarism. He hoped this little sortie was worth it.

"People of means such as myself—ourselves rather—are never so uncouth as to discuss it so openly." Gus drained his double shot of rum and realised he was trembling.

Tam snorted. "Well, aye, she did. *He* did, rather."

"I see," Gus replied, trying to disguise his glee. "That wasn't why I invited you up here, of course."

There was silence for a moment, then Tam said, "Any chance of a Lucozade?"

"Lucozade?" Gus had never tried the bright-orange stuff. He went to call Felicity, then remembered she'd cleared off.

"The true drink of athletes. Just ask Daley Thompson."

"How about an ale or a wine?"

"I told you, Mr Chairman, only slobs and Neanderthals drink. My body is a temple."

"Tea?"

"Oh, all right."

Gus fretted. He'd never made a cup of tea in his life. He didn't even know where the kettle was. He peered into the fridge. There was no milk, only mixers.

"How about a glass of lemonade?"

"Full sugar?"

"Indeed."

"Fine."

Gus poured a small can of Schweppes into a pint glass. Tam was still fixated on the box of pasties. He hadn't admired the pine panelling. The L-shaped sofa shipped over from Ikea. He hadn't even glanced at the bird's-eye view of the pitch when the second half restarted.

"I was wondering how much?" Gus asked, handing him the frosty glass.

"Now Mr Chairman, that would be telling."

Gus looked at his watch. He wanted to wrap this up so he could beat a path out of here before the final whistle and get to the helipad. He had better places to be. His sister was having her fiftieth tomorrow in Poole, and he had to pack.

"Listen, Tam, you know why you're here. The team needs urgent investment if we're to fight relegation. Who knows what it could do to our club if we went out of the league? Given the state of things, I don't think we'd be back. I'm not even sure we'd survive."

About this, Gus wasn't lying.

Tam finally took in the plush surrounds. "What about your own fortune?"

"Don't let the baked goods and soft furnishings fool you. I'm all tapped out on that front."

Tam rolled his eyes and grabbed another one.

"Just think." Gus waved his arms at the pitch where Bates was hitting a long-ball upfield which bounced out for a goal-kick. "If we could give the gaffer a proper war chest, he'd drag us up that table."

"You what?" Tam coughed, spitting a mouthful of lemonade all over the portrait. "I wouldn't give that man a wring of the sweat off my waistband if he were dying of thirst.'

"That's a bit rich."

"And so are you. I've heard quite enough. You, Mr Chairman, can stick your hospitality. I have a match to attend, and a team to support."

Tam pocketed the last pasty and thundered towards the door.

Part of Gus breathed a sigh of relief. He imagined spending every weekend cooped up in his beloved *L.A. Law*-styled office watching this specimen wolfing down God knows what and stinking it out. Still, he knew it was something that had to be done. To save the club. To save himself.

"How about a seat on the board, then? For a sizeable chunk of investment, of course. Director Bam—or Bamford, rather. Has a nice ring to it, don't you think?"

Tam stopped in the doorway. "You think I want to sit up here and break bread with you? Crunching bloody numbers. Wearing a shirt and tie. Bathing in the morning before games. Giving those prats out on the pitch even more money than they deserve. They should be paying for the privilege of pulling on the famous checkered Guff jersey."

"There's central heating. The best seat in the house. I'll organise Lucozade for you. I'll get a ruddy keg of it."

Groans rang around the ground. Both men looked and saw that the Rovers from Bristol had bundled in a third. There would be no way back now against their more experienced opponents. A maiden trip to Wembley would have been a boost for morale, would have done wonders for the coffers, but in all truth, it was never on the cards.

"I'll be off now," Tam said. "If you're not going to spend the money that everyone on the island knows you have after you've bled us dry, then I think you should do the honourable thing and leave as well. Preferably through that window."

It was a thirty-foot drop. Gus couldn't believe he'd been forced to stoop so low. To hold the begging bowl before this cretin. At least now he could do something he'd dreamed about doing since taking the reins of the club. "Fine. Have it your way."

"I will, thank you very much."

"But you are barred from this football club, Tam Bam. You are banned for life." Gus gathered the CB radio. "Nosferatu, come to my office immediately and evict this, this … bam from the stadium. Forever."

"Good," Tam said, chewing the last of his pasty and making his own way out. "I wouldn't work with you if you were the man who'd given me the £5M."

"What?" Gus dropped the radio to the floor.

He'd have dropped it if he'd found out Tam had £500K. But five *million*?

"I've got better things to do than waste a single red cent of my hard-earned money, or one moment of my time with you." And with that Tam slammed the door, sending the chandelier falling and shattering on the picture.

Tam was long gone by the time the steward arrived. Five million, hey? Gus sat and poured another rum, throwing it down the hatch.

He couldn't help thinking that he could have probably dealt with that situation a whole lot better.

12

Tam awoke to the sun bursting through the blinds, for a change. The sun never shone on Saturdays in winter. What a beautiful start to the first day of the rest of his life, he thought, as he yawned. The things he could do today.

The morning was gone, of course. It was midday, which usually was when he woke. But the afternoon and evening were his to come. No mother, no sister and no football. All the things which had been holding him back in life had been flushed away.

And on the first flush too.

As he heaved his heavy frame up from the sofa bed, he also realised this meant there'd be no fry-up. It gave him a moment's pause. Still, no mind. A man of his means could afford twenty fry-ups better tasting than his mother's at Vera's Cafe down the road. But that would mean having a wash, and a shave, and changing his Y-fronts, and, and ... ah, balls to that.

In the end, he settled for a reheated pasty. He lay back on the burst fold-out. The sheets could do with a spin. It was only now he realised his mother had them washed once a week. The smell of salty scrotum sweat was even getting to him. But he had no idea how to work the washing machine. The thing was like the TARDIS. Same with the heating. Same with the microwave which he'd only recently figured out.

What to do today? What not to do? He almost felt like a normal person.

He thought of watching a film. He picked up the greasy control. Crumbs and pubes had jammed between its buttons, meaning he had to push each one that bit harder. He scanned through BSB. A *Carry On* film was on with Sid James at the beach, chasing some tart with her boobs hanging out. He was hoping for an *Escape to Victory* or, at a pinch, *When Saturday Comes*.

He flicked through the usual channels. A home improvement show. Talk show. Ads. And news, bloody news. Floods in India, some crisis in East Germany, Maggie Thatcher touring an old mine site. A speech by that new American president, George what's-his-face.

His thumb wandered to the BBC and *Grandstand*. A feature on ice skating. He was drifting off just looking at it.

Still, no way was he going to give in to *Saint and Greavsie*. There was never anything about Guff Rovers, anyway. It was always Liverpool, Everton, Rangers or some other Billy Big Shoes club. Where was the fun in supporting that lot?

He finished the pasty and turned off the idiot box. He opened the front door and found the paper on the doorstep. There was a note from Mrs Singh stapled to the cover:

Dear Tam,
So sorry to hear about your loss. Please come in and see us when you get the chance.
Thinking of you,
Jasmin

Bloody vultures, the lot of them. Tam fumed. Wanting him to go in there so they could squeeze more money out of a poor bereaved man with his mother barely cold. That Jasmin lady had never so much as looked in his direction when he bought his *Shoot*, his Rennie and his Lucozade, admittedly belching and occasionally farting as he did so. But now that she knew he was the one in charge of the purse strings, in she swooped. This was another thing added to his pile, which he'd have to deal with.

Another bloody thing.

Tam went straight for the back pages, then stopped himself, remembering. Having already gotten more than enough news from two minutes of channel surfing, he dug into the supplements. New cars, skin tips. Pages upon pages about some Australian soap called *Neighbours*. Was this the hogwash that people who weren't into football filled their days with?

He turned the TV back on. Reruns of *Magnum*. *Antiques Roadshow*. *The Sullivans*. *Heaven help us*. Maybe the ice skating had finished on *Grandstand*. Perhaps there'd be something on about football. He could watch it for a few minutes. It wouldn't hurt to keep in the loop, so he had something to talk to folk about.

He clicked the number 1. Bob Wilson was at the desk. Arsenal v Sheffield Wednesday was later today. Celtic at Hibs. A full card in Europe.

This was more like it. Tam leaned back on the sofa. His breathing relaxed. Visions of that fry-up abated. Life was okay again. And then up it popped.

The Division Four ladder.

Guff Rovers, *his* Guff Rovers, floating a point above the relegation zone and the dark chasm of non-league football. Or what might as well be amateur football. Runcorn. Chorley. Kidderminster Harriers. He didn't even know where those places were.

Bugger that. Gus Pinkle was right about one thing. They might never get back up.

Tam's breathing became shorter as his heart bounced around his ribcage. He reminded himself that it didn't matter now. That football was in the past. Still, home to Torquay today. Almost a derby. He could buy a new coat, a mask from the joke shop, and sneak in the away end.

Guff had a good record against them. Won the last two, unbeaten in the last five. They had a good shout for the points if that Pullman prick could pull it together. He'd be better off in the stands, though. Preferably the stands in south London. That young Connor Whelan had done all right from what he'd seen of the Bristol Rovers tie. Got them playing a bit, gave that West Country lot a game.

Tam supposed he might as well get ready. But for what, he still wasn't sure. He hauled himself up. He peered into the shower and saw the black mould overcoming the ceiling. He couldn't remember when he'd last had a shower. He was more of a bath man, though his last had been before the funeral.

He gathered his crusty pink flannel, still damp at the corners, and gave his body the old father-son-holy-ghost, followed by a brisk how's-your-father.

The sink taps were caked in solid grey toothpaste and old soap. There were mounds of ginger hair clogging the sink. Janine's electric toothbrush stood tall in a plastic cup.

Janine.

The house was quiet without her. For the first time, Tam heard a bus power down the street. Normally she'd be singing or jabbering away about something or other that he could never make out, though his mother always maintained she could. To him, she made the same sound when she was happy as when she was supposedly sad. He'd always wondered what would have happened had she never been born, and he'd remained an only child. Maybe his mother would have been happier. Maybe his dad would have stuck around. Maybe he'd have made something, anything, of himself.

Tam heard footsteps and children's laughter from the footpath outside. He found the silence in the house unnerving.

Look after Janine, she'd told him.

It had been his mother's only request. Still, that hospital he'd found for Janine was a good one. The best on the island. She'd be well looked after.

He cleaned his ears with the corner of the rag. He applied Brut on the areas he'd bathed.

Perhaps he'd drop in on her. Take her a Lucozade and a Bounty. She loved Bountys. He'd buy two and give one to that wall puncher who worked there as a peace offering. Though he would probably be the one giving Tam a box of the things when he realised how much he'd tolerated from his sister during his lifetime.

He deserved a knighthood.

Tam put on his well-pulled fishing jumper and Umbro trackies, followed by the welly he wore six months out of the year. He only needed the one because he was still wearing the moon boot. Then his trusty lime-green mac and, finally, his treasured Guff Rovers scarf he was gifted when he saw his first game forty-two years ago. He would have to buy a new one, something plain to mark this new beginning.

He lifted his crutch and was ready. The things he could do today. Hmm, what exactly did people do on Saturdays? A round of golf? Clubs were probably in the loft or had been given away by his mother to that greedy church of hers. Like the Pope didn't have enough funds.

Tam hadn't played golf since he was a teenager. He'd still have a knack for it, of that he had no doubt. Although he didn't fancy it when there was a sheet of ice on the grass.

Shopping? Well, he did need a new scarf. He could do with some fresh Y-fronts. And sheets too. That would save him washing the current ones. But Saturday crowds? No, thanks. There'd be people there who knew him, who might ask about his mum, about Janine, about the money. And that he couldn't be doing with.

He sat back down on the couch. He loosened the scarf. He switched the channels again. More news. More *Antiques Roadshow*. Now ten-pin bowling from the States on *Grandstand*. That wasn't a sport.

Christ, what did people do with their Saturdays?

He'd have to do something about the empty fridge. And the state of the kitchen. And the bathroom. And the sheets. And the scarf, and, and, and …

He put some fresh milk in a bowl and laid it on the step for his cat, Alf Ramsey, in the hope it would one day return. It had been three years now. If he'd given it milk every day before it went missing, it might have stuck around.

Tam put on his vintage Cossack hat, which he reserved for special occasions. It was the only thing his father left behind. He stepped out into the cold. It must have been between two and two-point-two degrees. He still had no idea where he was going. But he knew he had to go somewhere.

"Bollocks to you, Gus Pinkle!" he roared.

His neighbour, Mrs Sampson, slammed her kitchen window shut. Even Tam had to agree that she'd heard it all before.

13

It had been the worst of weeks for Sam Statham. He'd been trying to track down Tam Bam since his little stunt. He'd called by his house and found the lights on, the TV blaring. He'd rang the doorbell until it came loose in his hands. He'd slammed his fist on the door so many times it started to hairline.

Noticing the lock was missing, he'd gone in, shielding his nose with his sleeve, making sure to keep his eyes wide open so he could dodge the odd shoes, socks and empty Lucozade bottles littering the hallway.

He'd found the bathroom lock intact. He knew the fat man was in there. He could smell him. Bam certainly wasn't bathing, whatever he was doing.

Sam had thought about shouting. He'd thought about breaking the door down but knew he'd already overstepped the mark by coming into the house and didn't want the police on his tail. He'd had zero assistance from them when he'd called, saying the Bamford woman had been abandoned. They didn't care. Though he knew that breaking and entering would be a different story. Particularly as it was him. The police did not like him and refused to believe he was reformed. The sergeant told him so the day he left Dartmoor Prison and returned to the island.

Sam had given the front door a slam and removed himself from the property. He'd got on his Triumph, put on his helmet, and navigated the wet and windy roads towards his work. He had lots of it, too much of it to do. Way too much without caring for someone with cerebral palsy. They were already overrun in the psychiatric hospital. Not enough funding, not enough staff. Always the way, or so his tutors had warned him back in night school.

Each one of the fourteen rooms in the facility was occupied, four of which had two patients, which was against every regulation. The two doctors were on sick leave, although he'd heard on the grapevine that they'd actually snuck away for a dirty weekend together in the Cotswolds. It had been left up to him as the most senior staff member, along with one other nurse and two students on work placement from the University of Plymouth, to keep things ticking over. He was no grass, yet he was struggling and called the mainland for help. He had to. But everyone in the department was too busy to offer a solution, promising to return his calls but never doing so. He'd even contemplated going to the papers to rally against the conditions, though he knew that would end all hope of him ever getting any sort of promotion or transfer away from Guff. And now, to top it all off, he'd had this woman dumped on him. No way could he put her in with one of these literal psychos. She wasn't a mental patient. These genuine nutbars would tear her up and spit her out the first chance they got. And as much as he despised her brother, he couldn't do that to her. Nor to anyone.

Instead, he brought in an air bed from home and placed her in the rather spacious broom cupboard. And he'd fed her. It was food the old cook, Bill, said he couldn't spare, and boy did he hear about this. Still, not everyone ate all theirs. No one, not even the certified insane, would eat all the crap that Bill dished out.

But Sam wouldn't bathe Janine, that was far outside his remit. And after a week, she really needed it. He helped her to the toilet and stayed outside while she relieved herself. That was the extent of his help. He was already going way above and beyond the call of duty.

So as much as he despised the man, and he genuinely did (although on the Isle of Guff he was hardly alone in this), he was glad to see Tam Bam stumble into the hospital that Saturday afternoon.

"I'm here to pay my sister a visit."

Sam looked up from the pile of paperwork he'd accumulated. "A visit? You inconsiderate pillock! You can take her with you right away."

"That's hardly my job. It's the bloody state's. That's what my taxes are for. And anyway, I left you a hundred-quid cheque. That oughta cover her for a few weeks at least."

"A hundred quid doesn't cover a day in this place, you moron." Sam noticed that his fists were clenched, his hands raised. He paused and tried to relax his shoulders. He had to remember who he was dealing with. Someone who in many ways was far more mental than the people he cared for. Especially with this daft Russian hat on. Sam thought of the therapy he received on the inside. He began his box breathing exercises. He exhaled so sharply he thought his nostrils would split. "And anyway, we're a psychiatric hospital."

"A psychiatric hospital?"

Sam fantasised about splatting Tam's big fat nose over his big fat face. "This is a looney bin, you daft bastard."

"Good. She's as nuts as they come."

"Are you sure you don't belong here?"

He had the gall to actually look offended! "I beg your pardon."

Sam leaned forward. "Your sister has cerebral palsy. She doesn't have a mental health condition."

Sam looked to where Janine was watching *Donahue* on the TV in the corner of the office. As pleasant as he'd tried to make it, the last few days had been harrowing for her away from her comfort zone. Her usual life probably wasn't much better, but at least it was familiar.

"Well, what am I going to do with her?" Tam asked.

"She's your kin. She's your responsibility."

"I'm an invalid myself."

Sam took a deep breath. It was about all he could do to stop himself from twisting Tam's head off. "Here, take this." He handed Tam a piece of lined paper with a phone number jotted in red ink. "This lady came by earlier looking for a job. She's not qualified to work for us, but you'd get a lot more mileage out of her with your hundred quid than you will here."

Tam saw the name 'Zabe'. "She's my mother's home help. Or she was. What's she doing looking for work in here?"

"You sacked her. That's what folk generally do when they're out of a job. They look for another. You wouldn't know much about that though, you work-shy git."

With a sniff, Tam said, "She's not qualified to look after someone with Janine's needs."

"And neither am I! She cared for your mother for years. It's the best offer you'll get round these parts."

Tam roughly folded the slip of paper, pocketing it. "I'll keep it in mind."

"Right, now take her and get out." Sam tried to unclench his jaw. "I've eighteen patients to care for and I've wasted enough of my time on you. Next time you pull a stunt like this, I'll be kicking down the doors at your gaff, grabbing you by the back teeth and dragging you here."

"Where are your superiors? I wish to complain about your complete and utter lack of customer service."

A piercing wail went up from one of the rooms, followed by a loud crash.

"Good luck with that. There's no bugger within a hundred miles who'll listen."

A few minutes and a bit of shuffling later, Tam clutched the handles of Janine's wheelchair. Her eyes hadn't left the TV where Phil Donahue and his guests were discussing adults who still slept with their childhood teddy bears.

"Could you give us a lift?" Tam asked, as nicely as he could muster. "No? Call us a cab? At least prepare us a packed lunch for the journey home."

It took everything Sam had not to laugh in the smarmy bastard's face. Or header it. "Here's your cheque. Organise your own cab. I won't make you run for this one."

"How kind."

"Now fuck off out of here." Sam shoved him and the wheelchair onto the street and locked the door.

Thank Christ that was over. Now he could get some work done. Sam finished his cup of tea, slapped on a pair of rubber gloves, and went to Harold's room to give him his daily enema.

He felt bad leaving the woman with that buffoon. He wondered how long it'd be before she'd be joining her mother on the slab. He thought about how long the pair of them would last. Still, there were only so many people in this world you could save. His job was to look after those in his care.

And if he had to pick one more person to help out on this island, it wouldn't be Tam Bam.

Harold was waiting. Sam gave him a friendly "Hello, Harold" as he lubed his index finger and pulled down the old man's pyjama bottoms.

The stress of this job was almost enough to send him back on the gear. Sometimes transcendental meditation wasn't enough. He liked his vocation. It gave him purpose. Earned him respect. But in so many ways, life was easier back when all he had to think about was his next rob and next fix.

"Assume the position please, Harold." The old man's back arched, and his bony arse pointed to the heavens.

Maybe Sam would call his old pal Amph in Wigan later on. He was out of prison now. Word was he was in a bad way. Just to see how he was getting on, of course. Not to do anything else. Maybe to ask if he fancied a trip across here. Not to do any of that shit, mind. No, nothing like that.

Just a catch-up, for old time's sake.

14

Barry Lennox liked Saturday afternoons a little after three o'clock in The Wick. Contrary to what people thought, this was the quietest time of the week. The lunch set had packed up. The shoppers were still shopping. The bulk of the nurses hadn't clocked off yet at the old hospital. And the football scores wouldn't come in for another hour or so. This meant an hour until the regular punters would stream in, one eye on the screen, the other on their usually burst coupons. And the evening crowd felt like a lifetime away.

Barry had never worked out what happened to his regulars on the weekends. The barflies with nothing to live for Monday to Friday would go to ground. Were they sleeping off five days' drinking? Spending time with their families?

Those people didn't have families.

Barry didn't care enough about them to dwell on it. He grabbed himself a bowl of soup from the kitchen, which had been left over from lunch. Old Bill also cooked in the mental hospital. He was half-blind and crippled with arthritis since he left the navy in the sixties. He smoked a pack of Regals and consumed a bottle of red.

And that was just while he was at the burner.

Guessing by the declining taste of his food, it seemed Old Bill had no taste buds or sense of smell. Barry was no foodie by any stretch. He was from the Isle of Guff, after all, a place where having brown sauce on your chips instead of red was viewed as exotic. Still, he swore this particular greyish concoction he was consuming wasn't anything near resembling soup. It was something so gluggy it could be used to fill potholes on the

High Street. This was why the majority of patrons, apart from the most hardened of bastards, ordered no more than a liquid lunch. Barry knew he should have sacked him years ago, but he always imagined Old Bill would retire or die in his sleep. Or worst case, at the stove.

Barry had tried to get Bill pouring pints. He ended up losing more beer down the sink and down the old cook's throat than he did into the glasses. Then he put him on washing-up duty, but it cost him more replacing the receptacles than it did in wages.

Barry dreamed of pasta, sushi and burritos. Pizza, tapas and noodles. Yet the few locals who ate here never complained about the food. Like him they were hardly used to experiencing culinary excellence in the smattering of restaurants and hostelries on Guff. Barry knew that the soup, as rank as it was, was one of the tastiest things for twenty-odd miles. And it had to be better for his waistline than gorging on endless packets of pork crackling.

Barry checked his answering machine. He was hoping to hear from men from the dating agency. Young men. The two potential hook-ups he'd made last week had gone to ground. Probably afraid of getting caught by their girlfriends, wives, friends or workmates, if they had any. It was always the way. He'd have to get the late ferry across to the mainland tonight if he wanted some thrills. Such was the life of a man who was, quite literally, the only openly gay man out of a population of around 40,000. Openly, because he knew the place was secretly crawling with them.

Repressed homosexuals made up at least half his clientele.

Barry jumped when he heard a man's voice behind the bar. "Who do I have to nosh to get a drink?"

Barry laid down his spoon and peeked around the nook. He was surprised to see Tam Bam in early. The clock read quarter past three. "What you doing in here? You lost your watch as well as your mother?"

Tam always came into the pub on a Saturday, but always after five o'clock. After he'd stayed back after the final whistle and remonstrated with the players, coach or whoever else wanted some, about the team's usually abject performance.

"It's not a crime to frequent your dank public house earlier than usual, is it?"

Barry poured him his customary Virgin Mary. By the looks of his pallid appearance, it was the only vitamins the big man got all week. Of all of Tam's foibles—his weight, his odour, his manner, his constantly foul mood, the list went on—he didn't drink alcohol.

About the only person on the island above the age of twelve who didn't.

"No, I suppose not," conceded Barry. Though in Tam's case, he wished it was.

Unlike the majority of people on the island, Barry didn't hate the man. As an outcast himself, he actually respected him for living his life on the fringes. Even if, unlike himself—trim, toned, close-shaved and always smelling as fresh as a bouquet from Amsterdam—he was on the flip side of the spectrum. Barry viewed them both, somewhat depressingly, as brothers-in-arms.

However, this was supposed to be his time. Soup, shot of vodka and a quick wank in the back toilet to the latest issue of *Blueboy* to get his Saturday kick-started. Fat chance of that now.

He noted that Tam didn't have his football scarf on. He was wearing some Hermès-type silk number with red robins on a green background. It looked somewhat Christmassy.

It looked downright queer.

It must have been a fake. This guy didn't know fashion. And it clashed horribly with his lime-green mac.

Nor did Tam have his customary copy of *The Post*'s sports section hanging out his front pocket. He looked remorseful, circumspect. Barry heard he'd lost both his parents recently, yet this was deeper. He sure didn't seem like a guy who'd inherited a large sum of money like everyone on the island was saying. For starters, he was still on the island. People stayed on the Isle of Guff because it was the cheapest place in Britain. Anyone with a few quid and half a brain would be off like a shot. However, it was doubtful that Tam possessed the latter.

"What's with you?" Barry asked, applying a flaccid stick of celery to Tam's tall glass, the poor excuse for a vegetable having sat in the back of the fridge since last week and maybe the week before that. "I have to say I never thought I'd see the day."

"What d'ya mean?"

"Rovers playing, are they not?" Barry had heard the usual grumbles from the ground across the street. It occurred to him they weren't quite as loud as usual. Now he knew that it was because Tam wasn't in attendance.

"I'm banned, aren't I?" Tam said, taking a generous gulp of his drink.

Barry remembered he hadn't added the pepper. Then again, Tam never seemed to notice if you forgot an ingredient or three. "What the heck did you do? Streak your fat arse across the field? That mob's desperate for fans."

"Absolutely nothing. It's a travesty. I'm writing to my friends at the FA to inform them."

Barry had no idea what an 'FA' was. He'd played rugby growing up, a game he enjoyed because it was the only contact his virile young body was permitted to have with other virile young men. He'd never been a football man. There wasn't enough physicality.

"Why are you in here then? You're free now. Heard you're worth a few bob 'n' all."

"Christ on the cross. Is there anyone who doesn't know that?"

"You should be travelling the world. Sunning your fat arse someplace warm. Drinking something more salubrious than this. Watching your Bayern Milans, or your Inter Madrids or whatever you call them."

"Hmph. I shall be. I shall be. Don't you worry about that. I'll show everyone."

"Sure, you will." Barry collected a dish towel and left the man with his drink and his morbid dreams.

What a queer bastard Tam Bam was.

Newquay it would be tonight to check out the scene. Some of The Wick regulars asked why he didn't move there. Or London, or Europe where it would be easier to be the way he was. But this was his island. He was born here. He'd visited London, taken the odd package holiday abroad, yet as much as he complained about this dreary sinkhole, he liked being on the Isle of Guff. Standing out, rubbing people the wrong way. You didn't get to do that in places where being gay—and outrageously gay at that—was acceptable. It could be that he was a born agitator. And at six foot four with a gym body, he could afford to be.

But if he was honest, the main reason he was still here was because he'd missed the boat. He'd never known his dad. He doubted if his dad ever knew about him. It was always Barry and his mum. She was forty-two when she had him. She struggled with her weight and her well-being. They were close, though. She was a good mother, and he wanted for nothing. When her health declined back when Barry hit thirty, he cared for her. By the time she passed away, he was too old to go anywhere else, or so he felt. Early onset baldness can sometimes do that to a man. So, yes, in a weird way, unlike the other inhabitants of the island, he got Tam Bam.

The football fans began trickling in shortly after the bookies crowd at around twenty to five. A good ten minutes earlier than usual. He could see by their long faces that Guff had been gubbed again. And he could tell by their reactions that they were as surprised as he was to see Tam on the premises.

Barry took their orders. He poured their drinks. Tam wasn't a betting man, but he was eyeing up the football scores on the screen like his life depended on it. In a strange way, Barry knew it did. Tam lived for this.

Football, Guff Rovers in particular, was his life.

Sure, Tam could go off the island. He could probably afford to watch Nottingham Forest or Ajax or Brazil, or whoever it was who was the best nowadays. But like Barry, this island was all he knew. He'd left it too late to try to do something different. To be someone else.

"See you, ya Bam," Ally said, approaching the bar. He was a younger, shell-suited regular who looked like he'd been glue sniffing all day with that pug nose of his. "It was another loss today, but that's the most I've enjoyed a home game since I was on my stepdad's shoulders."

"Is that right?" Tam answered.

"Aye, it's right. And you know why?"

"Indulge me."

"Because I didn't have to listen to your bollocks during it." His mates behind fell about laughing.

Tam was immune to such jibes. "You enjoy the losses. You sit back and revel watching old Pinkle doing what he likes and rinsing the club dry as he does so, while the likes of you sheep bleat away. Baaa. Baaa! That place will crumble without this voice of reason here keeping him in line." Tam doffed his big Russian hat. "It's a human rights tragedy that I've been banned."

"Fuck that,' the younger man cut in. 'It's the greatest triumph this club's ever had."

The kids behind predictably slapped his back in appreciation.

"All right, fuckwads, settle down. You've had your fun," Barry said, pouring the last of the four pints of snakebite and sending them on their way. He didn't mind punters having a go at Tam. Tam usually asked for it. But he more than most knew there was a line. Usually when Tam got so mad that he turned that violent shade of purple. The last thing Barry wanted was the big man keeling over in his pub and then having to give him mouth-to-mouth. And what if he died? He'd haunt the place forever.

The wider public already had enough reason not to come in here.

"Same again?" Barry asked.

The classified football results had begun. Tam normally nursed the one beverage, though since he'd come in early, he'd finished it, so he grunted a "yes".

Barry got to work. "Why don't you buy the club and take charge?"

"And turn it round? And make this lot of degenerates happy? I'd rather see it torched."

"You don't mean that."

"What would you know about what I mean?"

"Listen." Barry leaned in. "There's talk of this town expanding. We might even get back to what we had someday if Thatcher falls off her perch. The mainland's not cheap, and a few immigrants are knocking about now. Apparently, we've got one of the fastest-growing birth rates in the region. Admittedly, most of them illegitimate. I had a developer in here the other week from one of the big supermarket chains sounding me out about selling up and turning this place into a carpark. Now I'm a stone's throw from the ground, so if they've been in here, you can bet your bottom dollar they're heading in there." Barry nodded in the direction of Faery Meadow.

One of Ally's friends pushed the young man into the back of Tam. He spilled some of his Virgin Mary over his new scarf, getting more laughs.

"For once in your life, listen to someone," Barry told him, dusting

Tam down with a dishcloth. "I was the joke of the town. The amount of abuse you've gotten over the years is nothing on me."

Tam was tuned to the football results, giving a nod of appreciation upon hearing Exeter had lost. Yet Barry could tell by his rare silence that he was listening, and so he continued. "I'd had enough. But still, I didn't want to leave this place. It's home. So, what did I do?"

Tam shrugged like he couldn't give less of a shit if he tried.

"What did you do?"

"I pooled the few pennies I got from the inheritance, and I bought something."

Tam scoffed. "What did you buy, Queenie?"

"I bought one of the very few institutions that mattered here." Barry knocked on the wooden bar top. "And better than that—"

Another kid in a mop top and a sky-blue Aquascutum sweatshirt interrupted. "Four Malibu, vodka and cokes, and a Babycham when you're ready, please, Baz mate."

Barry whispered to Tam, "I bought respect."

He poured the drinks. The kid handed over a tenner. "Keep the change, yeah. Had a bit of a win on that Exeter result. I also owe ya for the other night. I was bang out of order, smashing that sink after Rachel left us. Sorry 'bout that. That's what pills made with Persil will do for ya."

"Thank you, Shaun. But it'll cost you fifty quid."

"I'll get it to you by next Sat."

Barry placed the money in the till, and the kid lifted the drinks. 'Lazyitis' by the Happy Mondays filled the room and a few of the younger drinkers cheered.

The landlord turned back to Tam. "I was a fucking joke before I got behind the bar. The only arse bandit between Merthyr Tydfil and Miami. But buy everyone's favourite drinking hole next to the football ground, promote cheap drinks and budget meals, put in a decent jukebox, and suddenly every tosser in a tracksuit loves you. And this, my friend, could be you."

He had Tam's complete attention now.

"Of course," Barry continued. "I put the ringleader of that Cardiff City crew in an induced coma after that cup-tie. And I ran a group of homophobic bikies off the island with a sawn-off and shot one of them in the arm. Might have had a bit to do with that, to be honest. But on the whole, I got the respect I wanted."

"So, what are you saying, ya bum pirate?"

"Are you actually that thick? Do I have to spell it out? Buy the fucking football team! Control the thing that people love. Make it a success. They'll love you for it."

Tam slurped his drink. He was contemplative. It was unusual for him.

Barry went in harder. "Of course, if you don't make it a success, they'll be the ones shooting you and putting you in a coma. I know enough about the game to know that. But that's the chance you take."

He left Tam in front of the football scores with that thought, groaning at confirmation of Guff's two-nil home loss.

Barry collected the empties. He joked with a few of the nurses who'd knocked off about how he would indeed be hitting Newquay tonight. He told young Gaz— a vertically challenged member of Shaun's crew— off for sprinting out the toilets with dinner plate eyes, looking like some giant white powdery caterpillar had lodged itself up his nose. It was the same as every other Saturday.

Rinse and repeat.

Barry looked to Tam. He was wearing that same expression as before, except now he was picking his ear and closely inspecting the remains. Ah, what was he thinking? That man would never get it.

Tam struggled over to the payphone at the edge of the bar and deposited some coins. Barry heard on the grapevine that Tam had splashed out on one of those new portable phones. Either that was bullshit, or he wasn't wanting to wave it around and give the punters more fodder about being a yuppy. Smart move. He'd like to think the call Tam was making was going to change his life, though he knew deep down it wouldn't.

He was probably ringing for a takeout.

Barry hoped that Tam would take at least some of his advice. If only so that Barry could get that hour back on Saturday afternoons. He missed his alone time. And maybe it was the shit-stirrer in him, but he'd love to see the look on the fans' faces if Tam the Bam was in charge. He cared not for the game, but he might even totter through the gates one Saturday just to see that.

Tam muttered a few words, then hung up. He finished his drink. He laid out a five-pound tip for the first time ever. "There you go, ya big brown piper."

"Cheers, Fatso."

It was how they'd always said their goodbyes. But for the first time since Barry had known him, Tam held his head high and didn't engage with the others, who were sniggering and gesturing as he beat a path to the door.

For the first time, he didn't say a thing.

15

Zabe Rwizi had never seen the house in such a state of disrepair. It had always been rundown; Mrs Bamford hadn't any money except the benefits she received which she had to keep two grown adults on. You'd be forgiven for thinking that it hadn't been redecorated since the Blitz, because this was the truth. However, inside, it was always well presented. No matter how Mrs Bamford was feeling, before Zabe arrived for work, the dishes were done, and the hoover run around the carpets.

Mrs Bamford would be turning in her grave at the sight of this, though. Zabe had gotten to know her well enough over the years to be sure of that. The bins were overflowing with pasty wrappers and fizzy drink bottles. The sink was full of dishes, the floors sticky, the carpets mucky. And there was that unmistakable whiff of sweat, filth, farts and who knew what else.

You'd think the woman had been dead for a decade instead of a month.

Janine was also in a bad way. She hadn't bathed in days. She appeared agitated and nervous, no doubt linked to her stint in the psychiatric hospital, a horrible experience for someone who'd recently lost her mother and who'd never spent a night away from home.

Not that the boy was doing much about it. While Zabe gave Janine a bath and washed her hair, the fat man sat on the couch and watched a rerun of *Songs of Praise*. Something was clearly the matter with him, even more so than usual. He always had the football on. And he hated anything to do with God.

"Poor baby," Zabe whispered, as she sat on the edge of the bath and washed and dried the woman's hair. Her mother was all she had. What would become of Janine now? There were no facilities for her on the island. She would have to go into care on the mainland, where she knew nobody. What she needed was love and dedicated care. There was zero chance of that coming from the boy. Zabe herself would happily do it, but she wondered how long she could last in Tam's employ. She hoped a while. She needed the money.

She'd worked for the family—or, more specifically, the mother—for almost ten years. Zabe had left Zimbabwe as a teenager to slip across the border and travel to the diamond mines in the Gauteng Province of South Africa where she worked as a cleaner. It was a relatively well-paid job which enabled her to send money back to her impoverished family. This was where she met her geologist partner, Clive. An older man by some twenty-five years, when retirement came, he decided to settle back on the Isle of Guff in the UK, where his estranged wife and grown-up children were. As she carried his child, Zabe came with him. It had to be better than life as she knew it.

And life for the first few years *was* better. Beautiful, even. They appeared on the BBC's *Gardeners' World* buying a rundown farmhouse where they raised landrace pigs, a breed she was familiar with from her childhood. They brought a beautiful daughter into the world, calling her Missy. They had very little to do with the other Guff residents, instead living remotely on the west coast, lost in their little oasis of contentment.

But all this ended when Clive suffered a brain haemorrhage bringing in the milk one Monday morning and died before he hit the mat. This left her alone with a five-year-old. Also, as they'd never gotten round to getting married, as he'd never gotten a divorce, Clive's actual wife and children took the lot, the farmhouse included. And as she wasn't a British citizen and couldn't afford a lawyer, Zabe was left with nothing.

She had nowhere to go. She'd been too long out of Zimbabwe and though she'd always sent money, returning wasn't an option. Her parents had passed away. To her brothers and sisters, she felt like a mere cash cow. When the money stopped trickling in, she never heard from them.

So, she took the advertised job with Mrs Bamford, and she stayed. The two women grew close, mainly because they'd both been abandoned by their partners, albeit in different ways. Poor Mrs Bamford was denigrated on the island by the actions of her son who, with his lack of people skills and lumbering appearance, stood out for all the wrong reasons.

But that wasn't Mrs Bamford's fault. The locals never understood what it was like to be a single mother to two highly dependent adult children. The girl, Janine, she couldn't help. That was a test from the gods. The boy, as Mrs Bamford often admitted, she could have done better with. However, it was hard with his father fleeing. Tam needed guidance in ways she couldn't give. But the woman had done her best as a mother and a homemaker, even though her chronic lupus never helped. Nor her depression.

Zabe helped Janine out of the bath and dried her. She blow-dried her hair and put her in her dressing gown, ready for the evening. The poor thing was already looking healthier and happier. What was that fool doing putting her in that hospital? She had a sharper mind and far more compassion than him. She just struggled to express herself. Luckily, Zabe could follow most of her cues.

"It's okay, little Miss Bamford." She took Janine's hand when she'd finished brushing her now glowing locks. "You won't be going back there. I'll make sure of that. Even if I take you in myself."

It wasn't perfect being in the employ of Tam, though there was little option. She received no unemployment benefits and had no way of covering the rent on their one-bedroom flat above the baker's (the not very good one). Or of funding her now fourteen-year-old daughter's schooling. With the fishing industry in decline, there were few jobs. When Tam called her the day before and requested that she come in immediately for a trial—despite the fact she'd worked for the family for nine years—she couldn't say no.

Zabe put Radio One on for Janine and helped her into her chair, positioning it in front of the overgrown back garden. She kissed her goodbye. She went through to the lounge and found Tam in his Y-fronts, chewing on a pasty and drinking Lucozade. The TV was showing an old Winston Churchill documentary with the sound down.

"It was a strange game on Saturday without you," she said.

"You go to Rovers matches, do you?"

"I've been a season-ticket holder for nearly fifteen years. I sit three rows back from you." As one of the few women in the stand, and the only one with a black face, he might have known. That, and the fact his mother had informed him countless times over the years that she was a fan.

It had been Clive who got her interested in Guff Rovers. He was originally a Swansea City supporter but living on Guff it made sense to support the local team. Zabe's brothers were mad about football (Tottenham Hotspur especially), as was her whole village. She'd never thought much about the game as it wasn't what women did.

But on the Isle of Guff, and not exactly flooded with recreational activities they could do together with a child, she went along with Clive and caught the bug. She never knew why, as the standard of football was terrible. Guff rarely won and were always struggling near the foot of the table. The food, facilities and weather were awful. Despite this, it slowly consumed her.

When Clive passed, she contemplated giving up her season ticket, then found she couldn't. Instead, she never missed a home match. It made her feel close to him. At great expense, she still bought three season tickets. One for Missy, who loved football even more than her, and an empty seat beside Zabe, which made them feel like Clive was with them.

"Hmph, well, those days are gone," Tam grunted. "I'm post football. The club and the game are dead to me." He belched loudly. "How … how was it?"

"Not good. There are rumours of administration. Ten points could be docked. That would send us bottom. The current squad aren't good enough to bounce back from that."

"Hmph," Tam groaned again as he raced through the channels. He landed on an Italian match—Maradona's Napoli versus Van Basten's AC Milan—but quickly changed the channel again, settling on darts. 'Did anyone in the stands mention the injustice I've been dealt from the dictator at the top? Were there demonstrations? Pitch invasions? A plane overhead dragging a banner bearing my name?"

"There was not." Zabe didn't want to tell him about the carnival atmosphere before the goals went in. How the fans chanted "Glory, Glory, Tam Bam's got a life ban" throughout, followed by "Tam Ban, Tam Ban, Tam Ban" to the tune of 'Here We Go'.

She couldn't remember the last time Guff fans sang about anything.

Zabe hadn't joined in. Although her daughter, along for the first time in weeks, had. Missy was still annoyed at how he'd had the audacity to fire her mother after all she'd done for the family.

Zabe was glad she hadn't joined in because when she got home, she got the call to be home help for Janine. She had sensed an edge of desperation to Tam's voice and, with the word out that he'd come into cash, managed to get him to void the trial and increase his initial offer of one shift a week to two. It was nothing like the four days she'd had before; however, it was a start and she'd somehow make do. Her daughter was applying for a till position at the Co-op which would help. Zabe knew she'd have to give up their season tickets next season, all three of them.

The phone rang. Tam didn't move. He never answered it. She always had, and she did now. "Hello, Bamford residence."

"Hello, Mrs Rhodes?" said a clipped voice.

"Ms. *Rwizi*." Everyone on the island seemed to forget that she'd never married Clive. She, though, would never forget. The poky flat she was now confined to. An end to cars which started on the first go. The holidays in the Greek Isles. The large farmhouse where they could easily afford to run the central heating all day. The fact she had to pander to arseholes like Tam Bam in order to survive. Every minute of every day was a constant reminder that she should have pushed harder for Clive to get that divorce.

"Sorry, Ms. Rwizi."

"Hello, Mr Treloar." She knew who it was. Her daughter's form teacher had often called here. "Is it about Missy?"

"I'm afraid it is. A member of the school staff caught her and her friends outside Spar trying to buy cigarettes."

"I'll kill her."

"The teacher went to grab them, but they made a run for it."

No wonder, Zabe thought. She knew who would have caught them. Mr Greg Dykes, the art assistant. Not even a real teacher. He'd already been reprimanded for allegedly groping a female student in a lake in Totnes during summer camp.

Zabe would have run too.

Still, she would kill her. This was the third time in three months Mr Treloar had called her about smoking and truancy. Her grades were falling: As had slipped to Bs, Bs to Cs. Missy had all but stopped going to the football. That had been family time. Zabe knew that fourteen was a difficult age, but she was realising she no longer knew her daughter.

"I'm so sorry," Zabe said, and she meant it.

"No, no, it's fine. Growing up isn't easy, we all know that. Especially with everything Missy's been through. We'll get her there."

"Thank you, Mr Treloar." He was one of the better ones. He wasn't long out of college and wasn't jaded just yet.

"She's outside my office studying. I'd rather not let her go home by herself."

"I'll be there right away."

In the time she'd been on the phone, Tam had microwaved another pasty. He stood before her munching it. As bad as it smelled, it was an improvement on the stench in the house.

"Did my mother let you take phone calls during working hours?"

Zabe held her tongue. "For the last time, I'm not working. I finished twenty minutes ago. That was the year head at Guff Secondary."

Tam's ears pricked up. "What have you done?"

"It's my Missy."

"Who?"

"My daughter." He didn't even know she had a child.

"And what's the little reprobate done, then?"

"She's a bored teenager. Lost. She's been like this since Rovers cut the girls' youth team. All the girls have."

Tam laughed a gross, messy laugh. "Women's bloody football? That's a joke if ever there was one. It'll never take off."

Zabe didn't respond. She didn't want to prolong the conversation.

She placed her handbag over her shoulder. "I'll be off."

"Off?" Tam glanced in the direction of the dirty plates and pile of old newspapers. "This house is a mess, woman. And what's for my tea?"

"You've employed me as Janine's carer. If you want me to cook and clean for you, that's a bigger undertaking." She looked at her watch. "And anyway, I was supposed to be finished twenty-five minutes ago."

Tam slumped back down, the foldout screeching under his weight. "Take, take, take. That's all this island wants from me."

"You could always do it yourself."

"I'm an invalid. And I've got more important things to do."

"And so have I."

She headed for the door before she said something she might regret. She'd never lost her temper in all her years on Guff. Through all the bad weather and covert racism, on top of the grief she'd endured.

"All right, all right," he called her back. "Five days it is. What was she paying you again?"

Zabe wanted to tell him to stick his job. To grow up. To do it all himself. But she couldn't.

"I want five pounds."

"That's above minimum wage. That's robbery. I'll give you a couple of quid and you'll be grateful for it."

"No, you'll give me five. Have you seen this place? Plus, from what I hear, you can well afford it."

"Two-fifty."

"Five."

They stared at each other. She knew it was a gamble, yet she also knew she was worth it. And she knew it would solve many of her problems.

Tam blinked first.

"Fine," he grumbled. "You can start now. There're pasties in that freezer that need defrosting and heating."

"No. I can start tomorrow. I told you, I have things to do today." She didn't really. Missy would be off with her friends as soon as they got home, despite Zabe trying to stop her. And her own flat, as always, was in good order. Still, she felt it important to stick up for herself and start the way she meant to go on. "I'll see you tomorrow at nine."

Tam flicked the waistband of his tracksuit bottoms under his gut and stretched out in the lounge room. Or the 'good room', as his mother would call it. It was the room taken up by Mrs Bamford's prized Welsh dresser and the photos of her ex-husband and her babies. Tam never used to go in it, happy to live in the semi-converted loft. Hence why it had always looked nice. Not anymore, though. Nuclear test sites looked better.

Tomorrow would be a long day, indeed.

"Is it actually true?" She hesitated in front of the open door.

"What is?" His pudgy face was squashed up against a velvet cushion as he watched another documentary, this one on Arthur Scargill.

"About the five million?"

"That's no one's business but mine."

"What about your club?"

"It's not my club anymore."

She lifted the Sunday newspapers, rolled up on the doormat. She opened the *Cornish Post* to a page where Gus Pinkle was pictured and read the headline:

'GUFF ROVERS CHIEF ADMITS CLUB IS ON THE BRINK OF EXTINCTION'

"Balls it is," Tam replied, not looking up.

Zabe read on. "He says the club's skint, that he's talking to Tesco about selling the ground, that the situation is killing him."

"He would, wouldn't he."

"That they can't even pay the hot water bill."

"Good. Those animals on the pitch don't deserve full amenities."

She read out the Gus Pinkle quote underneath. *"'The coffers are empty. We have a top-class manager in Gary Pullman, but he needs investment. I'd love to give him some proper backing and see what he could do for this club in the longer term.'"*

"That fraud!"

She had his attention now. Zabe had sat behind the man for enough seasons of mediocrity to know what wound his clock. "Someone should do something."

"Hmph." Tam focused on Scargill addressing a mob of miners.

"The fans had a whip-round at half-time to raise money for Roger Greenhill's consortium to buy him out."

"What?' Tam roared. "That's even worse."

"It's a good thing you don't care anymore."

She closed the door behind her, leaving him with that thought. As she walked to the bus stop, she heard that unmistakable sound of Tam flipping the TV set against the wall, smashing it.

Things were so bad at Guff Rovers that, as unstable and reprehensible as he was, Thomas Bamford might just be the man to save the club. Plus, for the sake of the poor deceased Mrs Bamford, it could be the thing to save the man himself.

16

The phone rang. This was the third time in the past five minutes. Whoever it was could wait.

Forever.

The colt felt good in Gus's mouth. Snug on his tongue, the steel cool against his inside cheek. He thought about how the bullet would feel as it pierced his brain. Probably the opposite of snug and cool, but that wouldn't last long. Gus had dusted the gun well. He wondered how many Jerrys his father had popped with it back on the beaches of Normandy. He hoped it still worked.

It had to work.

It had to blow his brains out cleanly. He didn't want to be one of those people in a wheelchair with half a face. He hadn't got much right lately, but this, *this*, he couldn't screw up.

Still, he didn't want to die. Not really. He thought of the things he'd wanted to do in life. Things that would never happen now. He wouldn't get to walk his daughter down the aisle. His daughter was a lesbian, he was sure. Those dungarees, big hands and short fingernails were a giveaway. Yet the way the world was heading, marriage could happen one day. He wouldn't get to be a grandfather to her children, either. Ditto, she could probably pull that off soon as well.

He wouldn't get to reconcile with Sabrina. He'd been such a stupid bastard messing about with Felicity. The younger woman had flirted with him for a job. He couldn't even succeed in having a functional affair. He should've waited until she gave him a clear sign before booking that weekend in Paris. He definitely shouldn't have paid for it from the joint account. That had bought him a year in the doghouse.

He wouldn't get to buy a yacht and sail around the world like he'd always dreamed. He wouldn't get to see Guff Rovers climb off their knees.

He'd never get to make his father proud, even if the old boy was ten years in the ground. His picture was propped against the wall. Gus spotted the pasty mark from last week, the film of sticky lemonade and the shards of glass puncturing it.

Gus had never been a quitter. A bullet to the brain was such a cop-out. But no, it was better this way, he reminded himself. He'd sneered at those who'd taken the old gas-pipe-in-the-car route. But bankruptcy? The indignation of having to sell his home? Maybe get a job? Join the real world? Hell, that would be much, much worse. And what would his fellow Masons say?

Gus removed the barrel from his mouth so he could finish his last dark and stormy. That felt better, a sweet contrast to the metallic taste. He wanted to finish the bottle. Didn't want to put the barrel back in. Still, needs must. That derisory offer from Tesco after they'd led him so far down the garden path—an offer which would struggle to pay his annual rum bill—was the final straw.

He put his finger on the trigger. In a few seconds it would all be over, and Gus Pinkle would be free.

Suddenly he heard deep footsteps. They were ascending the stairs. The front door was locked, he'd made sure of it. He'd heard these steps before. Definitely not Felicity's kitten heels. Nor Morticia Addams's knee-high Dr. Martens. Couldn't be Pullman's squeaky trainers. He'd seen the Londoner drive off hours ago, early as usual.

The door rapped. Gus lowered the gun. He sweated like a bastard on heat.

"Who is it?"

"It's your knight in shining armour."

Tam Bam. What did this basket case want?

"You're banned."

"Well, that's something we may need to reassess."

Gus stuffed the pistol under the cushion of his chair, dried his tears, cleared his throat.

"Come in then."

The door opened, and in it thundered. Looking as bulbous and sweaty as ever. But now wearing some ridiculous knock-off Hermès scarf instead of his grimy Guff Rovers one.

"Don't you pick up your phone anymore?" Tam studied the chairman behind the desk. "You look bloody awful, man!"

"Thanks for that." It didn't get much worse than being told by Tam Bam that you looked a sight. "Take a seat, I suppose."

Tam obliged, almost flattening the red oak piece Gus had imported from California (which had cost two grand for a pair).

"So, let me guess," Gus said. "You want to be a director."

"Nope, way better than that." Tam popped four Rennie from out of the foil packet with a satisfying crack, shoving them in his gob. "I've been thinking—"

"Here we go."

"I want to be the gaffer."

Gus laughed, slipping into a coughing fit at the same time. "You what?"

"You heard me."

"It's not possible. We have a manager in Gary Pullman, the best in the division. A man who has—"

Tam cut him off. "An arsehole of the highest order who's won one game in ten and taken us to the brink of relegation."

"It'd cost big bucks to get rid of him."

"Thanks to you, putting him on a three-year deal."

"Four years, actually."

"You bandit."

"It's done now."

"I'd sue him for gross incompetence. He'd get nothing."

Gus saw the determination in Tam's eyes and grasped for something, anything. "But you … you … you don't have the experience. The qualifications."

"I've already greased the right palms in Switzerland. Made the calls this morning. I can have the coaching certificates framed and on that wall by the close of business." Tam, arms crossed, nodded to the empty space behind Gus.

"That's impossible."

"No, that's Zurich."

"I … well … I have to think about it."

"You think about it all you want, but I didn't have to beat past many bodies on my way up here to make my generous offer."

"You haven't made me any offer yet."

"One hundred percent of the club. And I'll clear the debt."

Gus tried to laugh again. He found he couldn't. What choice did he really have? Guff were playing Hartlepool away on Saturday. The furthest-away fixture on the calendar, and one of the very few they needed a flight for. Back in his father's day, the club would make an event of a trip to the north-east. They would stay over in a hotel on the night before and the night after. It was a jolly. Nothing to do but eat, drink and philander. The football was secondary, and not being the chairman back then meant there was bugger all for Gus to do except get on it. And he did so with aplomb.

Those days were gone. Now they flew in on the morning and were out of there as soon as the final whistle sounded. Sometimes the players didn't even have time for a bath. Gus had already whittled the travelling party down to the bare bones. Players, manager, Jimmy Dolan. He didn't even go anymore. He wasn't upset about that in all honesty now that he'd grown up and seen a bit of the world. He knew that Hartlepool was a shithole, and the women were best avoided.

The women who hung around the Guff squad, anyway.

But these days it was his duty to make sure the team got there. The only thing was, and the thing that no one else knew (not even Felicity), he still hadn't booked the flights and now the price for a party of fifteen to travel was three grand. And with barely a pound to his name, there was no way he could afford it. And he had zero idea how it would happen.

Perhaps he could ring that mad fan Roger Greenhill. Guilt him into floating the cash for the trip. It worked last season. And the season before that. It was either that or the loss of the three points and most certainly a further point's deduction along with another fine, this one for much more than three grand. The FA loved to kick the little guys in the knackers when they were down. Gus really had no choice but to dance with the devil. Or Tam Bam, rather, which appeared to be the devil's nom de plume nowadays.

Then the realisation dawned on him that he could be free. Truly free and still alive. Visions of the ocean and tropical islands swirled inside his head. And suddenly the whole thing started to seem okay.

Gus Pinkle could be free from it all.

And just as the thought crossed his mind, the picture of his father fell face-first onto the carpet, landing on an upright tack, piercing his father between the eyes.

"Forty percent of the club is what I'll sell to you," Gus told him. As much as it was appealing, for the sake of the family name, Gus couldn't hand it all over.

"Sixty percent," Tam demanded.

"Forty-nine percent, then."

"Fifty-one percent."

"Fifty percent."

"Fifty-one percent," Tam repeated, giving him an iron stare. Gus had never seen him like this. "Fifty-one percent. You stay on as chairman, I get the manager's job. Or I leave this office right now and watch you lose the lot."

Gus paused. "Excuse me a moment."

He rose and went to the bathroom adjoining the office. He rested his buttocks on the lukewarm pine seat. He didn't feel like going, though he wished he did as he'd been backed up for days. But he had to think, and he couldn't with that mutant's face looking at him.

Pros: Debt free. And Tam wouldn't be a director and wouldn't be stinking up his office every home game. Gus could be left to his own devices. He'd no longer have to invite Sir House of Fraser or any other fuckwit with balls in his mouth up to his cherished pad, begging for scraps.

Cons: Who knew what havoc this lunatic would wreak on the touchline? The man was mentally unhinged. The club would be a bigger laughing stock. The fans would hit the roof.

But still, pros, pros, focus on the pros.

He could keep his house and wipe that six-figure credit card debt. Heck, he could start doing what he wanted to do with his life. He could finally follow his own dreams and not those of his father.

Cons, though. Who knew how far the club would fall and how low it would go? And that Pullman thug would literally twist his neck Millwall-style when he found out. He'd never wanted to come across here. Gus had to feed him all manner of lies about plans for a new stadium and a training complex, which Pullman had swallowed. He'd even bought a bungalow on the south-east coast of the island.

Ah, but who was he kidding? Gus held no cards here. He'd already taken his Bentley to the dealers this morning and scraped ten grand for it. A quarter of what it was worth. He'd even had to suffer the indignity of booking an economy ticket to Capri next week for his mid-winter break.

Gus felt a weight empty from him, and his bowels relaxed. He shat long and firmly. Hallelujah! It was as good as his first orgasm to that Jean Shrimpton pull-out in the *News of the World* back in the day. Gus wiped, flushed, scrubbed his hands, and stepped out into the great unknown.

He found Tam pacing his office, perusing the collection of fine rums. He was muttering unkindly, his face screwed up, as he chewed from a bowl of Brazil nuts that he'd found in the cabinet. "There's more value in here than the crap that's running around out there."

"I need this to entertain," countered Gus. "To show our distinguished guests what a fine, upstanding club we are."

"Bollocks you do. All this tripe should be housed in a tin shed. Your desk with you behind it as well. Everything should be invested on the pitch."

"You'd better not be having any ideas about kicking me out of here. You worry about what goes on out on the pitch. You leave me to deal with what goes on off it."

"So, we have a deal then?"

Gus thought of his father. The portrait of him was still face down on the floor. Stabbed, spat on, everything but shat on. He'd be turning in his grave if he knew this imbecile was about to run his beloved club. But what else could he do? Not use the club's funds to purchase the Bentley or his Spanish villa? Admittedly, that would've helped; hindsight is a wonderful thing. Still, what was done was done. And surely all this was better than shooting himself in the face.

"You call Pullman and tell him," Gus eventually said.

Tam smiled. "I'll tell him personally to his face."

"So, it's a deal?"

"Yes, we have a deal."

Gus was feeling a toxic mix of elation and dread. Relief and regret. His heart thumped to the beat of the multitude of possibilities and repercussions of what he'd done.

The men shook hands. Gus felt relieved that Tam hadn't hocked into his palm first, though judging by the amount of perspiration on it, he may as well have.

Feeling lighter due to the deal and his trip to the toilet, Gus sat back behind his desk. "Obviously, there are a few things to—"

BANG!

"Aargh!" Tam screamed, collapsing.

"Jesus Christ!" Gus froze. "I've killed the bastard."

His left buttock had hit the cushion and must have pulled the trigger. The headlines were going to be bad regardless, but they'd be a whole lot worse once the press got a hold of the story that he'd murdered Guff Rovers' biggest fan and newest investor.

What was even worse was that it was his only bullet. Gus couldn't now go ahead with his original plan and check out of planet earth.

He leapt over the desk. "Tam, Tam, are you all right?" The figure lay there, still as a freshly felled beech tree. Gus shook him by the neck. "Tell me you're all right!"

Tam brushed him off. "Of course, I'm not all right. You've assassinated me, you cretin."

Through the fat man's fingers which clutched at his arm, Gus could see a tiny drop of blood squeezing out of a small tear of the smelly green coat which the bullet had brushed. Beyond this, Gus saw the portrait of his father, Royston. The bullet had struck the door handle, bounced down and lodged itself in his heart.

Bullseye.

Gus examined the wound closer. "It's only a graze." Thank fuck for that. Gus felt like kissing it. It was only a graze!

Tam's neck arched up, Gus's words sending colour back into his chops. "You tried to murder me."

"A complete accident."

"I should call the police."

"Please don't." His wife and children did not need to know about this. Nor did anyone else on the island. "Here, I'll make you a cuppa."

"I need blood. I need an ambulance."

"You need a new coat, that's all."

Tam crawled to the door. "If you're not going to get me the appropriate care I urgently need, then I shall have to drag myself there."

"Okay, then. I'll drive you." He'd only had five, maybe seven rums.

"I refuse to go anywhere with my executioner." Tam latched on to the dented door handle and struggled up. "I shall call an ambulance myself."

"Fine, I'll book you a cab."

"It's the least you can do."

Gus dialled. "I'll see you tomorrow."

"What for?"

"There are contracts to sign. We'll have to announce this to the press."

"I imagine I'll be in hospital for a good while. Months, maybe. There's the wound, and the shock, and all the stress it's put on my heart."

"You're the boss. But can I ask you one favour?"

"What's that?" Tam asked, pinching the hole in his mac. "And hurry. I'm bleeding to death here."

"For the good of the club, please don't tell anyone I shot you."

Tam thought it over. "For the good of the club, provided I make it through this ordeal, I'll keep shtum until my autobiography." A horn beeped. "Till next time, Lee Harvey bloody Oswald." Tam turned and staggered down the stairs like he'd been popped with a magazine.

Gus slid to the floor. What a baptism of fire that was. He reached for the bottle of rum, unscrewed the cap, and took a much-needed slug, not caring if he was spilling it. Surely things couldn't get worse than that. Surely things could only get better.

Surely?

17

Transcript from Guff Rovers' press conference
Wednesday, February 1, 1989
11.08 a.m.

On the steps of the stadium entrance stand a shivering GUS PINKLE—Chairman of Guff Rovers, and PHIL GATES—Chief Sports Reporter at the Cornish Times.

GUS PINKLE: I thought there'd be more press here.

PHIL GATES: Think the radio has a few staffing issues at the moment. Where's the new guy?

GUS PINKLE: In the canteen. He's just realised that now that he owns half the club, he doesn't have to pay for grub. Not directly, anyway.

PHIL GATES: (*looking at his watch*) There's a sixteen-year-old one-armed rower I have to interview in Truro at midday.

GUS PINKLE: Can't you wait for the others? Isn't this bigger?

PHIL GATES: Not really.

GUS PINKLE: Okay. Fire away.

The reporter holds up his dictaphone.

PHIL GATES: Referring to the memo we received about you sacking Gary Pullman and moving Rovers' superfan Tam Bam into the hot seat. I have one question …

GUS PINKLE: Shoot.

PHIL GATES: Have you lost your mind?

GUS PINKLE: Mr Bamford is writing off the debt. The club's debt.

PHIL GATES: But have you lost your mind?

GUS PINKLE: We're now in rude financial health.

PHIL GATES: Yes, but have you lost your mind?

GUS PINKLE: I did it for the benefit of the club.

The reporter lowers the dictaphone.

PHIL GATES: What are you doing, man? He'll lead us—sorry, I mean, Guff—to rack and ruin.

GUS PINKLE: Point taken. But unless you have five million quid stuffed down your sofa, I have no choice.

PHIL GATES: Fair enough. Man alive, it's freezing out here. Any chance of a cuppa?

GUS PINKLE: Can't. Kettle's broke. We've ordered a new one from Argos.

PHIL GATES: Well, can we not go inside to the meeting room?

GUS PINKLE: Blue mould. Place has been condemned until the chippy arrives.

PHIL GATES: If it doesn't rain, it pours.

GUS PINKLE: Telling me. But seriously, where is everyone? I didn't sleep a wink. I thought they'd hang me for this.

PHIL GATES: Goes to show that no one gives a toss about the club anymore. I think you should count your lucky stars that your press release wasn't binned by me as well this morning.

GUS PINKLE: But there's no such thing as bad press. Is there?

PHIL GATES: With this mentalist in charge? You wait and see.

GUS PINKLE: It won't be all that bad. He's come into a bit of money, and I'm already seeing a change in the man. He'll rise to the challenge. I'm sure he'll be—

At this point TAM BAM comes out carrying a tray of pasties and a large bottle of Lucozade. He has a crude homemade Guff patch featuring the shipwreck crest sewn over his sleeve.

TAM BAM: Hoy, Pinkle. Get in there and get that canteen woman told that I own this place. She charged me fourteen quid for all this.

GUS PINKLE: Um, yes, Tam. Here, talk to this reporter. He wants to know your plans for the team.

TAM BAM: Keegan, Cruyff, Beckenbauer. I want all the greats gracing the turf here at Faery Meadow.

PHIL GATES: Have you been in a coma? Do you have brain damage? They were all put out to grass years ago.

TAM BAM: Class is permanent. Have you seen the princesses in this league that have the pomposity to call themselves professionals? Those boys could still do a job. They'd love it down here. The cosmopolitan culture, the fervent fans ...

A mob of TEENAGERS wander past. One with a hoop earring and a dark-blue Adidas tracksuit lobs a half-empty can of Special Brew. Tam has to side-step to avoid it as it lands and splashes the trio.

LAD: (*chants*) You fat bastard, you fat bastard!

TAM BAM ignores him and continues on.

TAM BAM: Then there's the weather.

A timely gust of wind has them reaching for a street lamp, nearly knocking them off their feet.

PHIL GATES: Why not try for Careca? Baresi? Maradona? I'm sure their model wives will be dying to leave the Med when they see the state of this shit-heap.

TAM BAM: No one's ever going to come here if you put that in your article. You need to talk us up a bit more. That's the problem with you lot. All doom and gloom. This is the greatest island in the world. The jewel in Britain's crown.

A randy bull clops wildly down the street. A police car races past in hot pursuit.

PHIL GATES: I call it as I see it. Journalist ethics and all.

TAM BAM: Is that why you did that puff piece when Pullman pulled up sticks here? It sounded like a bloody marriage proposal.

PHIL GATES: Tosh. The guy's a proven manager. It was a coup, someone like Guff getting him.

TAM BAM: Aye, such a coup that we're second bottom.

PHIL GATES: Hardly his fault. There's no money. Club even sold the carpark. I had to park four blocks away.

TAM gives GUS a sour look regarding this sore point.

GUS PINKLE: My office wasn't going to furnish itself.

GARY PULLMAN and his son JAMIE PULLMAN depart the building. The older man is carrying a cardboard box with his belongings.

TAM cheers and points.

TAM BAM: Take a picture of that, Mr Reporter. No matter what it's cost me, that image alone makes it worth every penny.

JAMIE PULLMAN—still on crutches—makes a run for TAM and is restrained by his father.

JAMIE PULLMAN: It'll be worth me ending you, ya fat fuck.

GARY PULLMAN: Leave it, you've already been inside once. Just remember the three hundred grand we're walking away with for doing sweet F.A.

TAM BAM: What's that?

GARY PULLMAN: You ask your esteemed chairman all about it. (*He turns to the others.*) Gentlemen of Guff Rovers, it's been an absolute pleasure.

The Pullmans get in their Range Rover and skid off, the younger man flipping them the bird.

TAM BAM: What's he on about?

GUS PINKLE: You wanted to dismiss him. So, I had to honour the remainder of the contracts. The both of them.

TAM BAM: You gave them three hundred grand of my cash?!

GUS PINKLE: It's £306,271.28 of the club's cash now.

PHIL GATES: And still, I can't get a cup of tea.

TAM BAM: What else have you wasted my money on?

GUS PINKLE: My Bentley needed a new battery and service.

TAM BAM: Thief!

GUS PINKLE: I'm the chairman. I need to get around.

TAM BAM: Get the bus. Don't you spend another cent until you run it by me.

GUS PINKLE: If that's the case, I'll be calling every five minutes. This is a professional football club, not the Hare Krishnas.

TAM BAM: Wasting my hard-earned coin. This sort of thing has been going on for too long round here.

PHIL GATES: (*cuts in*) I've got that one-armed rower to get to. Can I please have a—

GUS PINKLE: (*to Tam*) You could have settled for being a director, then you would've had a bigger say.

PHIL GATES: Please, I need a quick quote about your plans for the future, where you aim to finish the season, that sort of—

TAM BAM: I should sack you.

GUS PINKLE: You can't sack the chairman.

TAM BAM: My extra two percent of ownership says I can.

GUS PINKLE: And my solicitor says you can't.

At this point, PHIL GATES pockets his dictaphone. Amidst all the arguing, he doesn't bother to say farewell. He walks the four blocks back to his car and drives to the port to make his other interview, stopping to pick up a cup of tea along the way.

18

"I suppose if it were a five-a-side game we'd be all right," Jimmy Dolan said, peeling back the pages of the new Filofax his niece bought him for Christmas. He was a self-confessed Luddite and missed his old builder's notebook, the one that fitted neatly into his shirt pocket. He had no idea how to use this phonebook-looking thing, which took two hands to hold. The only thing he had any clue about was being a kit man and physio and chief scout for Guff Rovers, as that was all he'd known for the past thirty years.

And the groundsman as well—he sometimes forgot that.

"Gentlemen," the woman at the Land's End airport's check-in desk called to them. "The pilot informs me you have ten minutes before he takes off."

"Does that mean I can go for a quick fag?" Jimmy asked. He was choking for one. It had been at least a quarter of an hour since his last.

"God, no," shouted Tam. "Get on that blower and find my bloody squad."

Jimmy flicked through the book but couldn't locate the numbers. He should have brought his glasses. Should he find the digits he was looking for, he dreaded what to do with Tam's mobile phone which lay in wait in his other hand. He'd never even seen one before.

Tam appeared more anxious than usual, and Jimmy would know. He'd known him, or rather known of him, for all his years with the club. Jimmy first came across the man when he debuted in a cup-tie against Peterborough in 1955. Aged nineteen, Jimmy was new to the club.

The gaffer at the time, Peter Webb, had high hopes for him. However, when he ran out and took his place on the left-flank, it wasn't his more experienced marker who would prove to be his biggest obstacle. It was one of his own fans. A fat kid with a can of pop and a pasty, hanging over the rail.

Tam Bam.

From his very first touch, Tam was on him. "Whip it in ... Take him out ... Kick him in the kiwis!"

Jimmy had never experienced anything like it, and he'd served his apprenticeship at Liverpool where standards were the among the highest. Each time he collected the ball, he faced a commentary from the sidelines. Jimmy was already the nervous type, and the moment something went wrong—which was every single time—the fat kid was on his back.

"You're a joke, you short-arsed bastard. Where'd they find you, at the bottom of a cereal packet?"

Jimmy did fine away from home, laying on a few assists, and even scoring the odd goal. But when a home game approached, he'd have nightmares in the lead-up about the big overbearing kid with the booming voice. And then when game day came, he'd arrive short on sleep, even shorter on confidence, and couldn't do anything right. And he was so bad it wasn't long before the entire crowd was on his back.

He started drinking after each match, and then he started smoking. It began as a Saturday night thing to cheer him up after yet another below-par performance. Soon his love of port and Woodbines overlapped to Sundays, then Mondays, and then the whole week. He became useless at training, as well as games, and couldn't blame Tam Bam for this.

Peter Webb had little choice but to drop him. Then Jimmy struggled for consistency in the reserves until he was no longer picked for them, either. Too old for youth football, he was offered a move to non-league Yeovil Town. He didn't want to go away again. His family was on the island, homesickness being the biggest reason the former local golden boy hadn't made the grade in Merseyside.

Webb, who was a nice old man who'd always thought highly of young Jimmy, said he could stay on as kit man. Jimmy, who truth be told never wanted to kick a ball again, said yes.

Since then, he'd been happy in the role. Later, he branched out doing a masseuse course by correspondence. He was also handy with a lawnmower and hoe. Then subsequent gaffers noticed Jimmy had an eye for a player. With no budget to bring someone in, he found himself named chief scout.

Time went by, owner Royston Pinkle passed away, and his son took over. Costs were slashed further, making him officially responsible for all four roles. Jimmy didn't mind. He was happy to be involved. Still, whenever he saw Tam, he pondered what could have been had the superfan given him some encouragement when he played.

And now, with Tam Bam as the new gaffer, he would be seeing him a lot more.

Tam fronted up to the woman at the desk. "We're the island's football team. The meat in its sandwich, the cream on its cake. I'm not asking for a roll of red carpet, though that would be nice and somewhat fitting. But you can tell Biggles, that plane is going nowhere, or else I'll be marching into that cockpit and sitting on the bastard."

"You're actually not allowed to make threats like that anymore," she informed him. "That can get you ten years."

"PC bloody madness."

"Wait, wait." Jimmy waved his Filofax in the air. "I think I've got it."

"Give me that." Tam looked at the page:

RORY MCGRORY
864878

"Do you still want me to call him, gaffer?" Jimmy asked, eyeing the phone fearfully.

"I'll do it." Tam took the phone and carefully punched in the numbers. He popped yet another Rennie, his lips and tongue now turning a comical bright white. He paced loudly around the six players who'd bothered to turn up, waiting for his call to be answered. "This number doesn't work."

"What's wrong with it?" Jimmy asked.

"It's engaged."

"That's because I'm on the line to him," the woman at the desk said, holding a cordless against her shoulder with her chin as she typed.

"To whom?" Tam asked.

"Your captain."

"How'd you know his number?"

"I'm from Guff myself. It's a small island. Everyone knows everyone's number."

"And what's he saying?"

"That he and the others aren't coming."

"They're what?!"

She covered the mouthpiece. "He said they're on strike. They haven't been paid their last two weeks' wages."

"Pinkle, that ass! The amount I've had to cover this past week. Loan repayments, car repayments, horse dental bills. He's fleecing me every hour. Tell him I'll put it in the bank first thing Monday."

She continued typing. "He said they'll only start playing when they start seeing some cash."

"Mercenaries! We're late for a flight. It's Saturday. I can't get the bloody cheddar now."

"You mean we actually get paid for playing?" Darren Dangerfield asked, not looking up from *Astro Bomber,* which he was playing on his handheld Game Pocket. "I thought this was an amateur club?"

"I don't even have a bank account," keeper Lance Posobiec said as he noisily munched through a bag of Space Raiders.

"I forgot my PIN number," Zak Bates added, carefully polishing his boots, a proper pair, now featuring a left and right boot. "I haven't checked my account in months."

"In all fairness," the lady at the desk said hanging up. "I don't think they fancy it."

"He said that?" Tam seethed. "I'll sell them all."

"It's a bad line. But between you and me, I can hear seagulls, waves and an engine. If I'm not mistaken, I think they've made a day of it and are a few miles offshore."

"Jesus, take the wheel! Does no one else give a shit about this football club?"

"They went fishing?" Dangerfield put down his console. "Can we boycott the game and go too?"

"You're going nowhere, you." Tam turned to Jimmy. "Right, get the youth team's phone numbers." Jimmy skimmed through the Filofax as quick as he could. "I want them all here. It's about time we gave some fresh blood a chance."

Jimmy still couldn't make heads or tails of the thing. It was upside down for starters. How he missed his trusty old notebook. He didn't know what he'd do if computers and phones became the future, like the young folk all said.

The woman at the desk pointed to the clock above. "You have two minutes, gents."

"Give me that." Tam snatched the Filofax. Through with his fat fingers, he couldn't even open it. Frustrated, he pitched it at the

Rothmans billboard facing them.

The woman called back over, still cradling the phone. "Right, do you want the good news or the bad?"

"The good news," Jimmy said, collecting the Filofax. He didn't know if Tam could handle any more of the bad kind.

"I got through to your youth captain."

"How'd you manage that?" Tam asked again.

"I thought we'd already established that?"

"Right you are."

"Anyway, half the youth squad are on their way."

"Magic, we're on!" Tam punched the air. "Three points are in the bag."

"What's the bad news?" Jimmy had to ask.

"How long have you got?" she answered. "Last night was the captain's eighteenth. I'm well aware of that one because my son, Samuel, was there. A big bash at some rave in the woods. I've come off the phone to his mother, who I know from badminton. She's been through a lot lately, that poor woman. Husband left for a junior accountant he met at a course in Coventry. Used their savings to move there. Then her father had angina and—"

Tam sighed. "Can you please jump to the part of the story where I start caring?"

"Long story short, the boys haven't been to bed yet."

"Roger me raw!" Tam shouted. "And the nation wonders why we can't win another World Cup."

"Also"—she pointed out the window to where a small British Midland plane hurtled down the runway—"that's your plane."

"I ordered you to hold it."

She consulted her computer. "There is another one which leaves in just over two hours. However, that involves a stop in Bristol, then another in Dundee."

"Dundee?" Tam moaned.

"And that will get you into Durham Airport at 2.10 p.m. You should—*should*—make kick-off."

Tam stomped his moon boot on the tiles. "This is a bloody outrage."

"It's all I can do," she said. "Best of luck, boys. I'll be at this desk should you need me."

"What a mess." Tam slumped to the tiles. "Does this happen every away day?"

"More or less," replied Jimmy. "There've been Saturdays where we've had to take random blokes off the street and get them to pretend they're our players."

"That would explain our crap away record."

"The officials never know. We're hardly Juventus." Jimmy noticed Tam clasping a crisp blue passport. "You know you don't need that for a domestic flight."

"Of course you do. You need it every time you leave the island." Tam trembled so much that the book was twirling between his fingers like a hand fan.

"You want a cup of tea or anything, gaff?"

Tam was also perspiring more than usual. "You got a Valium or something?"

"I think there's a couple of aspirin kicking about the bottom of my bag. You have flown before, right?"

Tam began hyperventilating. "Shut up and get those aspirin." Jimmy didn't need to be told again. Tam forced them down with no water. "Excuse me, matron," he called to the desk. "Where is the bar?"

"There isn't one at this airport, I'm afraid. We're too small."

Tam leapt down the hall, his crutch swinging like a bayonet, as other passengers ducked for cover.

"Where you going?" Jimmy asked.

"I'm finding the duty-free."

"There's no duty-free. This is a domestic airport."

Tam froze. "What?!"

"You said you don't drink."

"Aye, and I've never been on a plane before either." And with that he turned, and he fled. "Hold the plane. I'm off to find the bloody pub."

Now Jimmy knew why Tam 'Superfan' Bam never annoyed him at away matches.

Jimmy shared a shy look of nervous despair with the lady at the desk. With her blonde bob and green eyes, she reminded him of June, his old flame. They had such plans. Him to make it as a footballer. June to make it as an actress. They got engaged in Liverpool. But when they returned to the island and his form dipped, the engagement was off. She told him she was off to London for some big assignment. She never came back. And he never did marry.

Jimmy took the opportunity to sneak out for that smoke. He saw Tam puffing and wheezing across the carpark in search of a drink, his moon boot having gathered a Walkers' salt and vinegar crisp packet along the way. At least Jimmy was fit. Lugging thirteen strips and twenty-six pairs of boots around the country saw to that. Never mind washing and ironing it all. Add to this all that massaging and mowing and scouting, and he was busy to the tune of a hundred hours a week.

He lit up and inhaled, satisfied. Jimmy never had time to meet someone else or mourn the loss of his June. He didn't have time to dwell upon how his life could have been very different if it wasn't for Tam Bam. He sometimes wondered what would have happened had Tam not jumped on his back all those years ago, and he could have made a real go of it in the first team. Liverpool would have come and taken another look at him like they promised. He could've played under Bill Shankly. He and June could've gone back there and made it work.

And if his uncle had knockers, she would've been his aunty.

It was good he was at Guff Rovers. The club needed him, and that was all that mattered. All through Jimmy Dolan's life, the club had been the only constant since his hopes of being a professional went down the plughole and June left.

He never did hear from her. He eventually found out what she was up to. It was on a weekday morning a few years later when he got to the club, had his cuppa and opened the front page of *The Sun*.

To this day, he still had that picture of her tits taped to the inside of his locker.

19

If this was the big time, CJ Adeyemi wanted more of it.

He'd heard of players swigging beer in the dressing room after matches, but never before them. Yet here he and his fellow youth players were, in the changerooms at Victoria Park, splitting a crate of Stella and passing a bottle of Buckfast tonic wine as New Order boomed out on the ghetto blaster.

All except Seth Graham, the skinhead with the big curly beard who some reckoned was one of those Amish types you see in the odd American flick. The keeper had never said boo since CJ first met him in the under-14s, never mind drink. He was in the starting line-up after first-team keeper Lance Posobiec was rushed to hospital with a suspected broken neck following a bizarre neck spasm when collecting his holdall from the luggage belt at Durham Airport.

The weird thing was that all this partying was out in the open. In fact, it was the gaffer's idea when they landed. With the majority of the six youth team players having not slept due to CJ's eighteenth birthday exertions, they'd been rapidly fading on the plane. The new gaffer, who himself was on his fourth miniature brandy, ordered that the first stop when they landed should be to the off-licence. He thought the best strategy was to let the younger players keep the party going until the final whistle.

What Tam really wanted was more St Agnes to calm his nerves. The drink seemed to have done the trick for him on the flight.

Sort of.

The air hostess had to tie him to the seat and gag him to stop him screaming and attempting to storm the cockpit and grab the controls to land the plane on the A38. It was either that or the pilot was turning the plane around.

As they changed into their Guff Rovers' first-team strips, CJ and his younger teammates were buzzing about making their league debuts. They were buzzing even more from the wrap of speed they'd smuggled onto the plane and snorted lines from in the toilet. This was something Tam and the other senior members of the squad did not know about.

The younger players were bouncing off the changeroom walls. They couldn't wait to get out there and tear into the opposition. All except poor Cal Mathie. The young left-midfielder was usually more of a loner stoner. While everyone else at the party had been ee-d out of their boxes, he'd been smoking bucket bongs and doing mushrooms and now he was not in a good place at all. He'd consented to a solitary can of Stella, something he usually never did, but it wasn't helping his paranoia. He knew he shouldn't have snarfed that microdot when they'd hit the tarmac.

He hadn't said a word since.

He couldn't look at anyone. He asked CJ when his third eye would close and his teammates would stop resembling Oompa Loompas from *Charlie and the Chocolate Factory,* a movie which had given him nightmares as a child. Or when Darren Dangerfield would stop looking like Skeletor.

CJ emerged from the cubicle following another fat line. He cracked open a can. He wondered if you could do this every game and get away with it. Probably not in the topflight. Then again, Besty did. Bryan Robson and Gazza, too, so he'd heard.

No, last night was a one-off. The greatest. He'd even scored a shag off Becca Rice. That had made his night until Meggsy told him she'd given everyone that for their eighteenth. And it would ruin his birthday if his girlfriend, Lyla, found out. Then again, she was the one who decided to go on a gap year to Jersey. Who knew what little surprises she'd bring back with her?

If he was honest, it freaked him out when Lyla called him right after he came out the bedroom with Becca. They were at a disco, Lyla told him. She wished him a happy birthday, though she seemed a bit cold, a bit distant. When pressed, she said there was something she wanted to talk to him about later. He knew it meant he was getting the flick, so fuck it.

CJ had dreamed of playing for the first team since he could kick a ball. Since he'd gone to his first Guff Rovers home game aged six. The fact it was a dull scoreless draw and he'd since forgotten who they played didn't matter. He'd turned down trials with Plymouth and Southampton to make it happen. When he signed youth forms two years ago, he made a hundred-pound bet with his stepdad that he would make his debut before he was eighteen. As his actual birthday wasn't until Monday, that cash was his.

There was a knock on the dressing room door. "Time, lads," came the ref's call.

Tam was still in the toilet. And given the ungodly sounds and odours emanating from the cubicle, he sure wasn't snorting lines. There'd been no team talk, no word about positions or tactics. They knew who was playing because they'd only brought over twelve players and now the keeper was in ER. The subs were two fifteen-year-olds they'd found on the way to the ground and told to impersonate Guff players for a tenner each, a large bottle of Diamond White and ten fags.

Tam emerged, wiping vomit from his lips with his ragged brown-and-pink Rovers scarf. He looked like he'd lost a few stone. What little colour he possessed had departed his bland features.

"Right, you lot," he said hoarsely. "You get out there and do your thing."

The Buckfast returned to CJ. He took a final swig. That speed was making him tingle nicely. He felt like he could run out there and flip cars. He made sure he didn't finish that last can of Stella, though. He wasn't a complete amateur.

They lined up at the door, shouting and geeing each other up. Tam removed the scarf from around his neck. It was so faded that it looked more dark grey than pink. It sure hadn't seen soap and water since Guff were briefly in the third-tier back in the sixties. CJ, standing three feet away, spotted flecks of green vomit around its tassels. He thought he could smell them too.

Tam unravelled the garment, holding it aloft in a 'You'll Never Walk Alone' pose. A tear abseiled down his chubby left cheek. "See this, boys. I want you to die for it. You've got to die for it."

They all nodded and roared.

"Fuck yeah!" CJ screamed.

"On the way into the tunnel, I want each of you to kiss my scarf."

The boys were not so enthusiastic about this last request, especially Cal Mathie, who thought Tam had said "arse".

Most of the kids were Man U or Liverpool fans. Growing up, their local team had never been more than an occasional joke and a constant source of embarrassment. But the sentiment was there and, credit to them, it may have been the drugs or the booze, but they all gave it a shot. Even Cal. CJ lifted a dreadlock and did the same. He was so pumped he'd probably have eaten the thing with a knife and fork had Tam requested.

And with another roar and high-fives all round, he sprinted down the tunnel. It was all he could do to stop all that Stella, Buckfast, gak and last night's ecstasy fleeing out of his stomach from the god-awful smell of that scarf.

He knew the drugs and alcohol wouldn't kill him. Not yet, anyway. But another minute in that dressing room with that stench just might.

20

Les McGarry thought he'd seen it all. In thirty-six years of management, spread over thirteen clubs with over nine hundred matches spent in the dugout, he believed there was nothing new under the sun in this thing called football. But he was wrong.

And this was why he was still involved with this crazy game. While his poor suffering wife, who'd never liked sport of any kind, pleaded with him to retire and dedicate time to her and the grandchildren, travelling the country in the campervan they'd bought last year, he knew it was football that was keeping him going. Now, he loved his wife and his family. He even loved the old Hymer, despite it being a money pit—how he resented shelling out for a new engine, having dropped three grand doing the interior. But he knew deep down that if he had to spend his days living for those things, he'd be dead by Christmas.

Les lived for football. The giddying highs, the punch-in-the-gut lows. Not that he told his wife or grandkids this, of course. That would be deemed heartless. And today's game was proving just why he loved the sport so much.

It was like nothing he'd ever seen.

Les always looked forward to the matches with Guff Rovers. He'd played for the club as a stopper back in the fifties, almost winning them a maiden promotion. He then went on to manage them from 1966 to '68, securing that elusive promotion in his first season and keeping them up in his next. He only left to take up a post at Grimsby Town so the kids could go back to their old schools. The Isle of Guff education system wasn't up to much, and his wife was homesick. She hated the weather, the food, the people.

That was saying something from someone born in Skegness.

Les had enjoyed the madness of living on the far edge of the nation. He liked the unpredictable, often cruel weather, and the oddball islanders. Well, most of them. The Isle of Guff was different from anything he'd experienced anywhere in the UK, and he was fond of his time there as both player and gaffer.

Now he was boss of Hartlepool and enjoying his current stint for different reasons. If you'd asked him earlier on in the week, he would have said this looked like a straightforward three points given that his team were sitting comfortably mid-table and Guff were 23rd. But things took a strange turn when their opponent's manager was ousted and a fan, Thomas Bamford, a man who McGarry remembered from back during his tenure (who could forget him?) made himself boss.

Football—what a beautiful, crazy, fucked-up game it was.

Through all the clubs he'd managed, and the other eleven he'd turned out for as a player, Les McGarry had come across countless colourful and eccentric characters on the sidelines, but none who stood out quite as loudly as Tam the Bam. Unlike most players, Tam had an unusually cordial relationship with him. Possibly because he was moderately successful during his spells at Guff and gave his all which, as a combative enforcer, led to him receiving four reds, something which Tam doffed his cap to. However, the abuse Tam gave the other Guff players who weren't performing was unrepentant. From verbal volleys to bed sheet banners with death threats scrawled on them, to threatening to 'Molotov' the guest house of a Soviet-born midfielder, to tossing bottles filled with piss at them—something he denied—Tam was unforgettable.

Today, though, would not be easy for Hartlepool. A gastro epidemic saw Les lose seven first-teamers and the entire reserve squad. The plumbers had to ship in a special truck from Newcastle to pump out the waste which had gathered in the pipes over the previous forty-eight hours.

After umpteen requests to the FA to have the match postponed (all of which were ignored), Les had to field five members of the under-18 squad. The lead-up to the game had been strange, no doubt about it.

Yet, what was to follow was far stranger.

Despite Hartlepool's own disrupted preparation, the kids on the pitch started brightly. Guff appeared to have their own player issues and were beginning the game with half a team who also looked like they hadn't started shaving. And the home-side took advantage, dominating.

In fact, dominating would be an understatement. They'd had about eighty percent possession at the break, hit the left post three times, the right post twice, struck the crossbar, had a goal disallowed and another effort hooked off the line. And somehow the match remained scoreless.

To Les, Tam didn't disappoint. Age nor wealth had tamed him. He'd fainted twice. He'd also displayed his lack of managerial experience and poise by attempting a double substitution on the half-hour mark, before realising he had no subs. He then bullied the referee to add on more minutes, accusing Hartlepool of time-wasting because they'd strung twenty-seven passes together.

It was Les McGarry's custom to open his office after every home game and have a glass of wine with the opposition boss, something memorable he sourced from the Bordeaux region each summer he caravanned there. In these cosy confines, they would exchange gossip. Which teams were good, which teams were crap, who was earning what, who was having trouble with whom, which managers were the biggest dickheads. But the thought of being in a small space with this man genuinely terrified him, and McGarry was an imposing six-foot-twoer.

However, deep into the second half, Guff were somehow hanging on. They say good management is mostly good luck, and at this rate McGarry thought his opposite number was on track to become the next Brian Clough.

What's more, from his dugout he could smell booze coming off the Guff players. It took him back to the sixties. Les couldn't believe the opposition still had it in them to harry and chase his boys like they did. The only one who didn't seem to be on anything was Guff's pious young keeper. With his military-cut and long beard, and how he would go down on his hands and knees and thank the heavens after every involvement, he certainly hadn't been invited to whatever debauched party the others had been attending the night before.

In the ninety-second minute, Hartlepool winger Rick Richardson conjured up an effort from the edge of the box. McGarry thought this was the moment he'd been waiting for as the twenty-five-yarder curled and curled and held up in the wind, heading right for the top corner. That was until the Guff goalie somehow spread himself and clawed it from the net.

As the young man thanked God above, McGarry had to laugh. And the gaffer did so loudly. It was all he could do to stop himself from crying.

"You'd do well to giggle, you would," Tam shouted across. "You lot have got out of jail here."

"Who has?"

"Your lot. Stealing a point."

"Have you been sniffing the liniment oil? You haven't even had a shot on goal. You've been up our end twice."

"Now who's high, McGarry? Or is it all that heading the ball you did over the years? Always thought you were lacking in the upstairs department. It would explain why you were so useless with us."

"I led you to promotion. I played a hundred and fifty-seven games. I came seventh in Guff's 'Top one hundred players of all time' poll'," McGarry pointed out. "If memory serves me right, you've got a tattoo of my face on your calf."

Tam pulled his leg away, the one without the moon boot. "That's never been proven."

The full-time whistle sounded. Tam jumped up, punching the air. Then he raced down the touchline, sliding in the mud on his knees. McGarry was amazed he was capable of anything other than a slow stumble.

And he was right.

"Aww, Christ. Aww, Jesus. Aww, Buddha. Aww, Allah. My knee's seized up."

As the players trudged off the rain-sodden pitch, Tam Bam was stretchered off.

"Will he be all right?" McGarry asked the lady from St John Ambulance.

"It's only a graze," she replied, administering Dettol and a plaster.

"Hurry up, woman," Tam moaned from his horizontal vantage. "I need to get in for my team talk."

"You want some advice?" McGarry offered.

"No," Tam replied.

"Be a bit more humble on the bench towards your rivals. You're not a daft fan anymore. Show some class."

"I don't need advice from an inexperienced amateur like you. I was born for this."

McGarry couldn't help but laugh again. He patted Tam on the

shoulder, then walked down the tunnel to talk to his own players. A smattering of fans had stayed behind to applaud him, despite the unexpected loss of two points.

"Well done, Les," said one. "Any other match, we would've won by ten."

"Chin up, gaffer, the play-offs are still in sight," added a kid in blue face paint.

He clapped hands with them. He was disappointed but wouldn't let it get him down. His senior players should be fit and well for next weekend's game. They had to be.

The old pipes at Vic Park couldn't handle another barrage.

Les watched as Tam was stretchered into his changeroom like an invalid from the Somme. The game needed nutters like him, they were the lifeblood of the game. But did it really need them in the dugout? No, it was all too warped. Maybe this was the way football was heading. Where those with money swooped down like vultures and ripped the heart out of the game. For the first time, he thought he might be better off living the caravan life after all and leaving them to it.

21

The players broke into a seven-a-side game. This was the happiest part of the training session. It meant things were winding down and they could have some fun and let rip by scoring some goals and letting the tackles fly.

Coach Connor Whelan was pleased with how the session had gone. The Guff players who returned from their weekend strike had put in a proper shift and appeared energised from their fishing trip. It was in stark contrast to last week's sessions where the lads hadn't been paid and Gary Pullman, who most of them were signed by, had been given the boot. The mood in the camp had been bleak. Today, the players had a spring in their step, the banter was back, and they seemed happy to be professional footballers again.

Part of that might have been down to the absence of the new gaffer, who everyone was dreading taking charge. They knew him well, of course. He needed no introduction. He'd been abusing every Guff player for the past forty years. What they feared was him now having the power to go ahead and do the things which on the terraces he could only threaten. Before this, Tam Bam was a figure of fun, someone the players would take the piss out of behind closed doors.

Now he was the boogeyman come to life.

The scores were 2–2. The youth keeper, Seth Graham, who Connor heard played a blinder on the weekend, was batting out shot after shot. If only he could stand up to his defenders a bit more, he'd have a future.

The other star of the weekend was moving about nicely. CJ Adeyemi. Connor knew all about him from the youth setup. He was a talent. He'd struck seventeen goals already for the under-18s from midfield and pulled all their strings. He should've been in the first team months ago. Would've been if he was more dedicated. Rumour had it, scouts from Southampton were sniffing around. Cardiff too. Undeniable ability, but he wasn't dedicated enough. Spent too much time on the rave scene and was too big a joker.

Connor was saddened by the reports that CJ, James and Meggs had lost the team at Durham Airport to hit the town. They didn't get back to the island until late Sunday night. They'd been charged with public drunkenness. James was wearing a plaster cast on his hand. Meggs lost two front teeth. Southampton and Cardiff wouldn't set foot on the island if they knew that.

Not even Accrington Stanley would.

Yet here CJ was, dashing around and breaking up tackles on one end of the half-pitch and creating chances up the other. And he hadn't mucked about once. He was the first one here this morning, which had never happened before. There was a seriousness about him which had grown overnight. *The Durham constabulary should collar him more often*, Connor thought. He could become a player — a major player— yet.

CJ frustrated him because he remembered another lad who used to score goals with ease from deep. A player who had even bigger clubs—West Ham, Leeds, Wolves—scout him. A player who would think nothing of going out on a Friday and drinking ten snakebites and starting a scrap. A player who was so confident he had the football world by the short and curlies that he gave up on school when he was twelve. A player who, despite the hype, amounted to absolutely bugger all.

A player by the name of Connor Whelan.

Connor watched in awe as CJ collected a stray ball, turned,

swivelled and put it through veteran midfielder Kenny Boddington's legs, then skipped by him. The bigger man grabbed the kid by the ankles, dragging him into a foreboding puddle on the waterlogged pitch to big cheers.

"That's child abuse," shouted CJ as he slipped, trying to find his footing. Connor feared the young man might try to clock him. He knew Boddington would knock him dead if he did, no matter how many players intervened. Instead, CJ took a quick free kick and ran onto the return, smashing a twenty-yarder straight into the net. And for a moment, just a moment, Connor believed the season might turn out all right after all.

But that moment sailed when a taxi pulled up in the middle of the training ground, beeping its horn.

Connor noticed the overbearing and all-too-familiar outline of Tam reaching across the driver, beating the centre of the steering wheel. Tam then forced himself out of the door before the car had stopped, limping as he landed.

"What's going on?" Tam yelled, hurrying over, dragging his crutch and moon boot through the mud. At least he'd had the sense to put a plastic bag over it to keep it dry. "What—is—going—on?!"

"What do you mean, gaffer?" Connor replied, carefully. "The boys are finishing training."

"It's a quarter to eleven. I'm over an hour early."

"Training starts at nine. The players get here even earlier for a rub-down."

"How can anyone expect to achieve anything in life waking up at that ungodly hour? And I thought a midday start was bad."

"You'll find it's the way most clubs operate."

"Well, not this one. Not anymore." Tam collected the cones which outlined the practice pitch, laying them out in a straight line.

"Also, some of the boys have afternoon jobs, kids to look after," Connor reasoned.

"You think Bobby Charlton had a bloody milk round? You reckon Pelé bothered having kids?" Tam turned to the players. "Right, you lot. Bring it in."

The players left their positions and edged towards the new man, their smiles wilting in the wind.

"Now I know some of you so-called footballers have never met me. That you don't know me from a bar of soap."

Is he actually serious? thought Connor. It had been a running joke through each Guff side—especially when he was playing—about how mental Tam Bam was. Each team had players trying to outdo themselves with impressions of the man. This team was no different. Rory McGrory's one with his holdall stuffed under his shirt was the best. He had the man's bowling-ball gait down pat.

They all knew who Tam Bam was, all right.

"I'm the man who puts food on your table, who pays your bills, puts your kids through school, ensures your wife can go to the hairdressers once a bloody week. I'm the man in charge. And I'm here to win. So, any of you who aren't winners, there's the door." He pointed to where a solitary elm tree stood, which was obviously lacking a door.

Dangerfield lifted his hand. "Will you pay out our contracts if we walk through that imaginary door?"

"You, ya big useless stick of rock. I can't believe you're not paying the club to get a game. You'll be getting nothing but my size ten up your arse. And that's me being generous. Anything else anybody wants to know?"

Lance Posobiec, his neck in plaster, spoke. "What's your masterplan for the club?"

"Short term—win games, beat the drop. Long term—European

Cup. Winning the thing." The players' eyes widened. Tam was even more deranged than they thought. He kept going. "No wonder this club is in the state it's in. Are there any more daft questions?" Nobody said a thing. "Right. I want a five-mile run from all of you followed by sprint drills."

Tam grabbed the ball they were playing with and booted it into the bushes.

"You won't be needing that for a while. You need to get fit," he said, his fat rolls rippling like a burst waterbed through his lime-green mac. "And anyone who complains will be doing double."

The players turned to Connor, desperate for a reprieve.

"Um, gaffer," Connor said. "It's just … the players have already been training for two hours. A solid shift too. We'd usually be wrapping it up now."

"Right, of course. I'm a fair man. We'll make it a four-and-a-half-mile run. Off you pop." The players slowly congregated, setting off at a casual trot, cursing as they did. "And what are you doing here, anyway?" Tam asked.

"I'm the coach," Connor said. "Well, not officially, but I've been helping out." He'd been doing so since his career ended.

"Why weren't you in Hartlepool when we needed you? Don't tell me you were out on the razz as well."

"You wouldn't pay my flight."

"Hmph, I see. So, are you my assistant then?"

"I could be. I haven't actually been getting paid. I'm doing my badges."

Connor had been on the dole for two years, living off a meagre lump sum from Guff's disability insurance. He'd been forced to remortgage his house while he studied sports management at Open University.

"We'll see if we can sort you out with a little something or other.

How does a tenner a week for expenses sound?"

"Right. Thanks. I guess."

Tam finished setting up the cones for the drills. On the far side of the park, the players dragged their heels through the puddles. "Move it, move it, move it, you useless lot!" He tutted to Connor. "What I wouldn't like to do with them."

"Personally, I wouldn't have them running their guts out this far into the season. I'd put my arm around them. I'd show them a bit of love and appreciation. They're not a bad bunch."

Tam watched as the players faded to walking pace. "No, they're not a bad bunch. They're a bloody awful one." Tam removed dumbbells and sandbags from his large training bag. "They teach you that hippy claptrap at coaching school, do they? No wonder England can't win anything. This is why you're backroom staff. You want to perk up your ideas if you ever want to be top dog, sunshine."

Connor saw the burnt-out car behind the goals which had been there since they'd made the public park their training headquarters. He got a dangerous whiff of decaying meat, vegetables and nappies wafting in from the dump next door. He wondered if there was any way of fast-tracking his coaching badges and course. If there was a way of getting off this island, and away from incompetents like Tam Bam telling him what to do.

He could do with that tenner, though. Things really were that tight. But a couple of zeroes at the end of that sum wouldn't go amiss.

22

Dear Fellow Faeries,

It would have been easy for me to ascend to the role of chairman and sit up in that ivory tower (or pine-panelled, as it turns out), and quaff gourmet pasties, and get gloriously rum-drunk off the back of you.

But those of you who know me know that isn't the man I am.

That's why this knight in shining armour has swapped it for bulletproof armour instead. And he's armed himself with a hand grenade or three, along with a machete or four, and joined the front line.

Viva la revolution!

And I want you, my loyal foot soldiers, to back me all the way. I can't do it all myself. That's why you'll notice I've lifted ticket prices and tuckshop items by twenty-five percent (and, as you'll see if you're reading this, fifty percent for the program). According to the lawyers, I can't legally squeeze any more out of you current season-ticket holders, but I implore you to follow your hearts and your conscience and make a donation to the club you love. Take out an overdraft, extend your mortgage or use a cheque book if you have to. The funds will go towards getting rid of the crap I—or rather, we—have inherited from our dangerously inept former manager and allow me to invest in a new type of player.

I shall bring the football greats to Faery Meadow, you shall see. But I can't do it alone.

And once we've got the right type of personnel, it's then that we shall climb that ladder. Imagine European football here. Close your eyes, take a long, deep breath, and visualise the likes of Dukla Prague, New York Cosmos or Santos coming to our glorious island.

I dare to dream.

I can see a flash new stadium. I can see tours of North America and Australia. I can see kids in Africa donning the famous brown-and-pink checkered shirt.

And I want you to dream too.

I know it's hard for us because we've been oppressed for so long, though fear not, Faeries. Just look at all the press we've gotten this week. It took a while for word to get around, but we're the most talked-about football club on the planet. Everyone from Troon to Tasmania is marvelling at how Guff could score me as a gaffer. As the song goes, "The good times are about to start rolling on in" (I can't remember which song it's from exactly. I accidentally sat on my new alarm clock earlier and the ditty was playing on Radio Cornwall. I should give them a call.)

Today we welcome table-toppers Rotherham United to our fair island. I don't care if they've lost bugger-all matches this season and have hit sixty-something goals. They're overrated. That 5–1 win over us in August was the most one-sided defeat I've seen, and I've seen a few. If we'd created a hatful more chances, defended a lot tighter and kept the ball, then that scoreline could have been very, very different.

I feel sorry for this lot, to be honest. With a woman on the board (A woman! And we thought we had it bad!), it's good their fans have had something to cheer about. And I'm not one to spark controversy within the ranks, but have you seen the number of kids in their team? I sure know what their manager likes to do in his spare time. Hang around local parks watching young boys, that's what!

And they only have one black player. The racists! Those days are gone. We have two and a half. This isn't the bloody seventies! And I plan to have at least three and a half of the buggers by 1990. That's how progressive I am.

Let's have this Yorkshire lot hobbling back to Coal Country (where they're all married to their cousins—probably) with their tails firmly between their legs and with zero points. The paedophile, incestuous racists that they are.

The nativity scene, VE Day, the moon landing and now my takeover of Guff Rovers and subsequent entry to the dugout. All great moments which reaffirmed man's faith in humanity.

I have a dream. Now join me on my quest.

Come on, You Boys in Brown (and Pink)!

Signed, Thomas Bamford.

Editor's Note: This is an edited extract from a 13,000-word essay written by Thomas Bamford. Views expressed are very much his own, and definitely not those of the editorial staff or the club.

23

Roger cuddled into his heavy fur-lined overcoat, bracing himself from the cold. He'd never seen so few fans in the ground for a first-team match. It would be lucky if there were five hundred people present, when the average gate was consistently two to three times that. Roger was well aware that the snow wasn't helping, but Guff Rovers fans were a notoriously hardy bunch. He knew they were boycotting. The majority couldn't cope with a degenerate like Tam Bam in the dugout bringing down the good name of their club. Tam getting rid of Gary Pullman so viciously was deemed the second-last straw. Significantly raising ticket, food and club shop prices on this struggling island was the final one.

Roger and his wife were supposed to be over in London, where their son was moving into his first flat following university. Also, Roger's sister was at the family holiday home in Madeira celebrating her silver wedding anniversary and had invited them there.

But Roger couldn't miss this game.

For better or for worse (even though he knew it was most certainly for the worst), this first home game since Tam Bam took over would go down in Guff Rovers folklore. And just like driving past a motorway pile-up, Roger had to see it.

"Do you want another cup of tea, duck?' he asked his wife, reaching for the flask. They always bought their beverages from the tuckshop to support the club. However, in protest at the price hike, she insisted they bring their own.

"I'd rather have a sangria," Rowena huffed.

"This is what supporting a team is all about. Through thick and thin and all that."

"Sitting in the snow watching a mental defective ruin the club you—*we*—love? This isn't sport. This is something quite twisted."

Roger poured himself a cup. He didn't want to give her the satisfaction of knowing she was right, although she usually was. He also didn't wish to snap at her about how it could be him in control of the club, if only she'd let him. Not in the dugout, of course. He would have kept Gary Pullman or found someone else. He had the means to buy it. The muesli had its biggest-selling quarter the one before last. But Rowena insisted that there was a line as a fan, and in no way should you cross it. In no way did she want Roger to do this, to do football, as a job. It would take up all his time and ruin his health, she said. They were doing more than enough for the island. And anyway, football clubs were money pits. The Greenfields may have been rich, yet they were by no means 'football rich'. Maybe a decade or so ago they may have been deemed so, but not in 1989.

Deep down Roger knew this. Instead, he fronted £100K and led the fans' consortium requesting that Gus Pinkle sell the club to them. They had plans for a new stand, extra funding for the youth team and a refurbished toilet block.

God, how the club needed it.

The current ground was so rundown that only a handful of functioning seats remained. The floodlights had died twice already this season. There'd been zero investment on the pitch. Gus Pinkle had even flogged the training ground and the carpark.

The consortium had clear, reasonable and achievable goals. But the token one pound offered, along with the clearing of an estimated £2M of accumulated debt via a low-interest loan, was not enough to entice the chairman. But the moment Tam came along with his thirty pieces of silver and the most bonkers plan going in the modern game, he gave the thing away.

Roger's wife wasn't even watching the match. She was knitting another brown-and-pink coat for their greyhound, McGrory, and planning on calling their son at the break for a blow-by-blow account of how dodgy West London removalists were.

And who could blame her? Who the hell knew what was going on out there on the pitch? By Roger's estimation—and he was no master tactician—the team was playing a 2–3–5 formation. He hadn't heard of anything like it since the tales his grandfather told him of pre-World War I football.

To make matters worse, the game was only a half-hour old, and Tam had already made his two substitutions purely for tactical reasons. Zak Bates was hooked after Seth Graham threw an innocent enough ball at him, and he lost his footing letting the Rotherham forward in on goal, fortunately screwing it wide. And captain Rory McGrory was dragged after he put the ball into his own net, trying to head it back to the keeper from three yards out.

By some miracle, that was the only goal of the half. Still, the locals were far from happy as the performance and tactics were all over the shop.

Old Dennis with his pink bunnet sat in front of Roger as he always did. He looked like he was about to have a stroke. "What's this shite you're dishing up to us, Bam? Put another man at the back!"

Tam heard him loud and clear, shouting back, "What I'm doing here is way outside your bollock-sized realm of understanding, old man."

Suddenly, from a Dangerfield long-throw, the ball landed in the packed Rotherham box and Kenny Boddington swung a shin at it. The ball bounced down and caught their centre-half's toe and swerved and bobbled, crawling over the line.

1–1.

The fans were on their feet. Everyone forgot what had gone on and who was in charge, and for a fleeting moment it actually felt okay to be a Guff fan. In fact, it was beautiful. Roger's wife even dropped her yarn, nearly stabbing him in the eye with her knitting needles as she wrapped her arms around him, kissing him on the lips.

It was all down to the kids. That CJ from the youth team was running the team's engine room like a young Bryan Robson, providing the side with much-needed dig. And this new (clearly God-bothering) goalkeeper, Seth Graham, was growing in stature. Literally. Roger could've sworn he'd gotten bigger during the game, as he now looked like the tallest man on the pitch. At seventeen, he manned the goal like a bearded Peter Shilton.

Then something really odd happened. Extraordinary, even. Graham belted a giant goal-kick against the wind, right down the guts of the park, a mammoth distance for someone so young. It bounced off a random shoulder and all of a sudden it was five versus three in Rotherham's final third. Dangerfield took a touch, a good touch, and then sliced the ball. It struck a defender's underbite and spun over the keeper and into the net.

2–1.

2–1 against the league's runaway leaders. Cue pandemonium around the ground. This time Roger's wife jumped him like she hadn't since their wedding night. Old Dennis lost his bunnet, and no longer was he caring.

When it all died down and the game restarted, Roger zeroed in on Tam, noticing that astonishingly he hadn't moved at all. He'd stood there motionless, chowing down more Rennie. Roger didn't think the man was capable of such restraint, especially at such a crucial moment against a top team.

And he was right.

As soon as the cacophony died down, Tam turned to the Guff fans.

"Choke on that, you sack of willies," he boomed, giving them a double v-sign. "Tam Bam doesn't know what he's doing, Tam Bam couldn't manage a packet of biscuits—is what you all said."

"No one would ever say that," joked Old Dennis in the pink bunnet and everyone within earshot laughed.

"And look at us now. Beating the leaders. Giving them the roasting of their lives. And it's all down to me. Me!"

A cheer went up from the small pocket of Rotherham fans behind the goal, which Tam didn't hear. "I'm at the wheel now, you degenerates. And a better gaffer you could not wish for, to lead you all to—"

"Sit down, you fat bastard," a stray voice shouted.

"They've gone and equalised," said Dennis's grandson, striking Tam right in the kisser with an overpriced pasty.

Tam clutched his mouth, turning in time to see Guff restart. If he was embarrassed, then the home fans didn't see it. Instead, he gobbled another row of Rennie. Even the most loyal Faeries couldn't help but find the comedy in the situation and share a few knowing smiles.

Tam Bam didn't turn around for the rest of the half.

Roger believed the only good thing to come out of this takeover was the exposure the club received. The section around the Guff dugout was packed with photographers and cameramen. Roger could've sworn he'd seen Des Lynam and Jimmy Hill up there in the old press box, which hadn't been used since Harold Wilson was in power. And earlier on *Saint and Greavsie,* the Guff Rovers saga was all they could talk about. Or rather, take the piss out of. No one on the show had ever mentioned the club before this. That all changed earlier when Jimmy Greaves dressed up in a fat suit and impersonated Tam. With the help of Ian St John, they acted out various scenarios of how the season could pan out for the club. Pasty shortage. Deadly meteor shower. A failed offer for John Barnes involving a lifetime's supply of Cornish fudge. Roger didn't get it.

He wasn't that big on comedy. But given the reaction of those in the studio, everyone else got it in a big way.

The previous evening on BBC's *Newsnight,* Peter Snow grilled Tam about how his actions may not only have brought about the death of Guff Rovers but football itself. Tam hit back by sending a message to Kenny Dalglish, telling him Liverpool's time at the top was up, before lunging at the camera (the interview was via satellite) and ending the transmission. Car crash TV at its finest.

Still, any press was good press, wasn't it?

Roger was stumped. He'd written to the FA enquiring just how someone like Tam Bam was allowed to take over a club so swiftly, but he wasn't holding out much hope. He'd even contacted Tam to arrange an urgent meeting with the fan-led consortium to mend bridges and get some idea of where the club was heading. Some realistic idea, that is.

Most importantly, he wanted to have some input. But given that as the half-time whistle blew, their new manager and majority owner was currently giving the entire Norrie Sutton Stand the middle finger, he held little hope for good relations.

Then Tam began coughing. His knees buckled, and he collapsed to the turf. The paramedics rushed to his aid as Tam clutched at his throat. He coughed, and coughed, and coughed again as the medical staff thumped on his back. They flipped him onto his side. The paramedic got two fingers down his throat, managing to dislodge the offending object (an undissolved Rennie) and get him breathing again.

The Rotherham staff in the dugout, their fans behind the opposition goal and their players exiting the pitch saw the funny side of this circus.

Guff Rovers were the biggest joke in football.

Roger Greenhill considered himself a smart man. A thinking man. But for the first time in his life, he didn't know what to do. And yet here they came for him, the fans fleeing from their seats like worker bees gravitating to their queen, desperate for guidance.

"What did you make of that, Roger?"

"You've gotta step in."

"We have to take back control of our club."

"Do something, do anything, but please, please, save us from this complete and utter psycho."

The fans were right, of course. Roger's forefathers would be turning in their graves at what this once proud institution had become. But Roger had no answers. Perhaps he should abandon it altogether and find something else to fill his Saturdays. Yet, this was all he'd known for almost fifty years. And on the Isle of Guff, it was too cold and windy to golf anytime except the summer.

His wife had told him to sell the muesli line. For them to get an apartment in London near the kids. Their daughter was also there with their first grandchild in the oven. Then there was the holiday home in Portugal. Rowena was always at her happiest there. There and in Malawi where they ran the foundation building schools. Those people needed them. And the little you did for them, they were so grateful.

But this island needed them too. The place was on its knees. The football club, once the pride of the rock, needed them.

"Oh, bollocks to this. Bollocks to the game. And bollocks to you." Rowena snatched her bag and headed down the steps.

"Where are you going?" he called after her.

"I'm going to get a decent drink. Something warm. And hopefully something strong."

"But what about the protest? What about the price hike?"

"And bollocks to that. I no longer care about anything associated with this, this … shit-stain of a club. I'm done."

And deep down in his broken heart he knew she was right, because so was he.

24

Tam hocked up something green and chunky from his throat, depositing it on the tunnel's concrete surface. Then he burst into the dressing room.

"You wankers, the lot of you. You walking abortions. What kinda piss is this you're dishing up now? That lot are shite, the most overrated bunch of tosspots I've ever seen near a football park. A gaffer with paedo glasses. A left-back with more hair on him than Chewbacca. And a striker with that many tattoos he looks like he belongs in the Gibtown Circus!"

He was in such a blind rage he hadn't noticed which dressing room he'd bounded into. When he heard the sniggers, he focused, suddenly seeing a mass of red and white shirts, the hirsute full-back and tattooed forward among them.

Rotherham United manager Sam Pettinger, who was stood by the door, offered his specs to the Guff boss. "I think you need a pair of these paedo glasses, big man. At least they help you see."

Tam's mouth gaped. His knees rattled. And for the very first time, he was lost for words. As the players' laughter bounced off the tiles, Tam spun on his heels and departed to his own dressing room, tail firmly between his legs.

"Normally I'd have the hump that some mug was trespassing and taking up valuable minutes of my team-talk," Pettinger called out to him. "But how on God's green earth can I top that?"

The Rotherham players cheered.

"There're still five minutes to go, but let's get out there right now and get into them."

The players put down their cups of tea and marched out, Tam's words ringing gloriously in their ears.

25

Transcript from Guff Rovers' post-match press conference
Saturday, February 11, 1989
5.27 p.m.

The room is filled with reporters from every news organisation in the country, along with international reporters from La Gazzetta, Marcos, Kicker, ESPN, *the whole lot.*

TAM BAM *faces this media scrum alone.*

THE GUARDIAN: Is this whole thing a hoax?

TAM BAM: Next question.

MAIL ON SUNDAY: What did you make of today's showing?

TAM BAM: The ref was a disgrace. One of their goals was offside. Another didn't cross the line. Four of their players should've seen red. I should be sat here talking about a deserved 3–0 victory via forfeit, thank you very much.

There are a few uncomfortable glances between the journalists. Is this guy high? Did he even watch the game?

ESPN: Do the players respect you?

TAM BAM: I think I scare them with my ideas, my approach. I'm an innovator. A maverick. Cloughie's suffered the same way. Anyway, I'd rather be feared than loved.

ITV: What will you do to turn things around?

TAM BAM: Each and every one of my so-called professional players is on the transfer list. I got the plumbers in to ensure they had hot water in the showers this week, and that's how they repay me? I even had an extra two oranges cut up.

HINDUSTAN TIMES: Who are you going to bring in?

TAM BAM: Only the best. If it kills me, I will take this club to the very top, to the mantle it deserves. And I will make sure that my name is mentioned in the same breath as Stein, Shankly, Busby and Dave Bassett.

SHOOT: And how exactly are you going to do that?

TAM BAM: I shall be on the phone to Alex Ferguson first thing.

MATCH: You're an acquaintance of Fergie's?

TAM BAM: More like a confidant. We were penpals as kids. Rangers were looking to sign me to partner him upfront in the sixties. But then I got a nasty case of gout during the game they were watching me in, and I had to be subbed.

DAILY RECORD: Are you going to resign?

TAM BAM: You get out. Security, deal with this man (*a young* GOTH STEWARD *does so*). I—am—here—forever!

CORNISH POST: But you're driving this club into the ground.

TAM BAM: I know you, and I shall speak to your boss.

NEW YORK TIMES: Do you not think, with all due respect, that with zero pro-soccer experience you're way out of your depth?

TAM BAM: You're the one out of your depth, Yankee. Fergie was about to make me his assistant at Man United until there was a visa issue, I'll have you know. I've watched this club for over forty years. I was one of the first in the area to have a satellite dish. The very first to have a VHS player. I watch four games of football a day.

THE TIMES: Yes, but you have zero people skills.

TAM BAM: I'll give you bloody people skills.

TAM BAM *rises and thinks about rushing over to the female reporter but appears to deem it too far.*

BBC CORNWALL: Have you ever had a real job before?

TAM BAM: Right. Get her out too. You're banned n'all.

BBC CORNWALL: Gladly.

The reporter leaves. The other reporters mumble and shake their heads. They collect their notepads, laptops and cameras and follow.

There is only one reporter left. A teenager with a middle parting and owl-shaped glasses.

TAM BAM: And where are you from, young man?

YOUNG MAN: *The Falmouth Anchor.*

TAM BAM: What sort of football paper is that?

YOUNG MAN: It's the Falmouth University student press, sir.

TAM BAM: Hmph. And what's your question?

YOUNG MAN: I'm more into the theatre, to be honest.

TAM BAM: The bloody theatre?

YOUNG MAN: I'm filling in because the sports guy's getting his wisdom teeth out. I have an interview for Channel 4 next week. I'm here to bulk up my resume.

TAM BAM: So, you're not a football man, then?

YOUNG MAN: No, no. Between you and me, I can't stand the game.

TAM BAM: You're barred too. Freak.

The YOUNG MAN *departs. With no one remaining, the* GOTH STEWARD *leaves as well.*

TAM BAM *sits there all alone. He takes a sip of Lucozade and sighs.*

TAM BAM: Well, this is nice.

When the door closes, he farts.

26

Connor Whelan did not like Vera's Cafe. It shouldn't have been called a 'greasy spoon'. He believed it should have been called a 'greasy spoon, knife, fork, cup, plate, condiments, tables, chairs, loos, the lot'.

The place didn't need cleaning, it needed condemning.

He'd never been a fan of fry-ups, probably the reason he went on to become a professional footballer. He was always into lean meats, rice, pasta and greens.

His eight-year-old daughter, Gillian, wasn't into that food, though. When he had to care for her, that kind of fare didn't cut it. With no Wimpy, Kentucky Fried Chicken or Pizza Hut on the island, on Saturday nights when he'd been away all day at the football, they came to Vera's to eat. It was the only day of the week he would do so. He would have a cup of tea and a cheese and tomato toastie (on brown bread, which Vera surprisingly had), and his daughter would have whatever she wanted, always with a ton of chips, swimming in salt and vinegar. Tonight, it was lasagne. If you could call the garish yellow and red sludge on her plate a source of food.

"Is that good, my darl?" he asked.

"Not as good as chicken nuggets," she said, her mouth crammed.

At least she was speaking to him now. She'd cracked it because he'd refused to buy her a shake to go with it. She'd already consumed a lollipop, three fun size Mars Bars and a packet of crisps at the ground. He wanted to monitor her sugar levels. Last year she had a rotten molar removed, and the paediatrician informed them she was overweight for her age.

His former partner, Tiff, was a piece of work. Yes, she'd had postnatal depression. Yes, she'd had suicidal thoughts. Yes, she was effectively a single parent with a job, but that was her choice. She'd recently left him and moved to the mainland, taking a position at an estate agent to fund her "new lifestyle". Whatever that meant. Despite this, did she really have to feed their daughter junk food Monday to Friday?

It wasn't all Tiff's doing that they separated. She was right in a few ways. He had been an unsupportive prick, insensitive to all she was going through at that point of her life. However, there was a reason. That over-the-ball tackle at Leyton Orient when he was twenty by the O's central-midfielder, Jamie Pullman.

That Jamie Pullman.

He'd received a three-match ban for leaving his studs in and taking out Connor's knee. The local press made a thing about Jamie visiting him in the local hospital, saying he was sorry. It never happened. He merely dropped off some flowers, a four-pack of Guinness and a well-thumbed copy of *Roy of the Rovers* at the desk, then skedaddled.

When Connor made it back, he was never the same. He couldn't manoeuvre around opponents quite so sharply. His acceleration from deeper positions wasn't so quick. And when he had to make a tackle, or when he was tackled, he would freeze up, just for a split second, but enough for him to mistime the challenge or give the ball away.

When he slipped on the sidelines on a frosty November morning at training three years ago with no one near him, he knew before he hit the deck that his knee had gone again. And this time there'd be no way back, no matter how many pilgrimages he made to Harley Street quacks.

Fuck the world.

It was time for Plan B. But what do you do when there's no Plan B? He'd never done anything else with his life. His spelling was atrocious, his maths worse. He couldn't cook or do anything handy. Couldn't turn on a computer. The only thing he knew was football. So, he re-mortgaged their house, enrolled for his coaching badges and a course in sports science. He was halfway through them when Tiff fled, and he had to spend his remaining cash on a solicitor.

Connor signed on the dole and took up a role with Guff Rovers as their coach. And given that football was now taking up so many hours, even more than before when he was earning a full-time wage, he only had enough time to work a casual position at the local Texaco. Financially, he was on his knees. And things got worse when Tiff confirmed there'd be no reconciliation, meaning family life as he'd known it was well and truly finished, and the only time he'd get with his daughter was fortnightly weekend visits.

Gillian had dusted off her lasagne and was finishing her chips. Connor hadn't even eaten half his toastie. She had her Walkman on and was listening to Rick Astley's 'Never Gonna Give You Up' for the millionth time. Like she was eight going on eighteen.

She'd shown zero interest in playing sport or doing anything other than lounge in front of the television or listen to her tapes. He'd tried to enforce a TV and music ban during mealtimes, but it was hopeless. Tiff let her do what she wanted morning, noon and night. Back when Tiff and Gillian lived on the island, the TV was never on.

With his daughter preoccupied, his thoughts drifted back to Guff Rovers and that thrashing they'd received from the table-toppers. Connor had been with the club since age eleven. Pulling on that brown-and-pink checkered shirt was all he'd dreamed of. He got offered trials here, there and everywhere, but his love for Guff, the club his grandfather had scored eighty-one goals for in the late forties when he moved over the water from County Cork, stopped him. His love for Tiff at the time was an even bigger factor. Plus, he loved getting pissed with his mates on weekends and occasionally during the week. His father urged him to escape the island when he got the chance, but Connor's heart was here.

That was until a few years ago when his career ended. And then a few months after that, Tiff left him. Like it was all his fault that he couldn't earn a wage and was in rehab every day. Like it was his fault he was depressed because, at age twenty-five, his career, his dream, his livelihood, his life was all over, red rover.

The front door of Vera's flew open. And into the near-deserted diner blew wind and rain and the all-too-familiar presence of Tam Bam. He had the physique of someone who ate Vera's cuisine every day, though Connor had never seen him here.

After a brief struggle, Tam managed to settle his large backside on one of the faded vinyl bar stools. "Could you fix us a Virgin Mary?" he asked Vera.

"A bloody what?" she shouted back. She was almost completely deaf and—stooped and dangerously thin—looked just as unhealthy as him. Connor imagined that they could one day make a good match.

"A *vir-jin meh-ree*," he repeated slowly.

"You what? Coming in here sprouting your religious profanities. What kinda establishment do you think I run here? This isn't Belfast."

"Just give me a banana milkshake, then."

Connor tried to hide his face behind the menu. This was his time, time with his child.

"That's £1.25." Vera slid the drink across.

"What's it got in it? Should be Moët at that price."

"That's a drop in the ocean for you by all reports."

"Don't you start as well."

"If you don't like it, you can go elsewhere. Good luck getting anything around here at this hour."

Tam took a sip. He didn't remark, but his eyebrows arched up, obviously pleasantly surprised by the taste. He slammed a fistful of silver and copper coins down on the grimy benchtop.

He took another sip and then leaned too far to his left. He began to fall. He grabbed the bench but only managed to spin himself on the chair. Round and round he went until he spun straight off, shooting across the floor.

The other few patrons, loners mostly, were too immersed in their newspapers, or their ashtrays, or their own heads to notice. Gillian, though, let out a huge giggle as Tam bounced face-first onto the floor.

It was way more entertaining than Rick Astley.

Tam jumped up as quick as he could, straightening his Guff scarf. "I should sue you for that," He wagged his index finger at Vera. "Bloody hazard if ever there was one. You'll kill somebody."

Vera was trying to hold in the giggles herself. "A thousand folk have sat there and never pulled off a landing like that. The circus is in town at Easter. You should join it if this football rubbish doesn't pay off."

Tam's eyes rested upon the little girl in the booth who couldn't stop laughing. He spotted her father, his face hidden behind the menu which he was holding upside down.

"I know you, don't I?" Tam said, sitting in the booth, his large frame squeezing Gillian so tightly against the wall she yelped.

Connor reluctantly lowered the menu. "I should hope you do."

"You work at the garage. You lot do a good pasty. Much underrated."

"I'm the coach at Guff Rovers. I've spent the entire afternoon with you."

Tam searched the younger man's eyes for sarcasm. "Of course, I know that. Just out of context is all. You know how it is." He winked at Gillian. "This your date?"

Gillian grinned back. Despite the lack of space and the musty odour he'd brought with him, she hadn't taken her eyes from Tam. Connor had never seen her pay this much attention to anyone.

"This is my daughter. She's eight."

"You're a family man, then?"

"You ever come close to settling down yourself?"

"Never met anyone who could tame this wild child." Tam thumbed his chest. "Besides, I think my standards are too high." Tam slurped the last of his milkshake, making a drain-like noise. What hadn't gathered on his chin had soaked into his scarf. Tam studied Connor. "Don't think I don't know who you are. One hundred and eighty-two appearances, twenty-four goals, thirty-nine assists. Thirteen bookings as well. Never a red."

"That's incredible."

"Capped for Ireland under-21s, n'all. Don't get me started on your grandfather, I'd be here all night. Unlike him, you never got a testimonial."

"Cheers for reminding me."

"But a great player all the same. And a tragedy what happened."

"Thank you."

His daughter had her headphones back on. Shame, Connor thought. She was yet to show any interest in her father's career.

A lot like her mother.

"Never seen you in here before," Connor said.

"Let's just say, the pub has become a place unsuitable for my patronage."

"Tough with the locals, huh? They can be a fickle bunch and let their hearts rule their heads at times. Don't let them get you down."

"What do you know about them?"

"After one hundred and eighty-two appearances, I'd like to think I know a wee bit."

"And a trial at Liverpool, I do believe."

"I didn't go in the end."

"I've had a bit of an affinity with Man United given my best pal Alex Ferguson is there."

"Tosh. I heard you've never been past Devon."

"I nearly signed for Rangers, I'll have you know."

"I know. Everyone knows."

"They do?"

"They do. This is the only club I've had eyes for. And I have the limp to prove it."

"I know, lad," Tam said, mournfully. "'You were a wonderful servant."

Connor smiled. It was reassuring that fans of the club, real fans—albeit mentally unstable ones—still remembered him.

"Go on, what should I do with this lot then?" Tam pondered. "I know you're dying to be asked."

"You really want my advice?" Connor *was* dying to be asked, but never thought it would happen. Gary Pullman had never consulted him for his views. He didn't think Tam was capable of asking anyone anything, never mind listening.

"Yes, I'm asking. That's what I pay you for, don't I?"

"You're paying my petrol."

"All right, I'll double it."

"How about you put me on a proper full-time wage? As you can see"—he nodded in the direction of his daughter—"I have responsibilities."

"What will I get in return?"

"An assistant. Someone with genuine experience. Someone who knows the club inside out."

"Fine."

"Really?" Connor's eyes widened. "Never, ever thought you'd go for that."

"Gotta have somebody. And your grandfather was one helluva player.

And you weren't too shabby yourself."

They shook on it. Connor was thrilled at the thought of quitting the graveyard shift at the service station. At being able to make football a job, a real job, once again.

"However," Connor continued, "as I'm an ex-player, a local, and above all that, a fan, I would've told you what I thought for free."

"Bollocks," Tam groaned.

"You have to show the players some love."

"Not in this lifetime," Tam retorted.

"They're young boys, uneducated boys. A lot of them from broken homes. Even when they're doing bad, they need to be told they're doing some good. They need to feel secure. So get them on your side. Take them out to dinner. Give them a holiday. Show them you care."

"Never gonna happen in a billion years."

"You could at least buy a new boiler for the dressing room?"

"I got that one fixed."

"Twenty seconds of warm water per shower doesn't really cut it."

"Cold showers are good for you. It's proven."

"And give them a bit of grub after the game."

"They're professional bloody footballers. They can afford to feed their own faces."

"It builds spirit. Also, three training sessions a day is too much. As is making them stay behind to watch a *Rocky* film every afternoon."

"Sure. I'll cut it down to one *Rocky* movie a week. Might even alternate it with *Rambo*."

"You could also cut it down to one training session per day."

"Hard work is the only thing that'll get us back on top." Tam thumped the table, sending the salt and pepper shakers jumping. "Hard—bloody—work."

"You did ask. And you are paying for my opinion."

Tam wiped the milk from his chin with a napkin. "A group of overpaid, over-precious, over-pampered pillocks. I'd rather swallow a pregnant giraffe than spend a weekend away with that lot on my hard-earned coin."

Connor wanted to smirk at the 'hard-earned' reference but managed to swallow it. "Football management isn't about them. Or you. It's about the club."

"I love the club. I hate myself. I hate everything and everybody. And I hate modern players even more. I loathe to think what they'll be like in a generation's time. Give me strength, will you ..."

Connor finished his tea. Gillian removed her headphones. She opened the back of her Walkman, trying to squeeze some more life out of the batteries.

"I'm no Kenny Dalglish myself," Connor said. "But I've been around footballers and been a footballer long enough, particularly at this club, to learn a thing or two."

"I'll take it on board."

Tam sighed, squeezing Gillian further against the wall so that she dropped the Walkman with a loud clunk on the table. This only served to make her laugh again. If it had been her father who'd done that, the brat would have stropped big time.

"If you're unwilling to do that with this group," Connor said, "then you might as well be true to your word and pay them off. Buy a whole new squad."

Connor had said it flippantly. It was meant as a subtle dig at some of the remarks Tam had made to the press. No one in their right mind would pay off an entire team, no matter how much money they had or how much they disliked them. And at this stage of the season, no matter what the budget, it would be impossible to buy anything more than a handful of quality players.

Tam moved in closer, suddenly all ears. "And how exactly does one go about doing that?"

Fucking hell, fretted Connor. *He might just be mental enough to give it a go.*

"First thing you do is contact an agent."

"And how do we do that?"

"Can we go now?" Gillian asked, blowing out her chubby jaws.

"I'll buy your girl a milkshake if you stay," Tam offered.

"Wow!" She nearly leapt off her seat. "Yes, please."

Connor nodded, unsure of where all this was headed.

Tam clicked his fingers. "Three milkshakes."

"That'll be £3.75," Vera called back.

"And a plate of pasties as well."

This could be a long meeting.

"So, young Connor Whelan." Tam removed the batteries from his transistor radio and carefully slotted them into Gillian's Walkman, winking to the kid. Then he leaned even further over the table, looking Connor deep in his eyes. "Tell me every single thing."

And Connor, feeling appreciated for the first time since his injury, did just that.

27

"Is this really it?"

"This is it, all right," answered the cabbie.

Claudio lifted his leather Gucci briefcase and opened the car door. The fare was three pounds, but he made sure to give the driver ten. He had lost all his hair and looked like he was suffering from a serious illness.

Everyone he'd met on the island looked like they needed whatever was going.

As a young man, Claudio had volunteered in the Horn of Africa with his then girlfriend, witnessing some horrific sights. Whole towns ravaged by famine and floods. Zero funds put into regeneration. He'd then spent a month in South Africa with his girlfriend's aunt. Though she was from a wealthy part of Cape Town, he passed nearby townships, and heard gunshots, and saw limbless beggars by shanty towns. He'd once seen an old man lying on the street who looked like he'd been burned alive, his clothes and skin charred and peeling. Claudio called the police but didn't hang around to see the outcome. The image had haunted him since.

Yet all this was nothing compared to this street on which the owner of Guff Rovers lived. As a football agent, he was used to meeting in tree-lined boulevards or plush skyscrapers. Private yachts or ocean-side restaurants. Here there were cars on bricks, windows boarded up, and litter and dog shit lining the cracked paths. A stray mutt with three legs scampered up and began growling, then commenced humping his leg. The dog scrammed when what sounded like a pipe bomb went off in the street behind.

What a wasted trip. One of his clients, Steaua Bucharest left-back Marius Filipescu, was wanted by Norwich City. He should be there. But no, his twin brother Luca, who ran the agency and dealt with Jean-Pierre Papin, Roberto Donadoni and Lothar Matthaus, insisted he come and meet the new owner of a struggling side in England's fourth tier instead.

Yes, he was hated by him that much.

Claudio knew he was in a race against time to establish himself at the firm and its new UK division Football First—which he was put second-in-command of—before their mother kicked the bucket and before Luca, who'd given Claudio a job only because their mother insisted, could fire him.

The rotted gate creaked as he tried it. He pushed, then pushed again, but it was only opening an inch. Not enough to squeeze his Yves suit pants through without tearing them on the exposed wire. He pushed so hard that the gate gave way and he launch landed right through it, sending himself flying, knocking his head on a dislodged brick. His entire suit landed in a puddle of mud.

Or the way it was smelling, something much worse.

He shook his head, climbing out of the sludge, cursing and grabbing a handkerchief from his pocket, wiping his chin and suit and wherever else there'd been contact. The man who'd been splashed across the sports' pages all week appeared at the door, waving him in.

"Welcome to paradise," Tam Bam announced.

Claudio forced a smile.

As a teen, he once travelled to England for trials with Ipswich Town. He was a promising striker who'd netted thirty-seven goals in a single season for Udinese under-16s. He had a good turn of pace and could finish. Inter and Roma were among the pack of suitors. But after a year, they all passed. When he hit eighteen, Claudio struggled with his weight or, rather, his love of pizza. He ended up signing pro-forms for Udinese; however, his speed was diminishing, and he only ever featured for the reserves. If he was honest, he liked football, though he never really loved it. He found the discipline side hard, sticking to a diet even harder. He loathed training. He was happier in the kitchen; that was where his true passion lay. When he was released, it made sense for him to open his own pizza restaurant instead of flogging that dead horse called football.

It was Luca who wanted to be the footballer. He would have given his right leg to score a trial for a Serie A club. He couldn't even make their school team. He was smaller and bigger boned. Instead of being happy for his twin, he was eaten by jealousy. Despite being a football obsessive who watched every game he could, Luca refused to watch his brother. On match days, Luca would set the alarm clock in their shared bedroom to go off in the middle of the night. When playing, Claudio often felt like shitting himself on the pitch, more than once soiling his pants, certain that his breakfast had been spiked again.

When Claudio's pizzeria went bankrupt and he couldn't find another job, their mother made Luca hire him. This was the last thing Claudio wanted. He hadn't watched the Azurri in years, Udinese either. But he had no other offers.

Losing his restaurant, his dream, was hard. Working for his brat of a brother was harder. He was put in charge of prospects, burnouts and injury-plagued reserves which nobody, not even the most hardened football fan, had heard of.

And he was forced to visit dumps like the Isle of Guff.

Claudio greeted Tam, then excused himself to the bathroom. There, he wiped himself down with a used towel in the garishly peach-themed room that surely hadn't been renovated since the war.

Nor cleaned since Vietnam.

Tam was waiting for him in the lounge, or what looked more like his bedroom. Claudio couldn't be sure because it had a TV and a dresser, and yet it also had a sofa bed, crumpled sheets, and football posters on the wall from some team he didn't know playing in brown-and-pink checkered shirts. Presumably, this was Tam's own team.

"Would you like a drink?"

This was exactly what Claudio needed. "What do you have?"

"Tea. Bovril. Lucozade." The fat man brandished a chipped Three Lions mug which, much like the man and his abode, looked like it hadn't had many lasting encounters with soap and water. Claudio was hanging for a Chianti or a Chivas. Clearly, Tam Bam's recent windfall hadn't stretched into his liquor cabinet.

"On second thoughts, I'll be fine."

"Take a seat."

Claudio noticed what he thought was a brown skid mark on the sofa. He sat anyway. His trousers were already ruined.

How could anyone live like this? In this filth, this depravity, this squalor. The man needed therapy and a visit from the cleaners. He needed a lot of things before buying a football club and splurging on players.

Claudio shivered. The place also didn't appear to have heating. Best to get out of here as quickly as possible.

"So, Mr Bamford, I hear you have some capital to invest? You have players you want to purchase, yes?"

Tam sat next to him, the sordid moon boot he wore accidentally grazing Claudio's right loafer. He would have to burn that along with his suit should he get off the island alive.

"I want the very best money can buy. From the continent as well. I'm a fan of the mentality of you lot. On loan, of course, for now. I'm not completely daft. I want players from Manchester, Milan and Madrid."

Christ, thought Claudio. This might be worth cancelling that meeting in Switzerland after all. How rich was this man? Claudio's bottom wriggled uncomfortably on the hard sofa bed.

He sure as hell didn't spend his loot on soft furnishings.

Claudio removed a series of folders, along with his new IBM laptop, and began thrashing away. "There's this rising Benfica star, Julio Belsis. A real terrier, all right."

"A lazy bastard, more like," Tam said. "I've heard about him. He's run six point three miles in his last four games. Even I could shift my arse further than that."

"Yes, of course." This man was smarter than he looked. "How about Antonio Lorenzo? An enforcer for Inter Milan reserves."

"Enforcer? Bloody lock-up case, more like. He's run up six yellow cards and two reds in his past seven games."

"He's had a few anger issues which I can put down to his miniature poodle being put down last month; however, I can assure you he's improving."

"I need somebody on the pitch, not fronting the disciplinary panel every week."

"Yes, yes, of course." Claudio sweated. This was going to be a harder sell than he imagined. He squinted, feeling the onset of a migraine. He hoped it wasn't a mild concussion from the fall. He removed a file and laid it on the table. "Rayo Vallecano have a young winger from Nigeria. Top scorer for their B-team and for his nation in the under-20s."

He showed Tam a picture of a teenager who, with his bulky shoulders and beard, could easily have passed for thirty.

Tam clicked his fingers. "Sign him up."

"Good. Great. Obviously, you'll be expected to develop him. You'll be seen as a stepping stone on his career journey."

"Just you wait until he sees this island. He'll be begging me not to send him back to Iberia."

Through the cracked windows, Claudio heard a gale roar and the gate slam. The rain lashed down horizontally. He'd always thought that was a myth about the UK.

"And here's a stopper at AC Milan. Maurizio Taratelli. They paid £1.1M for him from Bologna three years ago. He's been unlucky with injuries." Claudio hoped he sounded believable. Taratelli hadn't played because of crippling anxiety, a bladder problem and an allegation he had to settle out of court for having sex with his fifteen-year-old cousin—or fifteen and ten-and-a-half months, as the player liked to remind him.

"However, I can assure you he's good now. Been an ever-present this season on the bench and for the reserves. Wonderful reader of the game, terrific organiser and speaks English almost as good as you."

Though that wouldn't be hard, thought Claudio, as Tam mumbled something inaudible through the handful of antacids he'd popped.

Tam studied the picture on the screen. The player looked like a buffer version of Real Madrid and Mexico striker Hugo Sanchez who, Claudio had heard from his brother, happened to be one of the gaffer's favourite players away from Guff Rovers.

"Done deal."

"And there's Sven Svensson." He passed a folder to Tam. "Third-choice keeper at Sheffield Wednesday. Capped for his country seven times. He hasn't had a look in since Howard Wilkinson left, but he's fit and starving for action. Any kind of action."

Tam's lips prickled. "What are you trying to say about us?"

"Nothing, nothing at all. Also, his wife is a big fan of the south-west, so I'm told."

Yes, and they're also in the middle of a trial separation as Sven awaits gender reassignment treatment in the summer. Oh, and he hates to fly, which isn't great for a club marooned on an island. This is what Claudio didn't tell him as Tam admired the picture of the six foot five stormtrooper figure with burgeoning breasts.

"Sold," said Tam.

This was getting a bit easier. Claudio imagined he might even make the next plane to London. He could be in Bucharest by day's end and get that Filipescu deal over the line before his brother did.

"Wonderful, just wonderful. They will not disappoint," Claudio lied.

"They'd better bloody not."

"Now let me do the math for you."

Claudio took out the trusty old Casio he'd had since high school. He always got a bit sweaty on the palms when this moment arrived and liked something he could bash. Not that it happened very often.

"That's a £150K fee and £1K a week in wages. For Taratelli, it's a £250K fee and £3K wages. And then for Svensson, there's no fee but a £2K weekly wage. And that, until the end of the season, brings us to £500K even."

As Claudio spoke, Tam didn't say a thing. His face turned an odd colour. Not pale, not red, but a dull shade of green.

Claudio felt he should sugarcoat it. "They'll push you up the table, ensure your survival. Could even put another thousand or so on the gate."

"You want me to give you five hundred grand to borrow a handful of rejects whose fans at their own clubs have never heard of?"

"There's also my fee, which adds another £100K." Half of which would be hoovered up by his brother, Claudio thought. Hoovered being the operative word as Naples' finest would literally go up his nose.

Tam stared at him, his jaw frozen. Claudio wasn't sure if Tam had heard right.

"You don't have to pay it all upfront. You can pay it in instalments. Five of them. Or even weekly. Twenty-two of them if you like."

A more natural shade of off-grey gradually returned to Tam's face. "Get out of my house immediately and back to the pond you crawled out from you, you …"

"Please, Mr Bamford, don't be like this. There are other options. There's a winger from Panathinaikos who only wants £1,200 a week." Tam rose and stood over him. "A promising striker in the youth team at Monaco. He'll set you back £150K flat."

"Get off my island, you criminal."

"I'll even waive half my fee."

"I never should have involved bloody agents."

"There's only six weeks of the transfer window left."

"Six weeks to find an agent who won't bugger me in my own home. Some negotiator you are."

"No offence, Mr Bamford, but these clubs will not negotiate. If you were a Hull or a Bradford and their parent clubs knew their players were coming somewhere with good facilities, where they could play at a credible level, things might be different. We may even be able to get the clubs to cover some of their salary. But you have zero room to negotiate given your club's current, or rather permanent predicament."

"We are a sleeping giant, I'll have you know. These players should be paying for the privilege of coming here."

Claudio wished he'd asked the cabbie to wait. Out the window, a crowd of old people had congregated outside the house like zombies waiting to pounce.

"It's fair to say there are more salubrious surroundings in Western Europe where players can pitch up at."

"You posh, greasy bastard. I should run you out of town with a pitchfork."

Claudio sensed a real possibility this could happen. "Fine, I'll leave. I meant no offence. All I'm saying is maybe you should, as you English say, cut your cloth to suit your coat."

"I'll cut your bloody throat more like."

"Go after players in your league. Players you've seen, players you like. Players with the stomach for the battle."

The giant approached Claudio like a storm cloud about to burst. He placed a heavy arm on Claudio's collar. "Mr Pino, I am going to ask you to leave right away."

Thank you, sweet Jesus, thought Claudio. At least he would be able to breathe now.

"I'm leaving. But so that you don't waste anyone else's time, don't think Manchester, Milan, Madrid. Think Middlesbrough, Mansfield, Morecambe."

The zombies out on the street did not look inviting. He regretted not hiring a vehicle but hadn't seen them at the dock. Europcar probably hadn't reached the island yet.

Like penicillin, soap and running water.

"Could you call me a cab?"

"I'm sure you're perfectly capable of organising that yourself, Mr Super Agent."

"Well, the offer is still there, Mr Bam."

"Mr *Bamford*."

"If you change your mind, and want to get top players on board, and get up that table, and get Guff moving, then call me."

"Aye, and if you don't want to get sat on by a 350-pound giant, then you should go while your legs still work."

Tam lifted him by the lapels and dragged him to the door. He flung him onto the path, his backside landing in the big puddle with a dull splash, his head striking the same brick yet again.

The door slammed behind him. Claudio rubbed his head and looked at the mob of geriatrics crowded by the fence line, greedily eyeing him up. He must be dazed. Surely he was hallucinating. An old man had a dodgy wig, no front teeth, and a line of blood dripping from his nose. The old woman next to him (his wife?) had rollers in her blue hair and was drooling as her arms stretched out to reach him.

Claudio cursed his brother. He'd heard from Sophia in the office that Luca had taken the private jet to Paris as he attempted to engineer Chris Waddle a move to Marseille. Claudio crawled up, only to step in an even bigger puddle on the lawn. He felt the water seep through his loafer and into his sock. Despite the designer clothes, he hadn't received a single lira from his brother in two months, not since he negotiated that one-year contract extension for Roberto Sinagra at Fiorentina. And that was only for £9K.

It barely covered his rent.

"Who's this? He's a cheeky one. Give us some tongue, loverboy," the lady in rollers squawked as she descended on him.

Claudio saw a cab rolling down the street. He leapt in front of it before the crowd could grab him. He smelled rubber as the brakes jammed, the bumper stopping inches from his torso.

"The port, please," he said, jumping in.

"What was that, mate?" the bald driver replied. "You have to speak up."

The old people surrounded the vehicle.

"The port." Claudio spoke slower, using his best English. "The place where the boats leave."

"Oh, the port. I'll have to ask you to pay the fare in advance, I'm afraid. A policy we have for this area."

The old people banged on the windows and tried the doors. Claudio tossed his American Express to the driver as the old man in the wig climbed on the bonnet and began twisting the windscreen wipers like an angry chimp.

"Sorry, we don't do cards."

Claudio searched his pocket and found a twenty. "Here. But please. Please go."

"I'll get you your change."

"I don't want change. I want to go!"

The driver paused and turned. "No need to be rude. You big Euro types are always in a hurry."

"Just go!"

The driver tutted, and the car sped away, knocking someone (or something) off the roof. Then he turned on the remaining windscreen wiper and swished the man with the hairpiece into the gutter like it was an everyday thing.

This was all too much. This was not in the brochure.

As Claudio's head pounded, he decided there and then that he would quit this job and go back to Udine. There were a few pizzerias he knew who'd be glad of his services. It was a job he loved. An industry he was known and respected in. And when his mother died, his brother would have no chance of firing him.

When his mother died, Luca Pino would be a dead man.

28

"Get up, you son of a whore. Go, go. Go!"

Paddy bounced in front of the big screen in William Hill. Castle Royale, which had been leading the pack at the 2.15 at Doncaster for half the race, stumbled again, almost falling.

"Whore of a horse! Bastard whore of a horse!"

The others broke away from the pack, surging to the finish line. Castle Royale's jockey ceased whipping the mare as she slowed to a canter, strolling home second last.

"Useless fucking shitting, wanking, buggering donkey!"

Paddy knew he shouldn't have backed anything with 'royal' in it, the same as he never usually backed anything which ran in blue or orange. Particularly if it had a dash of red and white in there as well.

"Where's that fucking Jason?" he shouted. "Jason, where are you?"

The punters in the bookies were too busy watching their own money fritter away on greyhounds and donkeys in enticingly named places like Bendigo to bother replying.

Jason had given Paddy the tip on the 11/2 shot, and Paddy put thirty quid on it to place. He tore at the slip. He wanted to tear Jason's balls off when he found him. Ah, but who was he kidding? It was his fault. Jason was usually good to him. The kid with the computer and the first in maths from Trinity was usually right. Ninety percent of the time, anyway. But he was wrong every once in a while, the kid admitted as much. It was Paddy's fault for betting the farm. That was him, skint for the weekend.

Angie shouted from the cashier's desk. "Paddy, you've a call."

No one ever called him. Definitely not in here. His skin prickled. Someone was dead. He hoped it wasn't his daughter or his mum. His ex-wife or father he could cope with. Fuck, he'd probably enjoy that. But not them.

Paddy edged over, feeling the effects of the four pints he'd had with lunch. He normally had the two with his pie and chips in the local, the only meal he had each day. This time he'd bumped into Davie Lynch, his old neighbour, and they got chatting, and Davie was buying. Davie wanted to talk football, but Paddy really wanted to know how Davie's niece was getting on. He loved Davie's niece, Cassie was her name. She took after her Sicilian mother in the looks department. She was a beautiful, busty, brown-eyed girl who Paddy had banged several times on account of having once been famous and once having had money. Unfortunately, he wasn't viewed as marriage material. The first fella to come along with an education and a job and she was off. She lived in Galway now and had three children. Washed-up, alcohol-dependent, failed footballers were clearly not her thing when it came to committing.

"This isn't your office," Angie grumbled.

"I'd want a better carpet and a secretary with her own teeth if it were."

Given that he'd dropped forty grand in here last financial year (according to the taxman), he could've afforded somewhere a lot nicer. That figure wasn't worth thinking about. He did think, however, that it merited some level of customer service.

"If it's not women, it's bloody gangsters calling ya. I've had enough."

"So, is it women or gangsters on the blower?" He was serious. He wanted to know. It hadn't entered his mind that it could be the people he owed money to. Anything would be better than the police telling him his mother or daughter were dead.

"Why don't you fuckin' take it and find out." She thrust the phone so hard that it gave him a dead arm. What was her problem? He'd slept in her bed two nights before, had a grand old time. They weren't in a relationship, didn't need one, they'd both had too many bad ones. They agreed on this.

Ange's mood meant this must be a woman. Hopefully that one from Derry he'd met in Badger's Bar last Friday. His balls throbbed, his old fella in his boxers raised its sleepy head. As much as it could after four pints, half a pack of Embassy and a mouth like dry ice.

"Who's this?" he croaked into the receiver.

"This is destiny calling," came a deep voice with an accent he couldn't place. Destiny, who the fuck was she? He hadn't been at the prozzies for the best part of a year, he didn't have the readies. And this one sounded gruff as fuck. He'd bet the farm it was a man.

"And what would Destiny be wanting?"

"I wanted to tell you that I watched you in your debut for Manchester United against Derby. Seventeen years and two hundred and thirty-two days of age, so you were."

Paddy could barely remember this.

The voice continued. "Came off the bench and scored one and made two in a 5–2 win. Then after you moved to Newcastle, you scored a twenty-two-minute hat-trick against the Mackems."

He remembered this, all right. Paddy liked how the caller didn't mention how Newcastle went on to lose the match 4–3, and how he got sent off for an attempted headbutt on the linesman in injury time following a disallowed goal. That was silly.

He'd been five yards offside.

"And with Hibs, you beat four players and rounded the keeper at Ibrox. Then went up to the Copland Road Stand and whipped out a pair of rosary beads and started saying Hail Marys on the turf."

This he didn't like to remember. His front room windows got put in that night. That's when Di left with their daughter. In fact, things had never really been the same since.

"Are you fucking Michael Aspel? Am I on *This is Your Life*?"

"I bet you're in that betting shop right now."

"You know that, you mentalist. You fucking called me here."

"Bet you're skint, as well. Bet you've backed a load of losers."

"Who the fuck are you?" The voice knew him too well.

"Bet you don't even know where your next pint's coming from."

Far too well.

Paddy looked at the payphone on the far wall to see if anyone was at the wind-up. They weren't. He thought of who he owed money to. More people than he could remember, and Sligo was not a big town.

"I asked you once, I'm not going to ask you again. Who the fuck are you?"

"I'm the man who's bringing Paddy Conroy back to the big time where he belongs."

"What?"

"I'm offering you a four-month deal with Guff Rovers. Longer if you perform well."

"Who?"

"We play in the English Fourth Division. For now."

Paddy hadn't thought about football in so long. Even for an ex-pro, it was an impossible game to bet on. And as for actually playing the game, there was no possibility of that. Climbing the two flights to his council flat was a mission. He couldn't remember a day when he hadn't been in the pub. He'd smoked every day since he hung up his boots and a few years before that. He didn't even watch football. He was shocked when last week someone in the chippy told him that Frank Worthington was still playing, Wimbledon had won the Cup, and English sides were banned in Europe.

"Right, you, Mr Whatever—Your—Fucking—Name—Is. I'm thirty-five years of age. I haven't kicked a ball in the last five of them. I don't think I could run more than twenty yards without needing a piss, a fag or a lung transplant."

"You won't need to run. We have players who'll do that for you. We just need you wandering around the final third sprinkling your fairy dust."

"*Fairy what?* You're off with the fairies, you are." Paddy watched the screen as the pack of greyhounds waited in the traps. He remembered he had a tenner on Luca Brasi, the favourite. "Listen, a few years ago I might've done. But not now. I, my friend, have hit rock bottom."

"As much as it pains me to say it, where we are is rock bottom. You could outshine these no-talent ballsacks in your sleep."

The dogs shot off. Luca Brasi in the sky-blue coat made a good start, establishing a lead.

"Nice thought, but I'll be okay."

"I bet you're watching another race right now. I bet you're losing ground as we speak. And that'll be you spent for the week. It'll be Pot Noodle and stolen cans of Special Brew from the offie this weekend."

Paddy scanned the betting shop. Who was this? How did he know? But no one was so much as glancing at him.

"You're a madman. This is harassment."

"You're the madman for not sticking your arm down this phone line and ripping my hand off for this very generous offer. I am your Jesus Christ. I am your saviour!" The other dogs gained ground at the turn. "I'm offering eight hundred quid a week. Room and board in a cosy guesthouse by the sea, a hop, a skip and a jump from your beloved Emerald Isle. I'll even give you a five-grand signing-on fee."

"You fucking what?" Paddy almost dropped the phone. He'd had a few clubs contact him over the years, although admittedly not in the betting shop where all hope usually died. Most offers involved an unpaid trial. Some promised a couple of grand for an exhibition game. Then there was that short-term contract a few years back from a South African side for five hundred quid a week which he agreed to before he went on a bender in Cork and woke up with a broken ankle and a torturous case of the clap.

This, however, made his ears perk right up.

He must have paused for a while because the caller was suddenly shouting down the line. "Fine. Ten grand signing on, and a grand a week. And a bottle of Bells and a carton of Woodbines after every match, excluding the midweek ones. But that is it. I'm haemorrhaging cash."

Paddy watched every dog bar the last overtake Luca Brasi. Fuck that prick. That traitor was always his most hated character in *The Godfather*. The cheating, backstabbing bastard.

And fuck Jason too. Two big losses in a row. He was losing his touch. And when Paddy saw him next, the kid would be compensating him with some pounds or pints, or he'd be losing some teeth from that Colgate smile.

The door chimed. Paddy peeked out and saw one of the Kazam twins enter. Which one, he couldn't be sure. One was male, the other female, but the girl's five o'clock shadow was thicker than her brother's and both had the same squat, rugby-player build. Paddy hadn't seen either of them in months. He remembered the five grand he'd borrowed from them at the end of the summer. It was to pay his rent and cover a trip to Vegas for his brother's fortieth. He planned on having a few wins at the poker table and paying them back as soon as he returned. It didn't happen. He didn't even come close.

He lost £18K.

Now he was fucked. Properly fucked. And he knew from the grapevine down in Dublin, where they were based, that the Kazams are people you do not fuck with. Jason's neighbour had been in a coma for six months proving it.

Yes, they might have been Man U fans, but even his former status wouldn't save him. His head would be in a plastic bag by the morning, and that was if he was lucky. He had to get out of Sligo fast. But how could he? He hadn't a penny to his name.

"You have yourself a deal," he told the mystery caller.

"Right answer. I'll send the tickets. Be at the ground midday on Monday."

"Fuck that, send a driver first thing. I want to be there right away."

"I can arrange that. I love your enthusiasm, I have to say."

"One thing …"

"Which is?"

"Who's this club again?"

"The mighty Guff Rovers."

"Who?"

"The Faeries. From the famous Isle of Guff. The most celebrated club in the south-west. We've had the most goal kicks of any side in the football league for the past five years running."

Paddy didn't comment as he didn't want to appear rude to his new employer. "Where did you play, did you say?"

Tam slowed it down. "The —Isle—of—Guff." Paddy remembered playing in Bristol once but had never heard of this place. "Y'know. Off the Cornish coast in the Celtic Sea."

"Right. I see." Distance didn't matter. The further the better for Paddy at the moment.

"It's the most beautiful place in the world. There's sand, there's sea, there's fresh air. As good as anything you Micks can dish up."

"Sounds all right."

All right? You'll wish you spent your entire career here."

The Kazam twin was speaking to a few of the regulars. Ted, still wearing his painting overalls, pointed towards the cashier's desk. Paddy ducked.

"So, we have a deal then?" asked the voice.

"Could you wire us a few grand right now?"

"You haven't kicked a ball yet."

"It really is a matter of life and death."

"This is what I get for extending a helping hand."

"Please," Paddy pleaded. Ange was speaking with the twin out on the floor. Paddy didn't fancy playing with a bullet in his kneecap. He imagined this so-called Faery on the phone wouldn't either.

"How much then?"

"Say five grand."

Tam sighed. "Aye, I suppose that's how things are done."

Paddy recited his bank digits. He thanked the caller and hung up.

Ange re-entered the office. "Mr Kazam is looking for you."

"I know."

"Says he'll be waiting out the front until he finds you."

"I'm all good now."

"Tells me you went to Vegas instead of visiting your sick aunt in London. What a waste of space you are."

Paddy kissed her cheek. "Thanks for everything, Ange."

"You gobshite."

He stepped out of the office. "You mind if I leave by the fire exit?"

"We don't have one."

Paddy had to stop running and ducking. He could pay off his brother now as well. Buy his daughter a present for her birthday three weeks ago. He could go over the road and buy everyone a drink, everyone he'd patsied off since he quit football. And he could get really rat-arsed for the last time before training began.

When he hit the street and saw the twin coming towards him, he realised he didn't catch the name of the caller. That he'd never gotten round to working out how he was supposed to reach the Isle of Gak, or whatever it was called.

He couldn't even remember the name of the club.

Kazam shot him a smile. It was a foot long with that Chelsea scar attached to it. It chilled Paddy's bones. It was the boy, all right, and he was reaching for the inside top pocket, not giving a fuck about the men, women and children going about their business on the busy street.

Paddy hoped the mystery man had remembered to transfer those funds or there might be a body bag lining up for the team next Saturday.

29

Tam held the buckled Guff Rovers umbrella high over his head to stop the rain beating down on him, as he stood on the pavement watching the minibus of new players arrive from Swindon Town.

Fucking Swindon.

He'd desperately wanted half of Manchester United's youth team, but Alex Ferguson wouldn't return his calls. He knew this meant Fergie must be under pressure there. He always believed that going to Old Trafford had been the wrong move for him.

Tam called Nottingham Forest instead. He offered to pay the wages of their best half-dozen reserves players as part of a loan deal. He even bid twenty grand per player, then fifty grand. When he was told in no uncertain terms that it was not their policy to loan players to a fourth-tier side, Tam told them he'd never videotape their highlights on *Match of the Day* ever again, and that his signed Brian Clough unauthorised biography would be going straight in the fireplace.

Tam then contacted every other top-flight side offering the same terms and was told the same thing. Then he tried every Second Division club for their reserves (this time no fee, just wages). When he'd been blanked by twenty-three of them, Swindon Town finally said yes. They requested £25K per player. Tam grudgingly agreed. It was only when he hung up that he discovered their second-string side were anchored to the bottom of the Reserve League, with three wins in thirty-three games and a pitiful four draws.

Still, beggars can't be choosers, as he was fast learning.

Where was that BBC crew, Tam wondered? *The Mirror, The Sun,* the *Daily Mail* too. The only one here was that smart-arse reporter from the *Cornish Post*. He'd had Felicity order in a hundred bottles of Lucozade and a hundred pasties for the hungry hordes. He licked his lips at the thought of the food. This was countered by that familiar rise of stabbing heartburn which pierced his oesophagus.

"Where's the chairman?" asked Phil Gates from *The Post*, tucking into a pasty which he'd nabbed on the way back from the bathroom.

"He's not here." Tam didn't want to enlighten the little sneak that he had no idea where Gus was. That he hadn't seen him since he'd signed the cheque to take over the majority share of the club.

"Saw him on *Good Morning Britain* yesterday," Phil said.

"Hmph." Tam also didn't want to give the little twerp the satisfaction of knowing that this was news to him.

"Yup. Over there in Antigua preparing for some big yacht race. Has a shiny new thirty-nine-footer. Can't think of where he's suddenly got all the beans."

"Right you are."

"But you knew all this, didn't you?"

"Of course I did."

The bastard! Tam stewed. Sailing around the world like Captain bloody Cook on his coin when their club was sinking in the mire. Tam should have gone to the police and reported him for attempted murder after all, then taken the whole club off him for a song.

"These your new players?" Phil chuckled with his dictaphone at the ready.

All six disembarked from the minibus. One was on crutches, one looked almost as overweight as Tam. Another wouldn't have scratched five feet and looked around twelve years old.

The last of them got out, a beanpole wearing the same red tracksuit as the others which didn't reach his elbows, never mind his wrists.

"Thanks for lifting us," he said to the driver in a posh home counties accent. Then his neck spasmed, his eyes rolled back and he spat. "Fucking shit tit bastard!" He assessed his surroundings but struggled to control his tic. "Nice part of the world ... fucking bollocks! Can't wait to play for the team ... shit rubbish wanks!"

Phil Gates couldn't peel his eyes from them. "Looks like you've pulled off a masterstroke here, gaffer."

Tam thought about grabbing a rake, beating them away from the building and back onto the bus, and telling the driver not to stop until he reached the water.

He knew he was in far too deep.

Instead, he headed straight into the building. He grabbed a tray of pasties and locked himself in the toilet. He hoped the reporters wouldn't turn up. Not so they would miss out on the unfolding debacle, but so he could claim all the pasties which he'd need to cheer himself up for the rest of the week. There had to be some payoff from all this.

He drooled over them until another violent flood of acid singed his throat. Then he vomited into the pan beneath.

30

Down on all fours, Hans bit down hard on the hand towel which Darryl had wrapped around his mouth so he wouldn't scream out and wake the neighbours. He flinched as Darryl bucked and groaned and finally climaxed.

Hans knew what always followed. A slap on the bottom followed by a punch in the spine. Then a series of random thumps to the head until Darryl's lifeless, sweaty and middle-aged body collapsed onto Hans's black-and-blue back-end.

Aching from the blows, Hans squirmed out from under the larger man. They'd had carbonara for dinner, and Darryl had started on a second bottle of red. Hans doubted Darryl would rise before daybreak.

Hans hobbled to the shower. He turned on the warm water and scrubbed. This was the best thing about Darryl's apartment. The shower. He only had a bath in his sharehouse, which was clogged with all manner of man-filth.

What a life this was. Hans was in a rut so deep he needed binoculars to see the way out. He'd been hounded out of Leeds United when they discovered he was gay. A small section of the fans heard he frequented Bump, one of the local queer clubs. When his form dipped, mainly through a recurring ankle knock which the manager insisted he play through, the fans turned on him. He was called in by the board, who awkwardly asked if the allegations were true.

Was he gay?

He wanted to deny it like he had his entire career. Wanted to laugh it off. Wanted to tell them where to get off. But recently, he'd been feeling a change from within. Instead of mixing with the lads, he was reading Karl Marx, James Baldwin, E. M. Forster, Christopher Isherwood and Gore Vidal. He was suddenly feeling the need to break free, to be himself no matter what the cost.

So, he did it. Hans Schickler, in the middle of eighties' AIDS hysteria, told the club's owners that the rumours were true. He was gay.

Gayer than a bagful of butterflies.

It felt wonderful, so wonderful to feel that weight lift. The Leeds board said they supported him. Said they'd do everything within their powers to protect him from any backlash from the fans or the media. They even told him they were proud of him.

Two days later they put him on the transfer list.

Hans dropped down a division, signing for Bradford City for a cut-price £200K. The Bantams informed him his sexuality wasn't an issue. The fans welcomed him, their biggest supporters group stating they were proud to have one of the first openly gay footballers to play for them.

But every ground he went to he was hounded from the start of the game until the end with chants about cocks, balls and arse. He was no longer a 'Nazi bastard', he was now a 'Gay Nazi Bastard.' In all truth, he was never hounded until the end of the game because he never lasted a full one, the abuse from the players on the pitch and fans in the stands having the desired effect, meaning that he couldn't hit the proverbial donkey's arse with a banjo.

He was that bad that soon his own fans were on his tail, giving him even more stick than the opposition did. Their initial fervour for having a homosexual as a number 9 proved nothing more than a short-lived novelty.

Soon he was out on loan and moving down the divisions. Preston North End, Huddersfield Town, then Southend. But he never felt valued, the abuse never abated, and his form didn't improve. He fell out of love with football. He started doing more cocaine and drinking a whole lot more.

Before long, his contract was terminated.

He should have returned to Austria. Things were more liberal there. Everywhere, that is, apart from his family home. His dad was furious at the way he had sabotaged his own career by telling the world that he shagged boys.

Hans ended up working in bars in Yorkshire. Gay bars. It was shit pay, shit work, shit conditions, but at least it allowed him to be himself. And this was where he met Darryl. Darryl gave him a home, gave him money, let him quit his job. But Hans knew he served no other purpose than to be the older man's bitch.

Hans turned the shower off. He dried himself, being gentle around his bruised back. The phone rang. He put his hand out the door and grabbed it off the wall, even though it most certainly would be for Darryl.

"Hello."

"Hello, Hans Schickler?"

Hans took the cordless into the bathroom, locked the door and commenced brushing his teeth. At midnight it could only be the press or some prank.

"Who's this?"

"Thomas Bamford, manager of the famous Guff Rovers."

"Who?"

"Ahh, not you as well."

"Sorry, what is it you want?" The man had a thick accent, even stronger and more indecipherable than the people of Yorkshire.

"Do you want to come and play football for us, Mr Schickler?"

Hans hadn't played in a year. He didn't even have an agent anymore, never mind a pair of boots. "Which division are you in?"

"The fourth."

This was how far Hans had fallen. He had half a dozen full international caps for his country. He'd been on Bayern Munich's books as a kid.

"I don't think so, Mr ..."

"Bamford."

Darryl was awake. He tried the handle. He rapped on the door. "Hans. Hans, baby. Who are you speaking to?"

"Just someone in football."

"I thought it was all over. You told me it was all over. You need to concentrate on your new life. Our life together. I give you a good life, Hans."

The older man hated the game. If it had been tennis or cricket, then things might have been different. The thought of Hans getting back his independence, his confidence, would kill him. The thought of Hans leaving him would be worse.

And that's exactly what Hans intended to do.

He'd been jogging five miles each morning when Darryl went to the office. Kicking a ball out on the balcony in the afternoon and hitting the gym below the apartment complex every evening. Darryl didn't complain about this so much as he worshipped the younger man's body. At least until he battered it after sex.

"I can't go back down the leagues," Hans whispered to the caller. "I'll never get back." He'd been talking to agents and investigating opportunities in America, Australia and Japan. Places where people were more tolerant than the north of England. More tolerant than his family. Still, there were no concrete offers.

"With us, you will. We'll be playing European Cup football within five years. Cup Winners Cup within four. If we're not, I'll eat my moon boot."

This joker was either drunk or insane. Or both. "You know that no club in this country wants to touch me?"

"I used to watch you when you played for Leeds that first season. Twenty-nine goals in forty-eight appearances for a target man can't be wrong."

This joker may be drunk and insane, but he knew his stuff. "Best of luck with everything, but I don't think this sounds right for me." An intermediary for Winnipeg Fury said he would hear back soon. The same with Adelaide City and Kyoto Shiko.

"What would make you say yes?"

"Division One wages," Hans replied in a flash.

"How about Leeds United wages?"

Hans almost choked on his toothbrush. None of those other clubs had called. He knew deep down they wouldn't. Despite his fatigue, he weighed it up quickly. "And a twenty-grand signing-on fee."

"Mr Schickler, you drive a hard bargain, but you are on."

He was informed he'd hear more from the club secretary, and then they hung up. The knocking became louder. Hans really didn't want to play for Gubbed Rovers, or whatever they were called, in some footballing backwater. However, with this money he could buy his independence.

Hans wrapped the bath towel around him and nervously opened the door.

Darryl was pacing the polished floorboards in his black silk dressing gown. He'd poured himself another glass of red. "Who was that?"

"A football coach."

"But you don't play anymore." Darryl never liked to talk about Hans's career, unlike every other guy who he'd slept with who wanted to know every little detail. Darryl was into footballer bodies, and that was it.

"Where do they play?" he asked.

"The Isle of Guff."

"Where the heck's that?"

"Off the coast of Cornwall."

"I can't up sticks and move my operation there. What about my children? What about my wife?"

Hans smiled. Darryl's accounting firm. He could never leave it. Or the wife he always moaned about yet never spent any time with.

Hans was free.

"I guess this is it then?" Darryl finished the glass.

"I guess so."

"Well, get on that bed and get that pretty bum of yours greased and pointing skywards. You can give me a proper send-off."

Hans was free all right, just not quite yet.

31

The prison gates at Varonil Oriente swung open. Billy Wood had heard this same creaking sound at nine a.m. every morning and prayed for the day they would open for him.

He gave Mani's bicep a brotherly squeeze. It was all he could do to stop himself from weeping. He saw in Mani's nervous smile that the Mexican was emotional, too, as they, along with twenty or so other inmates, felt the breeze of freedom caress their cheeks.

As they took their first steps back out into the world, wives, girlfriends, children and the odd parent came into view. Mani rushed to greet his brood. His wife, Juana, a big-boned and large-breasted Latino woman who Billy recognised from the pictures which wallpapered their shared cell, wrapped her arms around him, kissing him. Mani's young boys, Carlos and Rafa, stood to the side, unsure of this man whom they couldn't remember ever living at home, only knowing him from Saturday visits.

With tongues flying and fingers gliding through hair, their greeting became an increasingly passionate one. Mani was convinced his wife was cheating on him with their neighbour, a dry cleaner with a chain of stores in the vicinity. Billy hoped the bulge in her tummy was from too many tacos and Tecate. If not, he knew it wouldn't be long before Mani exacted a bloody revenge on both her and the dry cleaner and was back inside Varonil.

After kissing both his boys on the head, Mani returned to say goodbye to Billy, who was leaning against a Pepsi machine and smoking his first Delicado as a free man. There was nobody to greet him.

"You sure you no come with us?" Mani asked.

Mani hadn't introduced him to his family. Billy knew it was a source of shame for him to be in prison, no matter how close he'd been with his fellow cons in the big house.

"I got my bus ticket, Mani. I'll be okay."

"You need anything, you call me."

"I want to get as far away from here as possible." Billy didn't want to tell his friend that apart from the stub in his pocket he had no other form of currency. The cartel still owed him his share of cash. He knew it was a long shot getting it after so long, and that there was a chance he would die doing so. But it was his only hope of getting some quick capital. Not that he'd warranted getting killed. He'd done the right thing. He didn't rat on anyone. Still, this was Mexico City and *loco* shit happened to those even with the best intentions.

If the plan didn't work out and he was still alive to tell the tale, then he didn't know what he would do. The Embassy might help him out, but he doubted they wanted him back in Britain. He knew his family didn't. He'd contacted his father, his ex, his other ex, his brother. No one had written or returned his calls.

The two men hugged.

"You take care, bud," Billy told him. "Don't do anything stupid. Remember how lonely it is back in there."

"You too, my friend."

Mani returned to the arms of his family. Billy hoped for the woman's sake she hadn't been stupid. Those boys deserved a mum and a dad.

Billy waited in the bus queue, lighting another cigarette. Mani had been a good friend to him. They'd bonded over football. Mani had been a goalkeeper in the Segunda Division, Mexico football's second-tier, with Nuevo Necaxa and various other lower-league outfits. But a recurring back injury and a failure to secure a new contract saw him drawn to the drug trade. The only industry in this fucked-up country offering a decent wage.

The pair had a mutual acquaintance in Rocky Diaz, whom Billy had played with for a season at Crystal Palace in 1979. Rocky had shared a home in Hampstead with Ossie Ardiles and Ricky Villa and had the same agent. Billy and Rocky partied together from time to time, though they were never huge pals. The Mexican's English wasn't up to much, and he was married, and very Catholic. But he was from the same village as Mani Fernandez, ensuring a friendship when Billy was on the inside. While Billy's own connections with the cartel ensured his safety.

The bus pulled up, its engine spewing ugly black smoke into the virgin sky, clouding this bright Monday morning.

"Does this go into town?" Billy asked the driver in his best Spanish.

The driver looked down at him, abruptly spitting on the step. The Madonna tattoos on his arm and the gold in his mouth told Billy that he knew the inside of Varonil very well. He stared at the cigarette. "You don't bring that in here, gringo."

"No worries, friend."

Billy took a final puff and was about to hit the steps when he saw a man in a button-up shirt and chinos wave from across the street. He hadn't seen that paunch, that overbite, or that mat of white-blonde albino hair since he landed on these shores. But he would never mistake them. Kelvin James. His old agent was coming this way.

What the fuck was he doing here?

"Billy!" His hand extended towards him. "Hope the fifteen months of ass pounding wasn't too enjoyable."

Billy ignored the handshake. "Well, this is awkward."

"Look at you, my son." He felt some of Billy's muscle. "You look fantastic. Better than when you went in. That is a relief."

"I'm not doing another job."

"If you remember correctly, I was the one who told you not to get involved shifting that shit with these wetbacks."

"Keep your voice down."

"Is that really a slur?" Kelvin whispered. "They say it all the time in the movies."

"You're the one who got me involved in the bung and put me on this path."

"Billy, Billy, son. Your memory is bent. Must be all that cut coke in there. I was exonerated from that. I told you not to go through with it. You stupid fucker."

This was Kelvin James. As shady as they come.

Billy had another agent from when he was a teen. Richard Fox— aka The Silver Fox. A Fifer. A true gent. He'd always looked after him, always been fair. Billy was in Chelsea's youth set-up and highly rated by Dave Sexton. He'd featured a few times for the senior side in cup games. England under-21s were watching. It was only a matter of time before he started in the league. Then Kelvin latched on to him one Saturday night in the west end. Gave him cocaine for the first time. Told him he was the best thing to come out of London since Bobby Moore. Told him that Richard was a dinosaur afraid to get his client what was duly his. That at nineteen he should be playing regularly, that he should be on triple the money. Billy stupidly listened to him. He stupidly believed every word. And more stupidly, he gave old Richard the flick and went with him.

Fast forward six years, three transfers and two failed loan moves later, and he became embroiled in a match-fixing scandal. Wimbledon versus Fulham. Fulham to win by two goals. Billy had pulled out of the deal at the last moment and played the game of his life in a 1–1 draw. Yet the FA still slammed him for two years.

His career in Britain was over.

Following that, it was a swift slide. With a three-hundred-grand mortgage, three kids to support and a soon-to-be ex-wife who wanted him fleeced, Billy had to get money from somewhere. He had no qualifications and, by his own admission, no brains apart from the ones in his feet.

Young, daft, impressionable. Billy Wood further utilised Kelvin's contacts and fell further down the slippery slope transporting Class A drugs in and out of Mexico under the guise of being a freelance football scout. He was stopped at Aeropuerto Internacional de la Ciudad de México bound for Heathrow with five pounds of cocaine strapped to his thigh and given six years, three and a half with good behaviour. Three and a half years which as a young father and footballer should have been the best years of his life.

But that was all in the past. That was behind him, and Billy was looking towards the future. Although what kind of future he wasn't sure.

He looked his old agent in his eyes, squinting in the sun, and could muster no hate for the man, try as he might. Only pity.

"Kelvin, I forgive you."

"Ah yes, I heard you got in touch with your evangelical side whilst in the clanger."

"That's true. But if you call me a stupid fucker again, I'll rip that pinhead from the top of your shoulders and shove it up your chocolate box."

"Classy."

"You coming or not, gringo?" the driver called. The bus had filled with prisoners who were as unpopular as Billy, with no one to welcome them.

"Anyways." Billy turned back to Kelvin. "I've got places to be."

"Where've you got to be?"

"Cut the shit, Kelv. Are you here to see me or what?"

"I'm hardly here to see the sights, you stupid fucker."

Billy fixed him with a stare. The man's colourless complexion was already singeing in the sun, and he was in dire need of a hat. For a split second, Billy considered making good on his threat. Though he knew it wouldn't be the best move with prison guards stationed metres away.

"Sorry," Kelvin retreated. "Listen. Let's start again. I was passing by and bumped into you. Let's grab a beer and a bite. Get some pussy if you're still into that."

"No, thanks." Billy slung his old Fulham kitbag over his shoulder. It contained his life possessions. A bible, a spare shirt, pair of Sambas, an old Walkman and his British passport. He stepped onto the bus.

"I've got an offer for you," Kelvin said. "A grand a week. Same again in relocation expenses."

Billy stopped. "I haven't played pro in five years."

"Doesn't matter. There's no trial. This gaffer really wants you."

Billy hadn't played professionally for five years, but he'd been a standout player for the prison's side, which had won their conference for the past three seasons. He'd played his best football. It was the reason he got food brought in from outside, a room with a view and was kept away from most of the other inmates.

He was treated like Bobby Moore in there.

Kelvin smiled. "Told you I'd look after you when you got out, didn't I?"

This was true. But Billy didn't want Kelvin's help anymore. Billy didn't want anything to do with him, had vowed as much when he heard The Silver Fox passed away last year and realised there was no chance of him ever making it up to the man who had taken him down to London and treated him like a son. The gentleman was the sole reason he even had a career in the first place. God only knows where he'd have ended up had he stuck with him. Although since he'd gone on to look after the likes of Frank McAvennie, Des Walker and David Platt, he had a fair idea it wouldn't involve a stretch in Varonil Oriente.

Billy stepped off the bus. "Who's it for?" The idea of playing for a top Mexican team appealed. He liked the weather, the women, and if he kept his nose clean (pardon the pun) he envisioned things could work for him here.

"Guff Rovers."

"Who?"

"In England."

"*Pendejo*!" the driver shouted. The doors slammed, and the bus chugged away.

"No, thanks," Billy told Kelvin. The thought of going back to Blighty so soon and facing his family, his friends, the media? That did not appeal.

"What else have you got going on? Hitting the pro golf circuit? Opening your own church?"

"I'm going to the cartel for the share I'm owed."

Kelvin laughed. "Those in that syndicate are either dead or have crossed the border. You've got about as much chance of getting your money as my Leicester City have of ever winning the title."

Billy reached into his top pocket for another cigarette and realised he was out. Kelvin lit one in front of him, taking a puff. "I'd shout you a snout, but it's not really in my best interests with you being my prized athlete and all."

"I told you, I haven't played in five years."

Kelvin took a step back and eyed Billy up as one might a prize-winning stallion stud or a high-class hooker. "You look good. Great, even. In fact, you've never looked so fucking fab. I'm thinking of getting down on my knees right now and showing you."

"That's because there's nothing else to do in there except work out."

"I guess so. If you don't include getting your face rammed into a showerhead and some wetback cock rammed in your jacksy every other day. Sorry, I meant *Mexican* cock."

Billy snatched the pack of cigarettes out of Kelvin's top-pocket and lit one. "You watch too many movies."

"You saying that shit's a myth?"

"How about I have a friendly word in the guard's ear and you can find out for yourself?" Billy nodded over at Javier on the gate. The guard gave a thumbs-up. He'd been the prison side's coach driver and their most vocal fan.

"I heard what you were doing in there," Kelvin said. "I know everything. Star of the fucking football team. The league's player of the year. Word travels even when there's no one in the stands."

"Shown on ITV, was it?"

Kelvin removed an envelope from his blazer pocket. "Fuck wasting your time with the cartel and signing your own death warrant. Here's your ticket home, sunshine." Kelvin handed him the envelope displaying the British Airways insignia.

Billy held it. Admired it. "You are keen. How much you making out of this?"

"Doing it out of the goodness of my heart."

"Yeah, right. You paid for a thirteen-hour flight to tell me this?"

"Bollocks to that. I got their daft bastard of a gaffer to pay for it. I'll take you to the airport, but you're going back yourself. I'll be on the other plane heading to Cancún for a fortnight. The prozzies there will be retiring with what I'm about to splurge. I'd invite you; however, you have bigger fish to fry, my boy."

Billy had to laugh at that. Kelvin would never change.

Was he really going to say no to a ticket back to civilisation and a guaranteed wage? He could start paying back the child support he owed. He didn't even know where the cartel was anymore. And if what Kelvin had said was true—*if*—then it was futile and dangerous to try to find them.

This was a gift from God, and though it was a strange messenger that Him Above had chosen, Billy couldn't look this gift horse in the mouth.

Even if it was Kelvin fucking James.

Billy pocketed the plane ticket. He reached out to Kelvin's top pocket and reclaimed the packet of cigarettes which Kelvin had taken back off him. "You can shout the cab."

Kelvin smiled and whistled to one waiting across the sun-baked road.

Billy knew that if things didn't work out, there'd be good money going for match-fixing, even at that level, away from the glare of the top-flight. Not that he would be actively seeking to do that again. No way.

Then again, prison wasn't so bad. Maybe he could request to come back to Mexico to do his stint. Star of the football team, burrito with the lot every night, decent room with a view. Not that he was thinking of going back there.

Not just yet ...

32

Zak Bates pulled his sock over his shin guard. He tried not to wince as his hand brushed his bruised fibula. He'd knocked it in last week's loss but didn't want to mention it to anyone. Looking across the dressing room at the six newly arrived Swindon players, he couldn't afford to. He'd be lucky to make the bench this weekend as it was, and he needed that appearance money.

He checked his pager. His brother put his bets on for him. He read the message. Barry Town were losing 2–1 to Bangor City in their Welsh League fixture.

Bugger.

Now he really couldn't afford to let on about the injury. Why had he put fifty quid on a home win for a team he'd never heard of, from a league he'd never watched? His fingers just burned to dial the bookies night and day.

He didn't even know where Bangor was.

And despite being a professional footballer, if he was honest, he didn't like football. Every player he'd ever met knew more about the game than him. Until recently, he'd always believed that George Best was an Arsenal legend and Pele used to play for West Brom.

Still, that was the affliction of being a gambler, he supposed. It was an illness. His doctor told him so. His bank manager too. He'd have much preferred if his tennis career had kicked on when he was a teen.

Unfortunately, he played more like Johnny Cash than Pat Cash.

Zak watched the Swindon players change. One had a headband on. One wore gloves. Another was wearing tights. Two of them were speaking Portuguese or French or whatever it was Africans spoke. It could have been Brummie for all Zak knew. Popstar looks, cabriolets in the carpark. The players looked like they came from Washington DC rather than Wiltshire. If Washington was exotic, that is.

Not that Zak would know.

He knew he'd be out of the team this weekend. He just knew it. Even by his own admission, he'd had a shocker last Saturday. It hadn't been helped by his fiancé paging him during the warm-up with a quote for a new carpet for three grand. The weekend before it had been wedding dresses which cost five. The week before that it was cruises to the Bahamas for their honeymoon. Another four grand spunked down the drain.

She was unaware he had an eight grand overdraft owing. Or that he owed sixteen grand on credit cards. She didn't know the waterside flat she moved into with him was a rental. That his Mustang was a loan from his cousin who was in America on exchange. Michele didn't know he had a child in Motherwell from when he played there for a year and was forking out twenty percent of his wages to support him or her.

Him or her, he could never remember which.

Michele didn't know he'd contemplated hanging himself last week but couldn't work out how. Turns out it's far more complicated than it looks.

She knew so little about football that she genuinely believed he'd be named in England's next World Cup squad and was already researching Italian day spas.

Zak winced as he stood. His hip was giving him grief too. That was another thing he'd have to conceal.

If he could get through this last training session, he had a shout for tomorrow's match. If only the gaffer didn't make them do the assault course that he'd built himself, featuring a bed of nails and hot coals to walk over barefoot, then he might be all right.

Or if he didn't make them finish up with a full-contact game of British Bulldog.

Zak heard those imposing steps boom from down the hallway. There was a collective groan from the players as they could feel the dark cloud approach. He wondered what tricks the gaffer had in store for them today.

Bull riding? Bungee jumping? Cage fighting?

A pair of lighter steps followed. *Please, God*, he thought. *Not more of them.* If any extra players were signed, then he really would be pushed to the margins.

Tam entered alone. "All right, you wage thieves. I trust you all had a restful night's sleep?"

Restful? Zak yawned. The ten-mile run the day before followed by two hours in the gym with Tam pacing around them like Sergeant Hartman from *Full Metal Jacket* cracking a riding whip. Zak had fallen asleep the minute he got in his front door. He hadn't slept fourteen hours straight since he started smoking skunk the summer he left school.

"And if you haven't and you're here to dick around," Tam rambled on, "then that's fine by me because I've three new players for you to meet."

Zak felt a shortness in his breath and wished he'd brought his Ventolin.

"These are in addition to the new lads from Luton who I'm sure you have already made your blood brothers."

None of the established Guff players had even managed to make eye contact with them over the past week, never mind shake their hands and welcome them. They were all too aloof. But at least the Guff players knew where they were from.

Swindon, not Luton.

Still, no one wanted to correct the gaffer. Not even the Swindon players who were too preoccupied. One was checking his pager. One was reading the *Financial Times*, two were braiding each other's hair. One was eating a salad and the tall, gangly one who swore all the time had nodded off.

"And I'm well aware there are no Oxbridge scholars amongst you. But even you lot of reprobates will be able to do the maths and work out that six plus three plus another three adds up to an entire outfield team, and then some."

Twelve new players? The silence in the dressing room was a heavy one.

"I would first like to introduce Ralph McInnes." The door swung open. The fact that the individual in question had a face resembling an overgrown potato wasn't what made their jaws drop. Or the fact he had to turn sideways to get his six foot six frame through the doorway.

No, it was what he was wearing.

"Gaffer, why's he wearing a skirt?" Rory McGrory asked.

The sniggers spread across the room like a Mexican wave.

"*Why's he wearing a bloody skirt?* he asks," Tam repeated. "A bloody skirt? That sums up the mentality around here, doesn't it?"

Ralph stood there in his red-and-black tartan kilt and grunted, seemingly unaware of where he was or what was going on. He sat on the bench, the impact sending Zak flying up and off it like they were on a seesaw.

"He's dressed like that because he's been training for the Highland Games. Night and day, might I add, because he's that bloody dedicated. You are looking at the second-best caber toss champion in the world."

The players didn't look at each other. Doing so would result in another fit of giggles, which none of them could stop. And the repercussions of that could result in the termination of their contracts or Ralf-Whatever-His-Face-Was ripping their heads off their shoulders and caber tossing them right back up to Scotchland.

"Gaffer?" Lance asked. "What good is a cabbage tosser?"

"It's caber toss, you hillbilly hick. Of course, he can't play football. Of course, he can't. But neither can you lot. What he can do, though, is throw a ball fifty yards. Every throw-in we get will be like having a corner. He's our secret weapon, our ace in the pack. We can't beat other teams at football, you've proved that. But we can beat them in other ways if we act smarter."

The players didn't have to look at each other to communicate the same feeling. They were collectively aware that this was the precise moment that Tam Bam had truly lost the plot.

"Percentage football, folks. The more times we get the ball in the box, the more chances we'll create, and the more goals we'll score. You don't need your Isaiah Newtons or your Alfred Einsteins to tell you that."

Tam joined Ralph on the bench, sending Zak skywards again. He was sure it would snap at any moment.

"I actually went for the number one caber toss man in the world—no offence, Ralph. But he's on the books at an American football team. That's how sought after their unique skill set is."

Zak heard Darren Dangerfield chortle. It was all right for him, Zak thought. His wife owned Hair Force One, the hairdressers in town charging fifteen quid the minute they pulled out their scissors. That jackass wouldn't be thrown on the streets by next Monday.

"I'd be lying if I didn't sniff some marketing potential in having him here as well," Tam said, with an arm around the beast. "He'll help us tap into the lucrative Highland market in the US, Canada and Australia."

Ralph grunted again. Zak wasn't sure if he was actually capable of talking. With jug ears and no neck, this Ralph fellow was no Joe Montana. Plus, he'd never heard of the sport, and he betted on everything.

Tam gestured to the door once more. "Anyway, boys, time is dragging away from us, much like this season, and we have lots to do on the training ground. So please let me introduce our next new player. Ibrahim Damn."

"Ibrahim Deng," the young African corrected him as he entered.

"Ibrahim Dang," Tam tried and failed again.

"Ibrahim Deng," Ibrahim corrected him even more politely.

"Oh, it doesn't bloody matter what we call you. The important thing is that you can play."

Zak was sure he'd seen the guy before. He racked his brain. There weren't many non-Caucasian people on the island.

"Isn't he the cleaner?" Ross Coyne asked, noting the mop and bucket.

"He was," Tam replied. "But nothing in life is permanent. Your next job, Sir Rosco, could be as a flunky the way you've been going. It may surprise some of you that even I was unemployed before I became a football manager."

No one said anything as no one was surprised. Every man and his dog in the town knew Tam Bam had never worked a day in his life.

"But while I've been staying back night after night when training finishes, burning the midnight oil and trying to work out how to kick you dunderheads into shape, I noticed the cleaner playing keepie uppie up and down the touchline during his designated break. Haven't seen skill like it since Alex Ferguson alerted me to a young Lee Sharpe. And I thought to myself, you could do that for me, son."

"Who did he play for before?" Darren Dangerfield asked.

"He made the under-17 squad for Gambia, I'll have you know. How many of you have ever featured for your country?"

Zak doubted this was the case. Ibrahim Deng appeared to doubt it even more as he looked down, embarrassed by the revelation.

"So, three cheers for Ibrahim Doo-wop, everyone," Tam shouted.

Nobody cheered as the man lifted his mop and bucket and exited.

"And last but not least," Tam continued, making a drum roll on the concrete wall with his fists. "I give you our new Turkish import, Mustafa Bilik." A man of around forty with a greasy moustache and a pot belly entered.

"I know him," Lance called out. "He runs the kebab van."

"Why, you really are a much more observant bunch than I give you credit for. Yes, he's a restaurateur. An entrepreneur. While you lot spend your time away from football drinking and playing your video games and racing your bloody sports cars, he's feeding the good people of Guff at all hours."

"And who's *he* played for?" Rory McGory asked.

"This man has an encyclopaedic knowledge of the world game from the Turkish and Romanian leagues, right on to the Arab leagues. His mentor was the great Tinaz Tirpin, and he's an expert on Schalker Kreisel football."

"What's that?" Ross Coyne asked.

"Who asked that? You're proving to me what philistines you are."

"But can he play?" Rory McGrory asked, taking in the man's not insignificant paunch.

"This man here can do anything."

The Turk was sweating just standing there. He might watch football, but Zak doubted he'd kicked one since he'd set sights on the big spinning stick.

"So make them all feel welcome on the good Isle of Guff," Tam told them. "Do whatever initiation it is you do for new teammates. Take them to the pub, set their clothes on fire, cling-film their cars. Whatever you decide, try and keep it legal."

Zak had never known them to do anything for new arrivals. Looking around the room, he noted that none of the established players were laughing now. They all had a similar numb smile on their faces, the type you might muster when your girlfriend says she's leaving, or your dog has to be put down.

Connor Whelan had his head in his hands. The assistant held some sway with the gaffer, so Zak believed that if he could remain on his good side, he might stay in the squad. He liked the young coach, they'd played together in the youths. And he was pretty sure he liked him too, as he was always encouraging him to bomb forward and beat his man. Maybe, just maybe, he stood a chance of keeping his place and scoring a new deal.

"And I don't need to remind you," Tam said. "You've got Darlington this Saturday, the worst team in the league. Even worse than you lot. Two points and one spot adrift from us at the bottom of the table. And with an even more atrocious recent record than us having lost their last eight. And they're in even more turmoil. Those unlucky buggers have no manager. Can you imagine that?"

That would be a dream, thought Zak.

"Gaffer," Dangerfield enquired. "You've brought a whole team in. Where does that leave the rest of us?"

"Wow, they can think as well." Tam praised the heavens. He was bursting with joy. "Very happy that you raised that, boyo. Very, very glad. You are professional players after all, allegedly, and footballers like to play. And with these new signings and the injection of zest which the youth players have provided, I no longer need you lot, do I? So, I offer you the chance, in fact, I urge you, I implore you, to go out and find another club."

"And what if we can't?" Zak, who never said a word, suddenly blurted.

"Then the curtain has fallen, and the fat lady has sung her final tune."

Zak felt his pager vibrate in his trackies. He sneaked a peek. It was his brother. It was full time in Barry, and Bangor had romped in with a 5–1 away win.

Zak collapsed to the floor, unable to breathe. He hadn't struggled with an attack like this since the Great Bristol Half Marathon back in high school.

"Create some space," someone yelled.

"Grab a puffer."

"Puffer?" Jimmy Dolan moaned. Zak sensed the physio rummaging through his old first aid bag. "I haven't had the budget to buy as much as a new zip for this thing since 1975."

Zak lay on the cold tiles gasping for air as they crowded round. He saw a bright light and wanted to follow it. There lay a safer, warmer place where there were no money worries, no football and definitely no Guff Rovers.

"If he doesn't pull through, just think, lads." As Zak drifted in and out of consciousness, he heard Tam's voice spoiling it all. "That's one less player on the transfer market vying for a contract. You young people are far too negative nowadays. You must always focus on the upside."

33

Zabe had never seen Janine this happy. Since last Tuesday when Zabe suggested they go to the football and support her brother and the team, Janine had grinned and rocked in her wheelchair at the mere mention of the game.

"Football today?" Janine had asked each morning that week.

"Saturday, Janine. Saturday."

And getting her washed and dressed, never the easiest thing, was for once a breeze. Zabe thought it would take hours to get ready and out of the house, but they were in the cab before one o'clock with Janine humming and cheering all the way.

Then when the game kicked off, she squealed with joy at every tackle, every pass, every shot. *She should've been coming to Guff games for years*, Zabe thought. It was a crying shame she hadn't.

Zabe was impressed by the disabled section. They had the whole area to themselves. Great pitchside view, ample legroom, easy access to all amenities. As word spread that Tam Bam was no longer frequenting the area, it might start to get popular.

If she could only get her daughter to start coming back, then Zabe would really be happy. But Missy and her friends said they were finished with the club after what had happened to the girls' team. It was a sin, that tight-arsed chairman scrapping the side. Zabe didn't want to think about what Missy was getting up to right now with the older group of fifth-formers who hung about the shops.

It had been a good few weeks for Zabe back at the Bamford homestead. Tam was rarely there. She doubted he realised what an undertaking managing a football club was. He was up and out when she started at nine in the morning, and he was still out when she left at five. And she could tell by how the place was almost exactly the same when she returned (sometimes there wasn't even an extra dish or stray crumb in the kitchen, often the foldout hadn't been slept in) that he truly was putting in the hours at Faery Meadow. Zabe knew this could only be good for him. Giving him some direction, some focus, something he'd never had before. His mother would be proud. She imagined that if he'd found some purpose when Mrs Bamford was alive, the old lady might still be here.

Tam's absence meant Zabe had the house to herself to cook and clean and care for Janine. As much as she missed Mrs Bamford, she found a certain peace in her new role. And she was finally getting to know Janine, discovering there was more to her than even she realised. She was bright, she was funny and she loved football.

Zabe and Janine may have been enjoying their matchday experience, but the other brave souls who bothered to turn up weren't. This was the smallest crowd she'd seen since she'd started coming to Guff games. They'd be lucky if there were four hundred here. The head of the fans' group and his wife who usually sat to Zabe's right were absent. So was the man in the pink bunnet. The fact that Tam followed up the gaffer's sacking by appointing himself in the role, then paid off the majority of the first-team squad, had not gone down well. The local paper and the radio phone-ins were jammed with disgruntled fans claiming their side were as good as relegated. Others claimed they wouldn't spend a penny on the club or set foot inside the ground until Tam Bam was sent packing.

Watching the match, Zabe knew that those absent had a point. The new players from Swindon Town didn't appear interested. The beanpole striker went off injured after biting his tongue just three minutes in following an outburst at the linesman. The Peruvian right midfielder in long sleeves, gloves and tights had barely moved, shivering near the touchline. At least he was moving more than their new Scottish signing, Ralph McInnes. He was so built he couldn't move at all. And each time he took a throw-in, he threw the ball so hard it ended in the opposite stand. Billy Wood, Guff's new centre-back, got his marching orders after twelve minutes for going through Darlington's striker like a knife through a bashed banana.

He wasn't just late reaching the ball, he wasn't even in the same postcode.

Paddy Conroy, out on the left-wing, displayed some nice touches but couldn't jog for more than ten yards without having to keel over, hands on hips, gasping for air. Zabe wasn't entirely surprised, as on the way into the ground they'd seen Conroy on the steps with Jimmy Dolan doing what her daughter once referred to as a "double lunger".

As the game wore on, all the players wilted, not just Conroy, who slumped to the turf after chasing down a ball which went out for a goal kick. He didn't get up again. Reduced to ten men presented an even bigger challenge than usual as every Guff player moved like they'd played two games midweek instead of having the week off.

The only player who appeared to have anything about him was Guff's new centre-forward Hans Schickler. Tam at least appeared to notice his ability as he moved him from the forward-line to help out in midfield. Then he shifted him to centre-back to cover the new Turkish sweeper whose distribution may have been sound, but who moved slower than a wet weekend on the island. By half-time, Hans had covered everywhere except between the sticks. It was a shame they didn't have ten of him.

The team displayed little energy. Very little shape. And with the incoherent ranting from the gaffer on the sidelines, and the continuing gripes from the fans in the stands, they had zero confidence.

After an insipid eighty-nine goalless minutes, and with the home fans rushing for the exits to get away from the horror show, the ball fell to Ralph McInnes at the edge of the Darlington area. He literally hadn't had a single kick of the ball all game, offering nothing except his rocket launcher throw-ins which landed far beyond the goalmouth. And his rustiness showed as he swung one of his giant hooves at the ball, hitting Row ZZ.

The referee lifted the whistle to his lips, putting everyone out of their misery. The boos let the players know exactly what they thought of the spectacle.

"What the bloody hell are you doing here?" Tam called over to the disabled section as he left the pitch.

"I told you, I never miss a game," Zabe replied.

He pointed to his sister, who was clapping. "But she's never been to one."

Even the standard of play couldn't ruin Janine's great day out.

"Yes, and she's never been happier. You should have brought her years ago."

"Football was my escape from the drudgery of my Struther Hill existence."

"And now it can be hers. We won't bother you."

"You better not. I've got enough worries. I hope she paid."

"Of course she didn't."

"That's more money out the pot. My funds are ever dwindling since the social cut off our benefits. A disgrace of a system, so it is."

"You've inherited millions."

"My father worked hard for that money."

Tam trundled off, the boos lingering from those who'd bothered to stick around.

"Women and football," he muttered. "It'll never work."

The smile on Janine's face would have thawed the hearts of even the most strident of misogynists. No one had ever smiled so much at what would have been a strong contender for the worst game in the history of football.

34

When Tam informed Connor Whelan that the young coach would be travelling with the side to the away fixture against Lincoln City, driving up the M1 during the biggest storm of the year in a rental Skoda and nearly flying off the road was not what the new assistant had in mind.

Tam hadn't uttered a word for the entire journey there, nor now on the way back. He sat in the passenger seat reading and re-reading the Little Chef menu while he tutted at everything Radio 2 had to say about football.

Despite keeping his footballer physique and being half a foot shorter than the gaffer, Connor barely had room to breathe in the moving sardine can, never mind steer. Connor assumed he would fly with the rest of the squad into Leeds on the morning of the game. Then Tam called as he was going to bed on the Friday saying the pair weren't flying. That Tam and the assistant were catching the dawn ferry, getting a rental car, and driving the near seven hours from Penzance in order to cut costs.

Connor had to tell Tiff he couldn't have Gillian over this weekend. He knew she'd made plans as she made veiled digs about how football was once again "put before their daughter". She would never understand because she had never, even in the ten years they'd been together, made any effort to.

She'd never even watched a game of football.

Connor didn't have a car and hadn't driven on the island in the two years since he sold his Reliant Robin to pay for his coaching badges. He thought at least they would hire a spacious new automatic. But no, it was a manual, and as far as driving skills went, he was way out of practice. And as Tam couldn't drive, there was no other option.

On the wings of angels, they got there in one piece. But now on the way back, with the darkness and the weather to contend with, Connor wasn't so confident.

The signs ahead told him they were passing Gloucester. He'd have to shatter the land speed record if they were to make the midnight ferry back to the island. That was if he didn't skid off the road and kill them first. An eighteen-hour day, plus the stress of a 1–0 loss, was all too much. Not to mention being stuck in the company of Tam Bam the entire time.

Connor felt his eyelids grow heavy and his body gently drift off to sleep. He slapped his cheeks. The intermittent belching and clearing of sinuses by his travel partner were the only things keeping him awake. That and how the heater didn't work, which meant he was anything but snug in the draughty automobile. Particularly as the soles of his Patricks were frozen tight to the pedals.

"Do you want to talk?" Connor asked. He realised when he said these words just how desperate he was.

Tam said nothing, instead slurping on the Lucozade he'd got from the second road service stop they'd made just an hour into their journey.

"About the game, I mean."

Still nothing.

Tam had the hump about something. Connor went for the jugular. "I think you should let me take the training."

"You what?!" The bottle slipped from Tam's pudgy fingers, splashing Connor's groin. Tam looked up from the menu. That had got him. "I am the gaffer!"

"You're still the gaffer. But it means we can bring the boys in earlier and you can have your lie-in. Come in when they're winding down and have your say. It's how the great bosses do it. Busby was rarely seen on the training ground."

"I've graduated from Bobby Charlton's Soccer School, you know. The oldest boy in their history."

"I have nearly every badge going, real ones, and I earned the things."

"Watch your mouth. I should bloody well sack you for blasphemy."

"I'm sorry, but it's true. Listen, half the team are dangerously unfit, and they need training, granted. But for the other half, it's too much for them. They were dead on their feet today. It was like they'd already played ninety minutes. That weights session was madness an hour before kick-off. You've got to go easy on them."

"You don't know what you're talking about."

"No, Tam, it's you who doesn't know what he's talking about."

Tam grabbed his assistant by his pink collar and squeezed. The car ricocheted across two lanes, missing the front of a National Express bus by half a car length before swerving around the tail-end of a scooter.

Connor screamed. Tam did too, finally letting go.

Connor braked and turned. The car skidded, barely missing a slippery road sign, coming to a halt in the breakdown lane.

"You daft fucker," Connor shouted. "I'm a father. You could've killed us!"

He held out his fingers and saw he was shaking. He half expected another attack from the much larger man. But Tam did nothing. He stared out the window, out of breath, watching the traffic shoot past. Connor saw that he, too, was trembling.

After a moment, Tam spoke, his voice breaking. "This was my dream. I only ever wanted to play for Guff Rovers."

"Me as well."

"And then when that dream died, I only ever wanted to manage them."

"Me too."

"I only wanted the best for the Isle of Guff."

Connor put a hand on his shoulder. "That's exactly what I want. Just let me coach. Tuesday to Friday. And you run the Monday one, if you like. It'll let you concentrate on being the best boss you can be."

Sports Report was covering the First Division title race. Their ears perked up when they mentioned their club.

"And now for some news from all the way down in Division Four. Reports are emerging from struggling Exeter City—Exeter, remember, topped the league back in September but have since fallen out of play-off contention, last month dismissing manager Chris Coles. They're saying that Exeter have appointed former Guff Rovers manager Gary Pullman as their new boss."

"What?!" Tam almost ejected himself through the roof and up into the heavens.

The reporter continued. *"And to make things really spicy, his first game in charge will be away to Guff next Saturday. The club he left last month in acrimonious circumstances."*

Tam turned the dial so hard it snapped off in his hand. He sat there for an age watching the rain tumble down. Then he finally spoke. "You coach the boys," he said. "But I'm picking the team and doing the team talk. I'm doing whatever it takes to beat that bastard Pullman."

Connor smiled. He switched off the hazard lights and got the car rolling, accelerating out onto the motorway.

"Can you stop at the next services?" Tam asked. "I'm starving."

"Sure," Connor replied.

It meant they'd miss the last ferry. It meant they'd be sleeping in the freezing Skoda on the docks of Penzance. But Connor was willing to do whatever it took to keep the gaffer happy, the car on the road and to get Guff Rovers ticking.

35

Jimmy Dolan sat on the steps of Faery Meadow, sucking his cigarette right down to the filter. He remembered the days not so long ago when they'd let you smoke in the changerooms. Heck, they'd even let you smoke in the dugout. Those days were gone.

Like so many other things in the game he loved.

He should have been in there rubbing down the players for the match, but he was useless if he hadn't had his quarter-hour fag, and the players knew it. Quitting had never been on the agenda for him. Ever since he'd hung up his boots, he'd smoked like a chimney. People reckoned that smoking killed you. Jimmy felt they were the only things which quelled his anxiety and kept him alive.

Tam joined him, pasty in hand. The gaffer himself should have been in there, in the players' ears from the get-go about what to do today. But Jimmy knew that Tam couldn't resist welcoming Exeter City to the ground.

Jimmy heard via Connor that Tam almost had an embolism on the M1 when he heard that their former manager had jumped ship so soon to Guff's biggest rivals. And it only got worse in the lead-up to their match.

Firstly, Tam was told he couldn't claim back the severance pay they'd handed to Gary Pullman as there was no clause in the termination agreement forbidding him from immediately taking up a new post. Tam hadn't bothered adding one, convinced that no club in a million years would want him.

Then the eleven players Tam released were snapped up by Pullman.

Once again, Tam never dreamed that any professional club would want to lay a finger on any of those 'degenerates'. But he was wrong. Whether it was spite or otherwise, Gary Pullman and Exeter City wanted them all.

The visitors' coach pulled into the space off the main street. Jimmy could tell Tam felt apprehensive by how the gaffer hadn't eaten the pasty. Instead, he was squeezing it so hard the pastry was crumbling, and the mince was tumbling onto the pavement.

The players in their new red-and-white shell suits exited the vehicle. They all wore headphones, and with good reason, because it meant they couldn't hear the abuse dished out.

"Traitors, one and all," Tam ranted. "Traitors, the whole bloody lot of you. This club clothed you, fed you, nurtured you, and the first chance you get, like Judas Iscariot himself, you stab us in the back. Every man, woman and child on the island you've shat on. Deserting us to our biggest rivals."

Jimmy, meanwhile, was shaking hands with the former players as they walked up the steps.

"Great to see you, Jimmy," Zak Bates said.

"Good luck today," Lance Posobiec added.

"How's your mother?" Darren Dangerfield asked.

"What the bloody hell are you doing?" Tam raged at his kit man/physio/groundsman/chief scout.

"They're only boys. I've known a lot of them since they could kick a ball."

"They are our sworn enemy now." Tam turned on them. "You cheating, thieving bastards have some neck coming here. Some bloody neck, I tell you."

"What did you expect us to do?" Rory McGrory replied. "Sign on the dole? You're the one who got rid of us."

"Yes, and on half-pay. I didn't expect you to jump into the enemy's bed the very next day."

"Bollocks to the pay, we want to play," Ross Coyne told him.

"It would be the first time in five years that you have done," Tam replied. "You never did when you had a Guff shirt on."

Jamie Pullman was the last player to head into the building, looking fit and fresh. He gave Tam a wink. "Oh, I'll make sure I play today. Don't you worry about that, fat man."

"You…" Tam's fist shook in tandem with his entire body.

"Calm it, gaffer," Jimmy told him, lighting another cigarette. "That stress will kill you."

"Those turncoat bastards."

"It's only a game."

"How can you say that?"

Jimmy wondered how he could say that. He'd never said anything like that before. For the first time he wondered what he was still doing here. The game seemed to be changing so much. The exorbitant wages players were on. The haircuts. That awful acid house disco music they always had blaring. How they all swanned around thinking they were Tom Finney when they weren't fit to cut the great man's toenails.

Then there was the media. The sponsors. And crazies like Tam Bam bursting in and making their mark just because they had the dough. Jimmy didn't know the game anymore. Maybe his time was up. Then again, what else would he do? This was the only life he'd known. But he suddenly felt so very, very, tired.

He stubbed his fag out in an old Dulux can on the step. "Anyway, I should go in. Got the kits to put out. And a few bodies to rub down."

"I don't bloody believe it," Tam muttered, as a familiar car pulled up and parked in its familiar spot right in front of the stadium.

The spot marked MANAGER.

Jimmy Dolan could very much believe it. There was little that shocked him now.

"What the hell are you doing in that space, arsehole?"

"Tam, Tam, Tam." Gary Pullman got out of his Guff Rovers' company Jag. "So good to see you."

"I will phone the police immediately if you do not remove your vehicle. Or my vehicle, rather, if you hadn't ripped us off."

"The spot says 'Manager'."

"Manager of Guff Rovers."

"You're the manager of Guff Rovers. Laughably. And you, my old chum, do not drive."

"Doesn't matter. Move the motor."

"It's a public parking space. Pinkle got Jimmy here to paint Manager on it when he sold the carpark to make it look official. You've no claim to it."

Tam turned to Jimmy to see if this was true. Jimmy shrugged.

"And if the police want to tow it, they can." Pullman smirked. "With the year my bank balance is having, I might just be able to afford it."

"I don't know how you've the stones to come here in that car with all my players."

"You sacked me. You sacked them. It's a game, after all. And it's a game you are losing badly, my old chum."

"Stop calling me that. You'll be lucky if the fans let you off the island alive."

"All right, Gaz, mate," a stray voice sounded out from a group of fans drinking across the road at The Wick. Some of them gave him a thumbs up. A few others applauded.

"Come back to us," called another.

"We love you, gaffer."

Then they broke into song.

"Oh, Gaz Pullman's magic,
He wears a magic hat.
And when he heard from Rovers,
He said I fancy that.
He said goodbye to Millwall,
Because they're full of shite.
And when Guff Rovers win the league,
We'll sing this song all night."

Pullman waved, setting off more cheers. Another young supporter approached with his autograph book. Pullman grinned as he signed it. "You're right, Bam. I shoulda brought the knuckle dusters, all right."

The fans at the pub then noticed Tam next to him and changed the chant.

"Tam Bam,
You're a wanker,
You're a wanker!"

Pullman's smile wasn't going anywhere. "I think you'll find you'll have more trouble leaving the stadium than me, old chum."

The former boss gave Jimmy a firm handshake. "Great to see you."

Jimmy blushed as he felt Tam's glare, though he was never going to snub him. Pullman hadn't done wrong by him. In fact, he'd been one of the best gaffers to work for. He invited him to his home for Christmas. Paid for his hip replacement. Bosses didn't get much better than Gary Pullman.

Jimmy had to admit that his old gaffer looked in rude health. Tanned, toned, Jimmy even thought his hair might have grown back. It was a wonder what a month away from the island could do for you. Jimmy wondered what might have happened if it was him standing there in Gary Pullman's shoes. He hadn't had a day off from the club in over thirty years. He knew this club would fall apart without him.

Pullman handed Tam a large gift bag. "Anyway, it's not like I've come visiting empty-handed."

"What's this tosh?"

Tam opened it. There was a sombrero, castanets, and an 'I Love Spain' t-shirt.

"Think of it as a peace offering. It seemed only right bringing you something nice back, seeing as you paid for the trip. My wife sends her regards. You're the most popular man in my house right now."

"You bloody—"

"The holiday wasn't all sun and sand. It involved a bit of business as well. I was buying a timeshare in Tenerife. I had a spare three hundred grand grand floating in my skyrocket and thought, why the hell not?"

"Bastard!"

"But hey, if you're ever travelling in *España*, you're welcome to stay. For a knockdown price, of course, since you paid for it. That is, if the owner at this joint ever decides to pull the rug from under you and ruin all your well-laid plans, and you have a free few months. Oh, but wait. That can't happen to you, Mr Fifty-One Percent, can it?"

Jimmy had only ever seen Tam angry. But he couldn't remember ever seeing him *this* angry. He was standing statue-still, holding the bag, eyes bulging out of their sockets like a Warner Bros character, making the type of gurgling sound he imagined a deer would make when you'd run over it.

"Anyway, chaps, we've a game to play. May the best team win." Gary Pullman left them to it, whistling 'Football Crazy' as he sashayed into the ground.

"We should go in as well, gaff. Gaff?" Jimmy saw that Tam couldn't seem to move his arms, his legs, his eyes or even his lips.

Tam Bam couldn't move anything.

"I'll get you in there, yeah?" Jimmy left him. The fat bastard chants had started up again from the pub. Jimmy, though, had a hundred and one things to do before the players made their way down the tunnel. He craved another cig but needed to get moving.

Jimmy wasn't sure if Tam would be alive by the end of the season, never mind still be the manager. If he was honest, he wasn't sure if the big guy would make it to the end of the game.

Some folk weren't built for a lifetime of this.

36

Father Gonzalez noticed his armpits were damp. Normally he'd be feeling the chill on the island even in April, but not today.

He knew it wasn't his new coat making him burn up. He could only afford a second-hand polyester number, providing little protection. And it certainly wasn't the football making him perspire. The game was scoreless, but Exeter should have been up by five the way Guff were playing.

Bishop Winstanley had called earlier to request a meeting first thing Monday. Father Gonzalez had always flown under the radar here. The bishop was more concerned with far saucier things going on in the mainland. But now word was out about Nora. Everyone knew about him and Nora. And as much as the bishop didn't seem to care about the Isle of Guff, the priest knew that he was on to him.

Father Gonzalez made up his mind to own up to everything. The bishop would be furious, but he would understand. The only reason he gave him the position straight out of the seminary was because no one else wanted to come here. Cornwall, sure. But Guff?

Not a chance.

The priest's three predecessors hadn't worked out at all. The first lasted a week before leaving the priesthood altogether and becoming a lawnmower man in Dorset. The second, Father Deans, who he'd once met at a divorce counselling course, threw himself onto the rocks near the bay. They couldn't prove suicide, instead citing death by misadventure as he'd been on magic mushrooms at the time. The third one, Father Harold Douglas, was committed at the age of fifty-three to the local psychiatric hospital after exposing himself to the congregation on Palm Sunday.

He was still there today.

Father Gonzalez wondered what would happen if he was defrocked. It could take months before they replaced him, and even then, it would be someone from the mainland coming across solely on Sunday mornings like it used to be before he arrived. There'd be no daily Mass, no one on the ground day to day providing assistance to local schools or the dying. Who would run St Vincent de Paul, and the food bank, and help the needy? There were so many of them.

This place would turn into another Beirut within a fortnight.

Father Gonzalez watched as Ralph McInnes controlled the ball (for once). Instead of blindly firing it forward like he usually did, he turned towards his own goal and passed it back to the keeper. However, he hit it so hard it rattled the crossbar, fortunately going out for a corner.

"This is no good," Nora told the priest. "I don't want to do this anymore."

"Neither do I," he replied. He took her hand underneath the brown-and-pink blanket which lay over her knees and looked at her earnestly. "Nora. Will you marry me?"

She squeezed his fingers and held him close. "You know I love you and what we're doing is wrong. But you leaving the church, you leaving this island? That would be a real sin."

As she said this, the corner came in. Seth Graham had his shirt cheekily tugged by Exeter's Darren Dangerfield as the ball missed the entire defence, looping into the top corner. Everyone in the ground but the referee and his officials had seen the foul, but the ref signalled to the centre circle and the goal stood.

Gary Pullman turned towards the Guff dugout with a solitary raised fist. Parents shielded their children's eyes, fans howled in protest, as

Tam Bam was restrained by his assistant, the physio and both subs.

When Father Gonzalez arrived here, all the island had going for it was its football team and the church. With Tam at the helm, and with himself on the brink, it would soon have neither.

The ref jogged up the sideline towards the Guff gaffer. "Get back behind the line, or I'll send you off." He blew his whistle, and the game restarted.

But Tam couldn't leave it there. "Lino," he called. "The ref has a bloody Devonshire accent, so he does. How is that fair?"

The linesman had a word with Tam. Father Gonzalez imagined he was explaining to him the decision-making process behind picking officials at this level who lived semi-local in order to keep overheads low.

"And you're from bloody Somerset," Tam moaned. "I can spot that monstrosity of an accent any day."

The linesman tried to usher the Guff boss back to his dugout.

"You're cheats, you're all cheats!" Tam wagged his finger at him. "I know you. You're Geoff Shanks. Former Exeter City midfielder. Nineteen appearances between 1975 and '78. You bloody scored one against us as well. Nearly got us relegated. This game should be abandoned." He turned to the crowd who were trying to watch the real action. "It's a bloody conspiracy!"

The linesman had had enough and called the ref back over. Tam used this as another excuse to let rip. "And the other lino only has one arm. And it's pointing in Exeter's direction."

Father Gonzalez heard the ref making light of the other linesman's predicament, joking that "In the second half, he'll be pointing your way."

"You bent bastards." Tam shoved the ref.

"Tell it to the card." The ref held it aloft. It was bright red, the colour of Tam's misshaped features.

"That sums you lot up. Bent as boomerangs."

Father Gonzalez hoped Tam would go quietly. There were children watching, after all. But then Gary Pullman started applauding and Tam went for him, this time knocking his new glasses from his face and getting his hands around his neck. "I'm doing humanity a favour," he boiled.

It took the whole Guff bench and the entire opposition one to pry him off and drag him down the tunnel.

The Guff fans were too embarrassed to boo the ref or cheer for their manager. Most of them covered their eyes, their worst fears about Tam Bam holding the reins coming true.

Nora kissed Father Gonzalez lightly on the cheek. "I'm leaving now, my love. We should no longer see each other."

Oh, how he wanted to whisk her away from this dump. Live in some far-off land where they wouldn't have to worry what other people, the bishop, the church or God himself thought. But he had work to do here. So much work. Until he was told differently, he knew it was the will of the man upstairs.

He squeezed her bony hand, not wanting to ever let it go. "Goodbye, my queen. I shall never forget you."

He tried to smile, though he knew it couldn't look all that appealing through all his blubbering.

As she shuffled down the steps cautiously, like any seventy-three-year-old woman would, the priest wondered if the local paper would let him post an ad for a trunk full to the brim of sex toys. There was about two hundred quid's worth in there, and if the bishop kept him on, he'd need the cash to finally purchase a decent coat for next winter.

37

CJ Adeyemi had never worried about much in his eighteen years. Nothing apart from which brand of boots to train in, or where to source his next bit of E, weed, speed or carry-out. But now things were different.

Very different.

So different, in fact, that the previous night he didn't join the lads at that warehouse rave on the Guff docks where Paul Oakenfold's cousin was rumoured to be DJing. He had too much on his mind.

Despite his fine form on the training ground, CJ was on the bench today. Since his impressive debut when he was up to his eyeballs on Buckfast and whizz, he hadn't had a look in. This was largely down to the gaffer bringing in a brand-new squad. Though he also knew it had a bit to do with Connor Whelan. He'd seen the assistant getting in Tam's ear. Heck, Connor had been in his ear all year telling him he had all the ability in the world but was pissing it away like so many before him on wine, women and song. And as the game approached half-time, CJ was beginning to see that Connor might be right.

With Tam banished to the stand—and Mustafa Bilik exhausted after keeping his van running until three a.m. outside the old warehouse— minutes before the break, Connor called for CJ to warm up.

CJ felt glad he hadn't joined his pals last night. It was good not to have a hangover or be coming down. Still, with the week he'd had, he wondered if he was in the right state of mind to take the field.

"Son, you're on," Connor said, putting an arm around him at the break. "How you feeling?"

"I'm feeling good."

"You weren't out last night now, were you?"

"I was in bed by nine." CJ didn't want to tell him he lay awake until three replaying how Lyla called from Jersey that afternoon and told him she was pregnant and that it was his.

And that she was keeping the baby.

"Good to hear," Connor said. "The gaffer has specifically stated I'm to play you at the back. You have the height, you have the pace, you have the strength. Above all, you have the know-how. Show us what you're made of."

"Sure thing, coach."

And he didn't want to tell him that Becca Rice, who he'd shagged on his birthday, had missed her period and was blaming him. Two kids by two different mothers, and still in his teens. This was not what he planned.

But he accepted it all. He had to make the best of it. He wouldn't run away like his biological father had. It wasn't like he was going to university. Even getting a trade wasn't an option. He'd failed to complete a full-term of secondary school. And given the local economy, he'd need a miracle getting a job.

Football was all CJ knew. It was vital he switched on. That he gave the boys (and girls) a wide berth, not just on Friday night, but every night of the week. That he break into the Guff Rovers first team— surely not that tricky, they were useless—and stay there. And then get Southampton, Cardiff, whoever, interested again. Score a big-money move and provide for his new family.

Or families.

He found Seth taping his gloves to his wrists. "Do you have your scissors and clippers here?"

"I never leave home without them."

CJ grabbed them from the keeper's hessian bag. At the sink, he cut his dreads off roughly one by one. He felt lighter, somehow older, with each slice. Then he plugged the clippers into the socket and shored the rest of it as close as it would go.

He stared into the mirror. He looked more mature. More serious. He felt it too. And this was exactly what he wanted.

He returned to the rest of the squad. "Nice one, Ceej," Seth said. Later CJ would think back and realise these were the first words the goalie had ever said to him. "Welcome to the straight edge club."

The other players didn't notice. CJ knew he could have returned in whiteface, high heels and suspenders and they wouldn't have cared. They didn't even know his name.

But he vowed that soon they would.

A loud commotion came from down the tunnel and Tam burst in the doorway. He whistled loudly to get the players' attention, not realising he already had it. Then he whispered, "If the ref catches me in here, I'll be banned for the season. Listen, if you beat this lot, I'll throw ten grand into the end-of-season kitty. Bugger it, make it thirty."

The players nearly lifted the roof off.

"Shush," Tam pleaded. "And you, son." He zeroed in on CJ. "You're a man now. Eighteen, so you are. You'll soon have the deep voice, pubes, the lot."

CJ had had pubes since he was ten. He'd been balling since he was thirteen. And he was about to father two children. He wondered if Tam was still a virgin.

"Go out there and play like a man."

"I will, gaff," he replied.

The ref rushed in with the steward who was that weirdo from back in school who was into The Cure and used to scrawl on his arms with a sharp compass and bleed all over the desk during geography.

"Get him out of here," the ref ordered. The guard sighed, taking Tam's arm.

"Sorry, ref," Tam said. "I thought this was where the pasties are kept."

He let the young steward lead him out gently, mumbling under his breath, towards the match official. "Devonshire bastard. Surprised you're not in the other changerooms giving them their team-talk."

The players lined up to go out. CJ hung at the back. Ever since under-11s, he always had to be the last one out. "You're not going out last," said one of the much larger African loanees from Swindon, taking his place.

CJ didn't argue. He filed in front of him.

Maybe it was time he started doing everything a little differently.

38

Transcript from BBC Radio Cornwall
Saturday, March 25, 1989
4.52 p.m.

EDDIE REAGAN: And now we're off to the Isle of Guff, where we understand there was late drama at the game.

(*Silence*)

EDDIE REAGAN: Joanne, are you there? (*beat*) Joanne?

JOANNE PLUM: Sorry Eddie, the real drama that's unfolding here is in my guts and soon to be my arse. I genuinely thought I'd been having a heart attack for the last twenty minutes. This is the unhealthiest place I've ever been, and I grew up in the Gorbals. Last night, I couldn't find anything healthy, so what did I have? Kebab. This morning I was searching for something light, Weetabix, fruit, that kind of thing. What was the only thing the guest house had apart from muesli with weevils burrowing through it? Fry-up. Then here at the game, all they've had is pasties. Breakfast was at eight a.m., I was starving, so I've had two. But oh my God, my guts. If I don't make it, please tell my kids I love them.

EDDIE REAGAN: Thanks for that, Jo. Can we get a few quick words on the game?

JOANNE PLUM: (*dry heaving*) The game? I'm bloody dying here and all you care about is the game?

EDDIE REAGAN: I'm sorry, but that's how our licence-payers generally prefer it.

JOANNE PLUM: (*hyperventilating*) Well, extraordinary scenes at Guff Park with the home side grabbing a much-undeserved point. Young substitute CJ Akinbiyi, in only his second appearance for the club, firing through a crowded penalty area from a half-cleared corner in the ninety-third minute to salvage a draw.

EDDIE REAGAN: High drama, indeed.

JOANNE PLUM: Gaffer Tom Bamford, who was earlier banished to the stands after being sent off for dissent, jumped up and celebrated so hard that he tumbled down several rows, landing on the pitch. Then he ran along the touchline, skidding on his knees in front of old Guff boss Pullman. It was high drama all right, but more so downright unsavoury as he struggled up, showing the whole stadium that he'd split the back of his pants. I think that was actually good for me because I vomited and brought up those two pasties. The fry-up is still there doing some damage, mind.

EDDIE REAGAN: A bit more information there than we needed, thanks, Jo.

JOANNE PLUM: I like to cover the game, warts and all.

EDDIE REAGAN: So where does this leave Guff now?

JOANNE PLUM: Two points adrift with four games left. If they can show the same fight they did in the second half then maybe, just maybe, they have a chance.

EDDIE REAGAN: And what was the mood like after the game?

(*Silence. Followed by a squeaky fart and then a projectile vomit into a bin*)

EDDIE REAGAN: Jo, are you okay?

JOANNE PLUM: You'll have to come back to me. Send for medical help immediately. Immediately! Remember to tell my kids I love them. I am not getting off this island alive.

(*click*)

39

If the Guff Rovers players thought they might get some reprieve by earning an injury-time draw, they were wrong. As if scolding the players for an hour after the match wasn't enough, here they stood on an icy Monday morning in the middle of the training ground (aka the public park) as Tam Bam waved a Remington hair dryer he'd brought along to rehash the same tired routine.

"You're shit. You're a retard. You're a spaz." On and on he went, pointing and waving the dryer, giving them 'the treatment', as Alex Ferguson apparently called it, as Connor Whelan stood aside, patiently waiting for the tirade to end and for his session to begin.

For Oko Mulumba, this repertoire had ceased to be funny. In the two months since he'd joined the club on loan from Swindon, he'd witnessed this charade every day. He already felt like he was coming down with a cold and being out here wouldn't help. He knew he should've worn a second pair of tights and gloves on top of the ones he was wearing.

Oko had such high hopes when he escaped the Congo for good in 1985 after scoring on a trial with Sheffield United. He did well in his fortnight there. The coaches were impressed with his game awareness and touch, and more so the strength and imposing frame of the bulky forward.

But when they found he was twenty-six years of age instead of sixteen, their interest cooled. The only club that would have him was non-league Bognor Regis. After netting twenty-four goals in his first season and thirty-one in his second, he earned another trial, this time with Swindon Town. A double in a pre-season tour of San Marino won him a two-year deal.

But turning pro wasn't all it was cracked up to be. The manager he signed for, Willie Byrne, got the bullet four games into the season and new boss Ivor Golag, a former Yugoslavian general, told him he'd never played a black player before and wasn't about to start now.

Banished to the reserves, Oko developed a love of real ale which lost him another yard or two of pace. In fact, his spendings in his local became so big, and his wages (without first-team bonuses) so low, his impoverished village near Kisangani had to wire him money to survive.

Eventually, he was thrown a reprieve with a loan move to Guff Rovers. The players seemed to have taken to him, nicknaming him affectionately—he hoped—The Ox. The island, though, made his malaria-ravaged Congolese home look like Miami Beach. The standard of football was worse.

And his new boss might not have been racist. However, he was even more unhinged.

"You wallies don't want to listen to me, then fine," Tam shouted. "That's why I've arranged for someone to grab you by the scruff of your brass necks and shake some sense into you."

An army-green Jeep raced across the pitch towards them.

"Let me introduce you to Drill Sergeant Trevor Duke," Tam said proudly. "A veteran of the Dhofar, the Troubles and the Cod Wars. Not to mention the Falklands which I'm told he reclaimed single-handed. Apparently, the SAS had to discharge him because he was that brutal. Now, you lot made me do this. Prepare to be beaten and bruised. Prepare to be humiliated. Prepare to be whipped into shape like the dogs you are."

A short man in tight jodhpurs and a violet paisley shirt skipped out of the vehicle holding a ribbon on a stick.

"Oh, I am sorry I'm late," he almost sang. He had a trim moustache which danced upwards and downwards and back and forth when he spoke. "How rude am I? But your ferry operator can be so unreliable. And I couldn't get a decent mocha. I was almost dead on my toes."

"Who the hell are you?" Tam asked, his face screwed into a tight ball.

"Drill Sergeant Duke. You booked me."

"I booked a drill sergeant. I didn't book you."

"I believe you did, sweetie."

"You're not a sadomasochistic war hero."

"You'd be very surprised what I'm capable of doing in heated situations." He looked Tam dead in the eyes. "Very, very surprised."

Tam edged back a little.

The sergeant faced the group. None of them had seen anything like him. "Hello, boys. I hear you're having a few troubles defeating the enemy. Well, have no fear because that's something I know a thing or two about. You see, it's all about preparation. It's all about training. Do you want to know what you need to start doing before you can annihilate your foes?"

"Weights?" CJ said.

"Steroids?" Ralph muttered.

"Giving a shit," said Oko, only half joking.

"Wrong, wrong and wrong, beautifuls. Though I do love your enthusiasm." He opened his hot pink sports bag, removing an armful of long, sparkly ribbons on sticks.

"It's rhythmic gymnastics."

He switched on a ghetto blaster and on came 'You Spin Me Round' by Dead or Alive. Under normal circumstances, a group of testosterone-filled athletes would tell this man, war hero or not, where to get off. But watching Tam's face on the sidelines grow more scrunched and purple by the second made them all want to join in. Plus, this beat the hell out of assault courses and triathlon runs.

"Grab one each and twirl, twirl, twirl," the sergeant told them.

So they did.

"To the left and to the right. Express yourself, boys. Higher, higher and higher."

The thing was, Mondays had never been this fun. They were laughing. They had never had any sort of fun since they'd arrived at the club. And this was proving to be a solid cardio session, the movement and stretching giving them a good all-body workout.

"Great work, boys. Great work. Such big strong boys you are," the sergeant said, circling the group, squeezing as many biceps as he could get his fingers on as Madonna's 'Vogue' came on the player.

"Right, that's it," Tam snapped. "Get off my training ground, you bloody fruit."

"Fruit? How rude. I have kids, I'll have you know. How many bubbas have you fathered, tubby?"

"Not the point. No wonder we don't rule the waves anymore. No wonder mainland Europe laughs at us."

"If you don't like this, wait till you see the tantric yoga session I've got planned."

"No, no and no." Tam snatched the ribbons from his hand. He tried to snap the sticks in half but wasn't strong enough. "Pack up your ballet dancing crap and go. The prime minister herself will be hearing about this."

"Okay, sweetie, tell Maggie I said hi. But I'm still invoicing you for the £400."

"I'll give you four grand if you get off the island right away."

"Done, Mr Cranky Pants." The sergeant collected his ribbons, returning them carefully into the bag. "Best of luck, boys. I'll be cheering you on from afar this Saturday."

"Just go!" Tam told him.

He blew them a kiss, leapt back in the Jeep, and drove off.

A crescendo of giggles spread throughout the playing group. Tam, though, was breathing heavily, clutching at his chest.

"Connor, you take over. I need a pasty, a Lucozade and a lie-down."

Tam got into his waiting taxi. Connor watched as the cab followed the Jeep onto the road and out of sight.

"Right, lads, fun and games are over. We've two games left and two wins to grab. You've done well today, so let's finish with a game of sevens."

They did just that.

Oko and the boys were happy. They'd only done the gymnastics for twenty minutes or so, but he was already feeling more supple, more flexible, than he had in a long time. That army man had been onto something. It looked like the others were feeling good too as they passed with a sharpness and precision they'd hadn't displayed since he'd got here. Oko exchanged a one-two with Hans and outmuscled his Swindon teammate Diego Caceras. He fired a shot in off the crossbar, so hard it toppled the portable goals. Oko celebrated like he'd scored the winner.

He celebrated like someone who hadn't scored a goal of any kind, be it in a proper game or in training, for six months.

He'd arranged to go for a pint after training with his second cousin, who'd come over from Glasgow to spend the week. But maybe he should give it a miss. Go to the library and get a book on gymnastics, a video if they had one, and do another session. Get back to feeling this way, playing this way, every day. It was the only way he could pick up his game and get firing again.

He knew it was the only way to avoid playing for shit clubs in shithole places like the Isle of Guff for the rest of his career, and to make his family proud.

40

Gus Pinkle packed his favourite rums into the suitcase, careful to separate them with the bubble wrap so they wouldn't break.

This wasn't his first rodeo.

He dusted off the Royal Navy Black Tot from 1970 and smiled. It was nearly empty. He got that for his last birthday and hadn't been able to resist cracking it open.

Then there was the Wood's Old Navy. He got it from … hmm … he couldn't remember where he got this one from. Probably from his father. He placed it in the case. Then he rolled up the portrait of his dad, careful not to damage it further. He placed it on top of the bottles. It needed some serious love and attention if it was going to survive.

Same with a lot of things in Gus's life.

He didn't want to return to the office, to the ground, to the island, but he realised he should. He hadn't been here in the two months since the deal. He couldn't stick around while that madman ran his family's club into the ground. Those media appearances? Those new signings? Jesus, help us! Admittedly, he had tried to get that African cleaner signed up. But when he heard there was no government funding for giving new refugees jobs, he pulled the deal. But a food van owner? A caber tosser?

Man alive!

Gus expected to feel a twinge of nostalgia, a tug at the heartstrings upon returning. But right now, he felt nothing. He hadn't even been following the side's results and had no idea how they were faring until this morning when he bought the local paper near the helipad. And it wasn't good. It wasn't good at all.

But what did Gus really expect?

The chairman braced himself as he heard the familiar rumble of what sounded like a rhino bounding up the stairs. He was glad he'd ditched the gun or else he might have been tempted to finish the job.

"It still exists, does it?" Tam burst in without knocking. "Where the bloody hell have you been?"

"Far and wide. Spreading the good name of Guff Rovers throughout the world."

"Bollocks you have. You've been sailing the seven seas, or racing them more like. I have a satellite dish, y'know."

"Of course. But for thirty-five hours per week, wherever I am in the world, I am dedicated to this club."

Tam sat down. A pasty almost magically appeared in his hands and quickly entered his gob. "Hit me with it. Since I've been slaving away on the football ground trying to knock that lot of shite out there into shape—at great mental, physical, emotional and financial cost, might I add—what have you been doing, Jacques Cousteau?"

Knocking them into shape? thought Pinkle. *Taking two points in seven matches?*

"I've been striving to find us sponsors, attempting to make us a viable commercial enterprise away from the pitch."

"So, who's gonna do our kit? Nike? Adidas? Lotto?"

"Well, Tacchi are keen to extend our deal for another year."

"And who the bloody hell are they?"

"A very respected Romanian garment manufacturer. They kit out a few clubs in the Indonesian top-flight, so I'm told."

"What about sponsors? As tasty as they are, Pete's Pasty Parlour is not befitting of a regal club such as ours."

"Good news on that front. A big player in the transport sector is keen to get on board."

"Brilliant work. British Airways, or is it Pan Am? Or is it from the car trade? Ford? Opel? Yokohama? Fergie tells me Man United's Sharp deal is worth a million quid. Is ours up there?"

"This is even better. This is an indefinite contract."

"Wonderful work, Mr Chairman. I knew you'd pull through in the end. How much are they paying?"

"You see, it's all about building relationships. You can't put a dollar figure on bonds such as these."

"How much?"

"Ten grand a year, but—"

"Who the hell with?"

"Guff Bicycles & Repairs."

Tam shook his fist. "You're a piece of work, you are."

"They said they'll offer a ten percent discount to all season ticket holders."

"This is unbelievable, even by your standards."

"It's a crowded market," Gus lied. It wasn't like he would know. He hadn't really tried.

"How about pre-season tours? North America. China. Australia. Taking on the local sides. But also, Celtic, Ajax, Benfica. The Guff brand must be spread far and wide."

Gus shuffled through some papers on his desk, which were mostly overdue bills. Tam was not going to like these at all. "I have a friendly arranged against Dungannon Swifts."

Tam's face fell. "Northern Ireland?!"

"I also have a contact in the Faroes who's president of a club in the second-tier. He said he would put us up if we pay our own way there. Reckons the quality of the lobster is worth the journey alone. Or there's a four-team tournament in Blackpool we could pitch for.

Apparently Partick Thistle have signed up."

"Scandalous! All that sea and air has ruined your brain. You need to up your game, Pinkle. And what about this midwinter break you were supposed to arrange for us?"

"It's April."

"Never too late."

"Well, good news on that front. You and the squad are off to Dunoon next week."

"Bloody Dunoon? Two pubs, a chip shop and a fag machine. That's even colder and more miserable than here. I wanted the south of Spain. Dubai. Florida. I have to say, this is awful even by your standards."

"Everyone's trying their best."

"Are they, though? It seems I'm the only one with passion and a vision for this club. Look at the brand of player I've brought in. Look at the know-how I've honed, the hours I've worked. Yet here we are, about to get bumped out the league. The lowest point in our ninety-nine-year history. Crowds sitting on half of what our average was last year when we narrowly avoided the drop."

"That's just the thing, Tam." Gus poured the rest of the Royal Navy into a tumbler and lowered his voice. "We're not Manchester United. We're not even Colchester United. We're Guff Rovers. A wart in the armpit of football."

"And? What's your point?"

"We're on a tiny island of forty thousand people. We've done nothing in the game except make the fourth round of the Milk Cup in 1981."

"Would've won the thing if Ipswich Town hadn't robbed us. If Kenny Boddington barely touched their forward for that penalty. Pfft! Spinal fracture, my toe."

"Bottom line is, this club has been wading through a sea of

mediocrity for a century. I'm not saying things won't improve, but you can't turn an ocean liner around in a few short months."

Tam looked to the carpet and sighed. "I only want the best for this club," he mumbled. "I only want what's best."

"We all do, Tam. We all do." He put an arm on the big man's lime coat. As unsavoury as it looked and smelled, Gus couldn't help but admire the stitching around the bullet hole. "Also, we're going to need some extra funds." Gus figured this was as good a time as any. "A couple of hundred grand should do it."

Tam's eyes stopped watering. They began burning. "I've spent nearly all my loot."

"Yes, on players, wages and fees. But we have to keep the lights on. There's water, gas, the cleaning bill as well. Nuts-and-bolts sort of things. You do understand."

Tam groaned. His fat fingers reached into the inside pocket and removed his chequebook.

Gus wasn't lying. All these things did need to be paid. What he wouldn't tell Tam was that he wanted a new drinks cabinet for the superyacht and an engine for the chopper. The common man did not understand that sailing around the world and keeping a helicopter did not come cheap.

Tam signed his name and handed over the blank cheque. "And you'll be with us on the Dunoon camp?"

"Ah, you see, I've got a good deal to chase in the Caribbean. Enormously lucrative. Could do wonders for the club. You know how it is."

A good deal of sailing, more like.

Either way, Tam seemed to buy this. "Right. But you'll be here for the run-in? It's crunch time. I can't do everything by myself."

Gus knew from the paper that they'd endured a torrid run. The final two games at home were vital. Two teams were to be relegated. Guff were second bottom, a point above cellar dwellers Darlington, and a point behind third-bottom Doncaster. They had to play Tranmere, who were already promoted, and then Carlisle United, who were mid-table and had nothing to play for.

"Yes, of course I will," he lied, locking the suitcase full of rum. By that stage he would be out of range somewhere on the Gulf of Mexico, while his old ship back here on the Isle of Guff sank without a trace. Gus would take no joy in this.

But he didn't want to be around to see it happen.

41

The players arrived on the shore like it was the D-Day landings. Some sprawled prostrate on the sand. Others held their sides, vomiting. A few felt their legs buckle as they dropped face-first onto the dirt. Those who were lucky swayed on the spot, dazed.

Jimmy Dolan, born and bred on the Isle of Guff, considered himself an experienced seaman, having caught the ferry back and forth to the mainland thousands of times. But as he violently brought up the cod and chips they'd had for lunch onto the rocks, never again would he attempt the ferry to the Shetland Islands.

The club was supposed to go for their midwinter tour exactly then—in *midwinter*. There were hopeful whispers about Portugal or the South of France. For a while it looked like the Channel Islands would be the more realistic destination. Then the trip was delayed, and delayed, then delayed again because of the takeover. Now it was happening. Dunoon was pulled at the last minute due to the lack of an available training ground. And so it was moved over a thousand miles in the opposite direction of the Isle of Guff.

It was Tam's call in the end. He thought it sounded rustic. Plus, Alex Ferguson had taken his Aberdeen side there the summer before they defeated Real Madrid to win the Cup Winners' Cup.

Summer, that is.

Fergie was smart. He didn't try it when they were barely out of winter. At least they could have flown here, thought Jimmy. But no, a boat it was. With a near gale force ten blowing when they were heading out.

What ensued was twelve hours of wave after wave. Anything the players had eaten soon made a reappearance. Those with families wrote goodbye messages to them and stuffed them into empty Irn-Bru bottles, tossing them overboard. Somehow, though, they made it. And now on dry land, they were still paying the price.

A four-seater Cessna circled the skies. Jimmy swore he saw Tam squeezed into it, giving them the thumbs-up. He'd wondered where the gaffer had been during the ordeal.

"Right, lads," Jimmy managed to say. As the most senior member of staff, he thought he should be the one to take charge of this shambles. Looking at the tourist map which the ferry's captain had handed him, he wiped the vomit from his mouth with a hankie and tried to get their bearings. "Digs are this way." He pointed north. "We can all die quietly there."

He was freezing. He only had a thin jumper on and no anorak. He was nauseous. His hands were cramping again; the carpal tunnel which had plagued him for the past few years was playing up in the elements. He needed a good kip. He was getting much too old for this.

The players grudgingly peeled themselves up off the sand.

"I hope you enjoyed the voyage," the captain said in his near indecipherable Highland accent. "Please come sailing with P&O Scottish Ferries again."

"You can stick your fucking boat, Blackbeard," Billy Wood told him, grabbing his Guff bag, and brushing past him as he made his way up the dunes.

This was meant to be a relaxing trip for the side. A time to bond, unwind, work on a few drills and sharpen their skills for their remaining matches, which would decide their league fate. What they didn't need was a twelve-hour bus ride followed by the ferry from hell with no break in between. Not at this point in the season. Not ever.

And they were letting Jimmy know all about it.

"This is taking the piss."

"Thought we were hopping across the water."

"We could get to Australia quicker."

"I know all that, boys," Jimmy reasoned. "The accommodation will be worth it. I'm sure there's some good reason why we've come all this way."

He led them up the bank. Tam had mentioned the chalets were by the ocean.

"What's that smell?" Hans asked.

"Smells like burning tyres," Oko said.

"Smells like my boy's nappies," Deng added.

At the top they looked down at a patchy grassed area with two paint-stripped goals either side. The pot-holed pitch was about as smooth as the turf at Bannockburn after a few days' battle. A team of shaved-headed, square-jawed young men were completing a passing drill at the far end.

"This is not our training ground," Paddy Conroy said, more out of hope than anything.

"And that better not be our fucking digs," Billy said, more forcefully.

By the side of the pitch were half a dozen log cabins that looked like they'd been transported from Siberia during the Tsar's last days. One had its windows put in. Another was half-burnt down, its busted roof filled with a hay bale.

Jimmy checked the map. This was it all right.

The boys started up.

"This is balls."

"I'd rather lay concrete than do this shit."

"I'd rather be on the dole."

"Lads, lads, I'm sure it's some mistake. Some easily rectifiable problem." Jimmy said this more out of hope than anything. It seemed every day he was saying the same thing. So much so that even he no longer believed it. And he could see in their tired eyes that the players didn't either.

"Where's the boozer?"

"Where's Wimpy?"

"Where's the airport home?"

Luckily, he wouldn't have to answer these questions, as from the bushes, the precise direction from where the Cessna headed, came Tam and Connor.

"Ahoy there, me maties." Tam beamed, wearing his Cossack hat. Connor couldn't make eye contact, clearly embarrassed by the situation.

Jimmy felt a dizzy spell hit. He needed a cup of tea and a nap. He tried to light a ciggie instead, struggling in the wind. "I was just telling the boys you'd sort out the misunderstanding."

"This shitehole here." Paddy pointed. "This must be some sort of joke."

"Joke?" Tam replied. "That team over there are Dynamo Grozny. Champions of the Chechen region's Third Division. Top-quality Euro opposition for us to sharpen our skills."

Connor did not know about this. "I thought the boys were here to train?"

"To train, to practise, to try out all the things we can't try out during the heat of competitive matches. And this is the perfect setting for it."

"I don't fancy this surface," Paddy said, poking the turf with his toe. "I've got bad knees as it is."

"There's nothing better to toughen you up," Tam said. "And you lot need it."

"You mean I gave up my triplets' birthday for this?" Mustafa tutted.

"And please don't say we have to stay in that place." Diego Carceras pointed at the decrepit barn-like structures. His expectations had been too high. He had a luminous yellow line of zinc across his nose, a beach towel draped over his shoulder, and wore Hawaiian shorts.

"You ungrateful bunch of babies," Tam replied. "Of course you're staying there."

"There's no room service," Paddy Conroy said.

"There's no hot tub," Hans added.

"There probably isn't even a telly," Billy grumbled.

"Of course there's not, you ingrates. It's rustic. It's real. You pampered puddings need some roughing up."

"I think this might be going a tad too far," Connor said, inspecting the setting closer. "This place makes Guff look like the Costa del Sol."

"Balls to that. Haven't you seen *Rocky IV*? I know you have because I've screened it six times since I've been here."

This much was true. While most teams would watch highlight packages of their opponents, Tam would still make them watch *Rocky*. At first, it had been a novelty, but after two months the players were over it and their requests to watch something starring Eddie Murphy or Michael J. Fox kept falling on deaf ears. The thing that Jimmy found funniest about Tam's *Rocky* obsession was how Tam thought Rocky Balboa was real. Along with Apollo Creed, Clubber Lang and Ivan Drago.

"So, get in those bloody rooms," he ordered. "Get stripped and get wired into these Bolshevik bastards. The season starts now."

Which Jimmy found even funnier as the season had two games left.

Jimmy watched the Chechens warming up. Their lads looked fit, strong and confident as they lobbed the ball about. They were shouting and revving each other up like it was a World Cup tie. Like their lives depended on it.

Jimmy joined the Guff boys, some of whom were still holding their stomachs, others their heads, as they mooched off to get unpacked in their rooms, and reluctantly get kitted-up for the latest wild chapter in their careers under Tam Bam.

"Call yourself warriors?" Tam taunted as he necked another handful of Rennie. "You're a lot of pansies. You've been mollycoddled for far too long."

Jimmy knew that being involved with Guff Rovers could be a lot of things. It could be disturbing, degrading and always bloody hard work. But one thing it wasn't—it was never dull.

And this, much like Guff legend Les McGarry, was why Jimmy could never quit.

42

Despite the sleeping pill he'd taken, Hans twisted and turned for what felt like hours on the plyboard bed, its foam mattress so eroded and eaten away by whatever else lived in the room that you could almost see through it. Then there were the exposed nails from the joints which threatened to crucify him at any false turn.

Hans didn't expect much when he signed with Guff Rovers, but he expected more than this. He clutched his bruised hip and battered shoulder. The Chechens had booted them from goal line to goal line during the friendly. *Friendly*, if you could call it that. Tam had done his usual talk about *Rocky* beforehand, and it turned out almost exactly like that. Their opposition was like Ivan Drago when he fought Apollo Creed.

And murdered him.

Hans finally drifted off into another uneasy sleep, not sure if he'd ever play again, never mind be fit enough for the league run-in. But after what felt like only moments in the land of nod, a strong arm shook him, scaring him out of his silk pyjamas.

"What the fuck?" Hans shot out of the bunk so quick that he clanged his head on the bunk above, believing he was being attacked by Bigfoot or worse.

A voice came out of the shadows. "Get your shoes and coat on. We're leaving."

The figure crept out of the room. Hans struggled up, his head throbbing, same as the rest of his body.

Guff Rovers had played like a side here for a holiday. Literally, some of them were. Diego Caceras had to play in flip-flops because he hadn't packed his boots. Then they lost two of the young lads to injury in the first five minutes. And then lost two of the Swindon loanees to a broken nose and two missing front teeth, respectively, after the fight that Billy Wood kicked off with a studs-first neck-high tackle. It was more like common assault. But given some of the challenges the opposition was dishing out, it was positively virginal.

The fight might have seen them all end up in hospital had it not been for Ralph McInnes. He had six of his brothers over to watch the game and they knocked half the Chechens out cold. In the end, the Chechens were the ones rushing to their minibus for cover. They were staying on the far end of the island, and their cube-shaped captain vowed they'd be coming back later to level the score on fighting terms.

Suddenly the signing of that big lump of haggis didn't seem like a bad move after all.

The game was abandoned with the score at 7–2 in the Chechens' favour. What that was supposed to do for morale, Hans didn't know.

He listened again for the voice. Was it a dream? He was in excruciating pain, was cold and hungry, but he wouldn't mind getting the hell out of here.

He wrapped the threadbare sheet around him and crept to the window, careful not to trip over the broken chair, bin and dog kennel strewn across the floor. He pulled back the curtain. There he saw the entire team out on the lawn.

"Hurry up, you lazy Kraut bastard," Billy Wood whispered. Hans could easily hear him because there was no pane of glass.

"Your chariot awaits," added Paddy.

Hans didn't need to be begged. He'd told Barry he'd call as soon as they landed but hadn't seen a phone box, and Tam refused to let him use his mobile.

Ah, Barry.

He didn't know what to make of the pub landlord. All he knew was that it was good. Hans confided in him that he was worried about what his ex would do if he should come across to the Isle of Guff and find them together. Barry told him not to worry. That he would deal with it. And given the size of him and his reputation, Hans was sure he would.

The forward threw on some pants and shoes, pocketed the paperback of *The Picture of Dorian Gray* which the players had been giving him stick for reading, grabbed his bag and was out in ten seconds flat.

"Where are we going?"

"Keep your voice down," Billy cautioned. "We ain't getting caught now."

"I'm not just heading anywhere with you lot," Hans said.

"Fuck this shitehole," Paddy said, waving a wallet in the air. "We're going to the mainland. I took the fat man's credit card. We've got the plane keys as well."

"Who's gonna fly it?"

"Mustafa had a licence in the Turkish navy."

"Is there even such a thing?"

"We're about to find out."

"Won't we be in an awful lot of bother?"

"He promised us a good trip away," Billy said. "And by hook or by crook, we're getting one."

"But isn't this essentially theft? Taking a credit card? Stealing a helicopter." Hans knew he couldn't cope with life on the inside.

"Where we're going, we'll be sure to make enough to pay him back," Paddy said.

"Where's that?"

"Perth Races."

"We'll get in trouble. This is more than a bit wrong."

"I got bitten by a fox that was sleeping in my bed." Oko pointed at deep teeth marks on his right calf.

"Jimmy had to give me nine stitches after I stood on a broken ashtray in the shower," Seth said.

"I have dendrophobia," said Benjamin Moshi, one of the other Africans from Swindon, peering into the forest and shuddering.

"What's that?" Hans asked.

"A fear of trees."

"How can you live like that?"

"I'm from Djibouti. There aren't any. And when you've gone your whole life not seeing them and then come across one … they're really fucking scary, man."

"I bet."

And with that, they were off. Hans worried what management would say, but he had to be loyal to his teammates. A group of players had never made him feel so wanted since … well, since ever. Even if what they were doing was erring on the side of shady. He didn't want to be seen as what the Yorkshiremen would call a 'scab'. And at the very least, he'd get to check back in with Barry, whom he was already missing.

Missing like he'd never missed anyone before.

43

If Paddy was honest, he was glad he was caught. He hadn't been near a betting shop since signing for Guff, despite the island hosting half a dozen of them. He'd also cut down on the booze (Saturday night, Sundays and Wednesdays only), was down to a pack a day and was getting to bed early.

If going to bed by two a.m. was early.

He worried about what another few hours at the races would do to him. Yet, it had seemed a good idea at the time. Going anywhere after Shetland did.

"You gambling, thieving lush." He felt a familiar clammy hand fall heavily on his shoulder.

Paddy was impressed that Tam had found them so quickly. Though perhaps they'd made it easier as they were the only punters donning fancy dress on this average Wednesday race day and the only ones with a light plane parked out front. It had been Billy Wood's idea that they stop off in Dundee to kit up. He was dressed as the chap from *Hellraiser*, acupuncture needles included. One of the Swindon guys was Mr. T—one of the white guys, that is. Pete Bennett, the beanpole forward, thought it was appropriate to boot-polish up for the occasion, despite the African lads telling him it wasn't funny. And Paddy was a leprechaun.

Tam grabbed him by his sparkly green bow tie. "Thought you could get away with it, didn't you?"

"It wasn't my idea, gaffer."

"Bullshit. You've been waiting for the moment when you could swan off to the pub and the bookmakers."

"I admit, it doesn't look good." And it didn't. He was perched there with a pint in one hand (his fifth or sixth, he couldn't remember), and a pina colada in the other. He also had eight hundred quid's worth of bets on and was precisely £809.99 down. He had a feeling a few notes had fluttered out of his pockets when he went to the bathroom.

"You're taking me to the others," Tam ordered.

"I could. But I quite fancy Black Dog in the fifth."

"Yes, and I quite fancy you not frittering away every cent I've given you since your comeback. Now find me those teammates of yours. You are bloody lucky I involved a private detective and not the actual fuzz."

Paddy didn't want to be the one who squealed but being midweek, it wasn't busy. If Tam weren't so lazy, he could have easily located their private box.

Paddy led the way to the top of the grandstand where they congregated. There were stains galore on their mostly superhero costumes. Drool, piss, vomit too. All the things that pointed to a good time had.

"You bloody cowards running away from a big team like that," Tam said, his voice raised. "Not to mention the homespun conditions."

"Ah, no," they groaned together. Although they knew it was inevitable that Tam would catch up with them, they didn't want it to be before the last race.

"We need to hit the training ground right away. The Chechen boys are still up there. I've got five grand resting on a rematch."

"I'll give you fifteen grand right now if we don't go," Billy said, looking terrifying in his costume.

"What about fitness? You're not getting fit here."

"You've had us running up hills and pulling weights and doing everything but marathons since we joined," Paddy said.

Tam looked to Connor who made his way into the box dragging their two suitcases. The young coach nodded. "He has a point."

"Look at the smiles on our faces," Billy added. "I didn't even know the names of Ox, Crusher and Boner before we got here."

"Who the bloody hell are they?" Tam asked.

"The lads from Swindon," Billy said, getting Boner (or Pete Bennett) into a friendly headlock and getting boot polish over his ear. "That's their nicknames. See, real teams have gotta have nicknames. We haven't had time to do that because you've been running the guts out of us."

Paddy plonked a large tumbler of Lucozade into Tam's hand. He sniffed it.

"Has this got gin in it?"

"It might have." Paddy winked.

"I'm the gaffer of a squad of professional athletes," he said. "Or so I thought. I don't drink, and neither should you."

Paddy cheersed him. "Get it into you."

"Let's go down the front for Race 5," Billy roared.

"What do I care about Race bloody 5?" Tam asked.

"If we win, we're gonna pay back all the money we took off your card," Paddy said. "New propellers are surprisingly dear."

"New what?! And what if you don't win?"

"Then you're down thirty grand."

"You thieving bastards."

"And champagne isn't cheap here."

Tam was ushered along by the mob towards the front of the grandstand. Paddy took this moment to break from the pack and sneak to the woman in the booth and make that bet. He wasn't walking out a loser. But either way, it was nice to be here, back with the boys, back in his element.

The football could wait.

44

"My brother's a businessman himself, you know," the cab driver told him. "He's in the muesli trade."

Sheikh Bin-Hassan nodded in the backseat, a handkerchief over his mouth. He didn't want to move for fear his pristine white robes would get even more soiled on the grimy upholstery. He didn't know what muesli was. He thought it might have been what the guest house he'd stayed at near the pier had offered him this morning as an alternative to the crispy bacon rashers on burnt bread which he couldn't eat.

How he missed the five-star hotel the family owned back in the United Arab Emirates.

"Are you sure I'm in the right place?"

"This is his island, all right," the driver replied. "For better or for worse."

The sheikh hoped the vehicle didn't break down. He couldn't believe anyone would live here, never mind a multi-millionaire. Dilapidated factories, houses with roof tiles and windows missing, graffiti. And a wind that cut through you like a *khanjar*.

He'd seen the Gaza Strip as a child, and this was worse.

The taxi stopped at the crosswalk. A group of teens smoking outside a shop spotted his attire and laughed. He didn't recognise the strange signs they were making with their fingers, but they didn't look appealing.

The taxi eventually pulled up outside a stadium. If it could be called that. It looked like it had been air-lifted from Chernobyl.

"Do you think he's there?" the sheikh asked.

"Lunchtime kick-off today."

"I've been calling him for days."

"They've been away on some training camp. They're back now. He'll be there. He's always there."

The sheikh got out. He looked around to make sure those kids weren't lurking. "Can you wait here?"

"For four hours?"

"Perhaps. However, I shouldn't be that long."

"It's your money, mate."

The sheikh couldn't imagine the driver had anywhere else to go. He walked carefully across the cobblestones in his sandals, the damp setting in between his toes. With two hours to go before kick-off, the front door to the stadium was still locked. He rang the bell.

"Coming, coming," came a man's voice. The door opened and there Tam stood, breathless and dishevelled. "You don't look like you want my money," Tam said. "You look like you're one of that Saudi mob here to give me a ton of it." He paused, appearing to think for a second. "You're not actually here to buy the club, are you? Keep your oil money and get back on your camel. We're not for sale at any price."

He began to close the door. The sheikh stopped it with his travel bag. "Not exactly."

"What exactly are you here for then? I've things to do, you know. This club isn't going to reach the top-flight if I'm wasting my time arguing with Yasser bloody Arafat."

"I believe we have something in common."

"And what is that, Mr Ayatollah?"

"I understand Gordon Bamford was your father?"

"For half my life he was. The other half I don't know where he was or what he was up to."

"I may be able to help you there because for the other half of your life I do know where he was and who he became."

"Where was he exactly?"

"In Abu Dhabi."

"And you're telling me this why?"

The sheikh felt another blast of cold knife right through him. He wasn't dressed for this weather. He heard a loud screech and saw the kids had followed him. They were torturing a cat in the middle of the street with a nine-iron and electrical tape. He shivered. "Can I come in?"

Tam thought. "I don't know. Can you? You could be a spy. You don't know how low some of the clubs in this league will stoop to decipher my tactics."

"Please. I've come a long way."

Tam eyed him from head to toe. "S'pose we could sit out in the stand."

Tam led him down the corridor and out to an area overlooking the pitch. They sat on the old benches, both of which were creaking under the weight of the two large men. The groundsman was making fresh markings around the goal area. The scene looked pre-war. The sheikh still felt the chill, but within the empty stadium he felt safer.

"Make it snappy," Tam told him. "I've a match to prepare for."

"I understand that."

"So, who was Gordon Bamford to you?"

"He was my father."

"No, he was my father."

"Indeed. And he was mine, also."

"But ... but you're a bloody Arab."

"Technically I'm half-Arabic. My mother is from the ruling Al-Fahali family. My father—*our* father—worked for them. They met and fell in love. They married and had me." The sheikh took in Tam's garish lime coat. He'd never seen anything like it in Abu Dhabi. "To be honest, I thought you would have done a bit more with fifty million."

"What? I only got five. Three mil after inheritance tax. How much did you get?"

"Oh, the same, the same. Of course, it was the same." The younger man was a terrible liar. He hoped he'd gotten away with it. He had received ninety million and didn't know what inheritance tax was.

"Hmph. So, I imagine this is an emotional thing for you. Being at this footballing Mecca."

"What do you mean?"

Tam pointed out to the patchy turf. "You must be a huge fan of Guff Rovers if your dad was supposedly my dad. He loved this place."

"Um, not exactly.' The sheikh had never heard of the team or the island until a month ago. His father never spoke of it. He'd got him into football, Division One to be specific. Not whatever league this was.

"Who do you support?"

"Chelsea."

Tam nearly fell off his chair. "He raised you a Chelsea fan! He must have lost his mind. The things I might have done with my life had I not been subjected to Fourth Division football." Tam looked out, sadly. "Had he maybe not subjected me to football in the first place. I bet you had a good education, n'all."

"You could say that. I attended Cambridge."

"There you have it. I was at the local comprehensive. Had to leave at fourteen because of my weight. And the bullies."

"I'm so sorry."

"Bet you never went without food. Heating. Replica shirts. Bet you had it all."

"I was not as wealthy as some of my cousins. There's a funny story, actually. One year we were visiting New York, and we had to stay at the Four Seasons instead of the Waldorf as our butler forgot to make a reservation. Now that was embarrassing." He could see from Tam's blank expression that the man found it anything but. "No, no, you're right. When I was born, my father, your father, *our* father, was a wealthy man. He married well and made many informed business decisions."

"Would have been nice to have heard about them earlier. Would have been nice if old Mother dear had reaped some of the benefits."

"I didn't know you existed until the will was read. Then I had no way of finding out where you lived until I heard about you on BBC World Service."

The sheikh stopped talking. He heard a low rumble, so loud he worried the island may be situated along a fault line.

Tam gripped his stomach where the noise burst forth. "Could I interest you in some food?"

"Please. I haven't eaten a thing."

"How are you operating, man? I can't go an hour without some fuel. I'll call across to the shop and get us a pasty."

"What's a pasty?"

"*What's a bloody pasty?* International cuisine at its finest, is what it is. Forget your curries and kebabs and whatever else you fussy buggers eat. You've never tasted anything like this."

The sheikh was surprised that Tam had a mobile phone. He'd ordered one last month and was still waiting.

Within minutes a small hunchback woman was struggling down the steps with a boxful of food.

"Thank you, Mayvis," Tam said, as she laid down a tray of what looked to be pies, featuring a braided decoration of pastry. "I'll call you about five to bring up my dinner."

"No problem, Mr Bamford," she croaked, the sheikh noticing she didn't have a single tooth in her head.

"Dig in, sunshine," Tam said when she'd gone.

"Is there cutlery?"

"*Is there cutlery*? I'm sure you don't always have cutlery in the bloody desert. Open your cakehole and dig in."

The sheikh did so. He found the pastry dry, and the meat overdone with far too much onion. "Is there sauce?"

"You don't need sauce, either. Not with that flavour."

To say it was the worst thing that the sheikh had ever tasted would be an exaggeration. Once at Eton, he competed in a dressage competition, and his horse threw him off the saddle, and he landed face-first and mouth open into a lump of horse manure. That shaded it.

No wonder Papa escaped from this place and never looked back.

The sheikh placed the offending matter down, lying, "On second thoughts, those oysters I had last night on the plane were most filling."

"Suit yourself." Tam grabbed it and shoved it into his mouth. "More morning tea for me."

As he chewed it down, the sheikh studied Tam's features. The pale skin, the large red nose, those beady eyes. There was no way he could be related to this man—his supposed brother. Surely.

"So, what are you here for?" Tam asked.

"I'm not really sure." He trailed off. "Listen, I'm sorry, but I think this has been an awful mistake."

Then Tam shot him a grimace, showing off an overgrown canine poking down from his top lip. The sheikh's heart sank. He himself had the very same teeth, just like their father. He even had the shock of ginger hair and shared Tam's whale calf body shape.

"Come here." Tam lurched over, smothering him in a cuddle. "Never had a brother before. It's got to work out better than having a sister. Today you are my guest of honour. We can use the chairman's office to watch the match. He's never here."

The sheikh plucked at his own overgrown left canine. It had a small oat on it from that bland bowl of whatever it was they gave him for breakfast that morning. English food really was the worst. He thought he'd gotten used to it at boarding school and university, but this part of England seemed to take it to a new level.

Tam belched so loudly that the few fans streaming into the ground ducked for cover. "That pasty did not land well."

The sheikh turned away, clutching his handkerchief to his nose. No, there was surely no way he was related to this oaf.

And then a loud belch escaped from his own mouth, completely unexpected, which he couldn't disguise. His heart sank. There was no need for a test.

He knew it was true.

45

The first half of the lunchtime kick-off had been a nightmare; Guff's shape was a mess, and so was their confidence. Yet somehow the game remained scoreless. This was all down to Seth Graham who, from a goalkeeper's perspective, was having the perfect game. He was catching, punching, clawing, beating, and tipping all of Tranmere's goal-bound efforts away to safety. At the end of the forty-five minutes, the entire ground, even the Tranmere fans, rose to give him a standing ovation.

If it wasn't for him, they would have been five down.

Tam's team-talks were usually based on mockery, bravado, and clichés from Sylvester Stallone movies. But this one before the game had been the worst yet as he belched and shivered and puked into a bucket, in between ranting about undercover Middle Eastern operatives who'd poisoned him in an attempt to sabotage Guff Rovers' season. Connor Whelan tried to interrupt him but found himself repeatedly blanked. As a result, no one knew what they were doing, or even who was playing, as thirteen players took to the pitch, the referee luckily (or unluckily) noticing seconds before the start.

Seth had read in the local paper that second division Watford were interested in his services. What Seth wasn't interested in doing was moving to London. Seth was part of the largest Amish community in Britain, with over thirty families situated on the Isle of Guff's north-west coast. Aged just eighteen, he was engaged to be married to Meredith—a local girl from the community—in the summer.

This performance wouldn't help the speculation about his career.

Seth knew they needed a win, at minimum a draw, to keep their hopes of avoiding the drop alive. He knew today was his day, and he wasn't going to let the fans down. He wasn't so confident, however, about the players in front of him or his gaffer.

Unusually, Tam hadn't made a sound all half. There was little surprise when the players entered the changerooms at the break that he wasn't present, and Connor Whelan was the man in charge.

There was no surprise—only pure joy.

It was the jump start they needed. Connor put his own mark on the team by gambling and using his two substitutions. He dragged Ibrahim Deng and Mustafa Bilik, both of whom hadn't kicked a ball, and threw on Paddy Conroy and Ralph McInnes. It was bold, it was brassy. It was precisely what was required.

And it worked. It worked so well that the biggest challenge Seth had for the bulk of the second period was keeping warm and ignoring the chants of "Beardy Bastard" coming from the small section of away supporters who'd obviously forgotten applauding his first-half heroics.

Guff were dominant. Billy Wood was winning anything and everything in the backline, and CJ was running the midfield. And upfront Paddy Conroy may have been moaning a lot more since he kicked the fags and booze, but his performance was benefitting because here he was springing, ducking and weaving, and displaying the type of form which once made him a First Division star.

Guff had struck both posts and had a shot cleared off the line. They'd had an effort disallowed for a questionable offside. But entering injury time, there were still no goals. And a goal was crucial.

Guff had a corner. The crowd was on its feet and firmly behind them. Connor gestured for Seth to stay back in goal, despite wanting to join the attack.

Paddy swung in the set-piece. The Tranmere centre-half reacted first, heading the ball clear into space. Their forward latched on to it, and Guff were caught short. Suddenly it was two against one. He slipped the ball past an out-of-breath Billy Wood onto his strike partner's path, which saw him bearing down on goal.

In the heat of the moment, Seth made a decision. He committed. He knew he wasn't going to reach the ball. He was well aware it was wrong, sinful even. He'd never fouled a player in his life, never mind been booked or sent off. Still, he knew if he didn't make a challenge, it would be a Tranmere goal and relegation for Guff Rovers.

Seth went with it. He followed through. He missed the ball, and the player went flying over his shoulders. The referee whistled. The referee pointed to the spot. The Tranmere fans cheered.

Seth looked to the heavens. He knew he'd done wrong. He picked himself up. Head bowed, he began the long walk to the dressing room.

"What the fuck you doing, Amish?" Billy yelled.

Seth looked to the ref. The card wasn't red. It was yellow. The ball must have been moving away from the goal when he struck. He'd never been yellow carded before, and it felt awful. But it sure as hell felt better than a red.

Thank you, God.

When he made it back to his goalmouth, their striker had already placed the ball on the spot and was ready to run up. Seth liked to psyche his opponent out, eyeball him, get the ball moved off the spot. Try to read his body language about where he was going to put it. There was no time for any of this. All he could do was pick a side and go as hard and as fast as possible.

And in the back of his mind was the horrible truth that if the ball hit the net, Guff Rovers were done for.

Seth went left. The ball did too. It was beyond him, but he found the strength within to stretch that little bit further. He got a finger to it. The ball sprung away, striking the post. He heard the hollow clang of leather and air on steel. The ball shot out.

Seth crawled up and saw two, three, four white shirts waiting to pounce on the rebound. Where were the Guff players?

Without a thought for his own well-being, Seth dived head-first onto the ball. He felt an avalanche of boots, studs and bones crash into his skull. The pain was unbearable.

Despite escaping a red, Seth wasn't hopeful of getting anything else from the ref. He might have been dazed, but he knew his bearings. His teammates were nowhere near him. That must mean they were further upfield.

With the ball in his hands, he struggled up. He moved his neck and looked out. Vision blurred, he could just make out Paddy Conroy free to his left. Oko unmarked to the right. And through the middle, with a ten-yard start on the sweeper, was Hans Schickler. Seth threw the ball into the space behind him. Hans was off like a rabbit.

All the big Austrian needed was one touch to line it up, and then with his next the ball was nestled in the far corner of the opposition's onion bag.

Faery Meadow erupted. The Guff players ran to Hans to celebrate. The only thing better than saving a penalty was saving a penalty then in the next play setting up a goal. Seth wanted to join in but was too sore.

He spotted Connor give him a thumbs-up on the touchline. Up in the director's box, Tam was cheering while at the same time vomiting into a wastepaper basket as a man in full Arab dress applauded next to him.

Was he hallucinating?

Then he looked to his feet and noticed a pool of blood gathering, dripping from his head. As he crumpled to the turf, he noticed a man in a blazer with a yellow-and-red striped Watford tie behind the goal, applauding and nodding his head, and looking most impressed.

Despite the searing pain, Seth wanted moments like these. But he didn't want them to mean he was moving to London.

People could say what they wanted about his island, but he'd rather play house with Beelzebub than live in that place.

46

In all his thirty-three years with the club. Jimmy Dolan had never witnessed anything like this. When the whistle sounded, the fans invaded the pitch, chanting Connor Whelan's name like they'd won the FA Cup. When in actual fact, all that happened was they'd taken league survival into their own hands. After Doncaster's loss at Rochdale and Darlington's relegation after falling to Rotherham, Guff Rovers were two points clear of the relegation zone. A draw next week against Carlisle would ensure their survival but wouldn't be required should Doncaster fail to win.

The young goth guard had his work cut out. Showing strength and restraint Jimmy didn't think he had, he managed to get the players and coaching staff into the tunnel unharmed from the enthusiastic mob.

Once there, they partied like they'd won the treble.

A crate of beers appeared, and the recently bonded team got stuck in singing and chanting along to the Smiling Tuesdays or whatever the pop band was called playing on the wireless. Then when Tam Bam came into the room, chalk white with a blanket wrapped around him, they threw him in the bath with his lime mac still on. Jimmy thought the gaffer would hit the roof, yet even he saw the funny side of it.

"You bastard lot, you've flooded my moon boot. How am I going to dry the thing?"

"How about taking the stinking thing off for once?" Paddy shouted.

Tam perked up and cracked a Lucozade. "Drink this in, boys. Once we win next week, you watch us go. I had a very important person watch us today. One who turned out not to be a spy after all."

"Whatever, gaff," Billy Wood said, hitting him square on the nose with a rubber duck.

"Whatever, yourself. You're looking at a man who is about to laugh longest."

The players cheered louder and began shouting

"Championeees, championeees, ole, ole, le."

All except for Connor. While the others sprayed each other with froth, the young coach sat in the corner studying his notes, no doubt preparing for Tuesday's training session. His headphones were on, and he was listening to the radio. Jimmy always suspected that the young man would go places. This confirmed it. Guff weren't out of the woods yet, and young Connor Whelan knew it.

Jimmy didn't feel a part of things, either. A bunch of kids and blow-ins celebrating about getting off the foot of the ladder didn't seem right. And anyway, he hadn't drunk in a decade. Doctor's orders. Smoking was different, though. No matter what the doctors told him, he couldn't be giving that up.

"You all right, Connor, lad?" Jimmy asked.

Connor took out the earpiece. He looked up like he was about to cry. "Something bad's happening at Hillsborough. Really bad."

Jimmy didn't know what he was on about or what the FA Cup semi-final had to do with Guff. It had been a while since he'd thought of Liverpool and his time there.

He slipped outside to his usual spot and lit up. The cigarettes always felt better after a win. Just a pity they were as rare as a dry summer's day.

Jimmy watched as the fans made their way out of the stadium. For the first time in a long time, they had their heads held high and spring in their step. He saw the April sun break through that dense, black cloud which seemed to perpetually hang over the island. He saw mates together, dads with their kids, grandfathers with their grandkids, and knew that this coming together was what football was all about. Jimmy had no one to share this moment with. His niece and her kids were away to Torbay for the week, his mother was in the hospice. He would go home tonight to nobody, the same as he did every night.

Behind him lay his true family. The pitch, the stadium, the players. He fretted about how the surface wasn't as good as it could be, how today some of the players' shorts had grass stains on them from the previous week's game. He thought about how Connor had stopped sending him to look at other teams or asking for his notes, preferring to do it himself or get some younger freelance scout on the case. Jimmy knew it was because the notes in his Filofax were too muddled. A lot like his mind these days.

Jimmy inhaled, wondering what would have happened if he'd made it as a player. Maybe he'd have had time to have the wife and the kids and now the grandkids, and a proper life away from the pitch.

He thought about how his life might have gone had he never kicked a ball to begin with. Maybe he'd have discovered a trade, a skill, and made it off this island and had a different life altogether. A better life.

The "Championees" chants were getting louder from behind the dressing room window. Jimmy lit another cigarette. Fuck it, he was celebrating. It had been a full life. It was not the life he had planned; still, it was more than most people got.

"There's been a crush," he heard a passer-by say.

Jimmy found himself nodding off and couldn't stop.

"They reckon scores are dead."

His head felt heavy. And yet, this was a peaceful weight.

"This'll change football forever."

Jimmy slumped against the wall and watched his cigarette burn to the end as it dangled from his lips. Unable to move, he slowly drifted to the tarmac along with all the ash.

This time Jimmy Dolan knew he wasn't getting up, and he no longer cared.

47

Phil Gates sat in his stationary hatchback. It was covered in takeaway wrappers, Coke cans and empty cigarette packets, just like any respectable journalist's vehicle should be.

His eyes drifted to the training ground, covered in dense cloud. He'd been all set to fly to London to cover the one-armed rower in his final qualifier for the Paralympics. Then his editor put a stop to it after Guff Rovers did precisely what no one dreamed they would.

They won a game.

His editor said Phil had to follow the build-up to the biggest game in Guff's history instead. And now his wife hadn't spoken to him in days because she'd booked a ticket to come with him and hit the sales.

It didn't matter, though. Nothing really mattered after Hillsborough. At least he wasn't there covering that. Football, sport itself, suddenly seemed unimportant.

So here he was. Yet the ground was empty. Tam Bam must've given the squad the day off following the sudden death of their kit man, masseuse and chief scout groundsman. But that would be most unlike him. The players hadn't had a single day off since his tortuous reign began.

Phil saw the goth magically appear from behind a crowd of trees. The kid looked both ways. When he was sure he wasn't being watched, he got in the car. He was wearing ridiculous knee-high cherry-red Doc Martens, his jet-black attire decorated in chains and safety pins. How he'd gotten a job at the football club, Phil would never understand.

But as a snitch, he was second to none.

"What you got for me?" Phil asked.

"Tam's had me investigating the source of his food poisoning," he said, getting in, his voice so small, Phil always had to lean in. 'I'm no forensic scientist, but given the hygiene practices of his favourite bakery, I'm surprised he hasn't dropped off the perch by now."

"And why are the players not here?"

The goth helped himself to the can of Lilt and packet of Scampi Fries he'd requested as part-payment.

"The gaffer has half of them laying new turf at Faery Meadow," he replied. "The other half are washing the strips."

"No way. There are out-of-work gardeners in this town. There's a launderette too."

"He reckons it will help them focus for Saturday."

"And they're actually going along with that?"

"He told them it was Jimmy's dying wish that they do it."

"Are footballers really that thick?"

"It would appear most are." The goth munched. "But Paddy Conroy and Billy Wood told him to shove it. Paddy's gone on a bender. Billy's gone to see one of his illegitimate children. He only has three, but Tam hasn't worked out yet that this is the fourth time he's left the island for his kids' birthdays since he's signed."

"You're good, Frankenstein, I'll give you that. Does The Bam know anything about Pinkle using his money to buy a castle in Casablanca?"

"I don't think so. Though he did order me to put a hit out on him last week."

"He wants him dead?"

"It would seem so."

"You would actually do that?"

The goth wiped his greasy fingers on the upholstery. "I'll give anything a go. I need the money to go to a music festival in Whitby."

"So, Bam must know."

"Nah. It was because Pinkle billed a new gold filling to the club."

"Imagine if he knew the actual truth? It would strike him dead."

"Do you want me to tell him?"

"God, no. I'll print it next week. There's no way my editor will let me push something like this through before such a big game."

"Fair dues."

"Is Tam over his food poisoning?"

"Apparently. Every time I see him, he has a pasty in one hand and a Lucozade in the other."

"No shock there. And what's the word for the match this weekend?"

"He hasn't discussed it yet. I know he asked for the game to be put back a month in memory of Jimmy, but that was rejected by the JA."

"You meant the FA?"

"Whatever." The goth slurped at the last of the can. He crushed it, dropping it on the mat. Then he helped himself to a Regal. "Everyone's down about Mr Dolan's passing, but the gaffer seems surprisingly upbeat."

"Why do you reckon that is?"

"Keeps going on about some mystery investor and how the club is on the verge of joining the European elite. Whatever that is."

Phil laughed. "He has more chance of winning an England cap."

"There was an Arab tycoon I had to accompany out of the ground last Saturday."

"Is that right?"

"He seemed pretty shaken by his matchday experience. He told me he couldn't get out of Guff and back to the Gulf quick enough."

The rain was coming down hard now.

"Can you blame him? Dresden '45 would've been prettier than here."

The goth's pager beeped. He read the message. "I should go. Gaffer has me on chief scout duty. I have a box of tapes from the Vanuatuan football league he wants me to scour for a new left-back."

"Do you even know what a left-back is?"

"Course not. But he's paying time-and-a-half. Speaking of which." The goth held out his salty palm. Phil handed over the twenty.

"Be sure to check in again with me on Friday."

"Same time, same place. I know." He got out the car, pulled the hood of his Sisters of Mercy jumper over his head and escaped back into the bushes.

What a complete and utter weirdo, thought Phil. The likes of him would have been strung up if he'd been found near a football ground back when he started in the press. Though if Phil was honest, the goth's introduction to the football club was one of the more normal things to have occurred of late.

But all said, the Siouxsie Sioux kid was up there with the best informants he'd had. And the way he'd seen him deal with Guff fans, and, more vitally, Tam Bam, he'd earned Phil's respect as a hardy little so-and-so.

And after the way he'd managed to fleece three hundred quid out of Phil in the three months since he'd started working at the club, a shrewd little bastard as well.

48

Father Gonzalez looked in the mirror as he patted down his creased cassock. Spring was here, summer was coming. It was easier wearing only three layers instead of his customary four, sometimes five. As dreary and gloomy as the island was during the winter (make that two-thirds of the year), the late spring and most of the summer when the clouds parted and lit up the horizon were up there with what his beloved Columbia could dish up.

The priest peeked out at the congregation. There wasn't a seat in the house. All standing room at the back was full with faces he didn't even know existed on the island.

He felt the butterflies in his gut. He'd gotten used to saying his sermon to the same half dozen (dozen if it was the weekend) regulars. He hadn't felt this nervous since he was ordained, and his entire village travelled to Bogota to see it.

Father Gonzalez slipped the bolt and opened the door of the sacristy to let in some fresh spring air. The mourners waiting to pay their respects snaked around the block. There must have been half the island positioned in and around the church, most draped in Guff colours, a few with Liverpool scarves or shirts. All silent, all respectful.

The priest smiled at the serene scene. This was why he had heard God's call. For the first time, he was thankful that the bishop had turned down his request to leave and marry. Nora was right. They needed him here. Though he still couldn't bear her being back in Romania. He prayed for her to return. He knew it was wrong, but he so wanted her in his life. The church wasn't always right on these matters. Bishop Winstanley had a different woman in each port, all the priests knew that.

"What do you mean I can't get a lawnmower man in until next week?" Tam Bam circled the chapel, arguing on his oversized phone. "There's a bloody game on. The biggest in the history of the club. We can't be playing on shin-length grass … Someone from the mainland? … We'd end up with a spy … And how much will that cost? … You offering, are you?"

He was so loud that those queuing rolled their eyes at the man's total lack of respect.

"Tam," Father Gonzalez whispered. "Will you please keep your voice down?"

The priest was most surprised when Tam actually did.

"I can't get anyone to mow the turf," he whispered to the priest. His eyes were bloodshot. He looked like he hadn't slept in days.

"Come in here." The priest led him through the back door. Anything had to be better than him ranting amongst the mourners.

"And then there's the strips," Tam continued. "Those players were no help. Heaven help them if they had to get proper jobs. Jimmy could at least have had the decency to put them in to soak before he fell off the perch. Four trips I've had to make to the launderette already this morning. And they're still not dry."

"All we can do is our best. This is a tough week."

"The pitch needs relining n'all. But did he care? Did he balls."

"He did a lot for the club, for the island. I think we may all be realising just how much. You are really missing him, aren't you?"

"Missing him? The inconsiderate blow-hard. Dying this week of all weeks."

This wasn't working out how Father Gonzalez planned. He might have known. He didn't need this now. Not minutes before his biggest mass. He had to try a different route. "Do you ever wonder what they'll say about you when you're gone?"

"I've never given a toss what people have ever thought of me. Least of all the reprobates on this island. Why would I suddenly care when I'm pushing up the daisies?"

"I see." Father Gonzalez knew that Tam would never get it. But he had to help him contain his ire for an hour. "I would love to continue this discussion. However, I must ask you to go back outside. I have a very important sermon to do and—"

"That's right, Father. You abandon me in my hour of need. If you really cared about the island, you'd be down at the ground with a whipper snipper and an ironing board."

The priest attempted to usher him out the way he came in. "Yes, yes. Now if you'll just—"

"Chucking me out onto the street as well?" Tam pulled his arm away. "What happened to 'give me your tired, your poor and your muddled masses', hey? You'll burn for this."

Father Gonzalez got Tam out, and the door shut and bolted. He did not need that *idiota* in his life. He looked at his watch. It was three minutes past eleven. The priest wet his face under the tap. He looked in the mirror, touched up his hair, and said a quick Hail Mary.

You've got this, he repeated to himself.

As he took to the altar, the congregation rose. The priest's knees had never knocked during a sermon. He was on home turf, but this felt like an away game. He knew the vast majority of those in attendance wouldn't be Catholics and probably didn't even believe in the man above.

As the choirboys finished 'Abide With Me', the priest cleared the tickle in his throat and a hush fell. "Everyone connected to Guff Rovers, everyone who lives on the island, knew who Mr Jimmy Dolan was. Everyone respected him. You couldn't meet a person who didn't like him. Jimmy was selfless in the way he served his community. You could not measure in *pesos* the work this man put into his football club or his beloved Isle of Guff."

You could have heard a pin drop between the sentences. Well, you would have if Tam wasn't stomping up and down the aisle. He made it to the front row where Jimmy's niece and her family sat, squeezing himself onto the end of the pew.

Father Gonzalez tried to make light of his actions. "I think Tam here knows it would have cost him millions to purchase a team player like Jimmy."

The congregation chuckled. Tam hadn't heard the quip because he was on his mobile phone. All the priest and the mourners could hear from him were the words "grass" and "strips" and "bastard" as Jimmy Dolan's niece tried to shush him.

The priest worked through the sermon as best as he could. At the end, the Guff Rovers' theme song to the tune of 'Football Crazy' by Robin Hall and Jimmy MacGregor played loud and proud. Father Gonzalez hummed along. Despite going to almost every home game for the past two seasons since arriving, he still didn't know the words.

The pallbearers lifted the coffin, draped in a Guff Rovers' flag and a Liverpool scarf. Jimmy's brother, his next-door neighbour, new club captain Billy Wood and Dennis from the stands (who was without his pink cap) got into position. A few steps along, Dennis gasped and clutched at his back. His grandson leapt over and steadied him, leading him back to his seat.

"You take it." Dennis wheezed to Tam through the pain. "You were his gaffer. It's what he would have wanted."

Tam put his phone away. He hesitated. His first reaction to anything was always to say the most belligerent thing imaginable. Instead, his bottom lip quivered. Father Gonzalez could see he was touched by the proposal.

Tam lifted his corner of the coffin with ease. Father Gonzalez led them through the heavy doors of the church. The Guff fans held their scarves aloft, singing 'You'll Never Walk Alone'. The pallbearers paused there, the sun shining, as the throng broke into a standing ovation.

Father Gonzalez looked behind and saw Tam's knees buckle. The priest quickly reached up, taking some of the weight from the casket.

"Are you okay?" the priest asked him quietly.

"Of course I'm bloody okay," Tam snapped, removing the priest's hand off his shoulder and regaining control of the pine box. "Stumbled is all."

But the priest saw his eyes were wet. And he could tell for the first time that Tam Bam finally understood what Jimmy Dolan had done for the club. And he was understanding what the club, the fans and the entire island meant to him.

And in what had been one of the most difficult weeks in the game's history to be a fan of the beautiful game, Father Gonzalez dabbed at his own tears as he realised he was thinking the exact same thing.

49

It was two o'clock on a Saturday afternoon at The Wick, and Barry hadn't had time to purchase this month's issue of *Blueboy*, never mind think about pleasuring himself.

He was too busy dusting, mopping and vacuuming the premises, making it look better than it ever had. He'd even told Old Bill to have the weekend off. He'd contacted a hospitality agency in Penzance who'd shipped him over a temp chef for the ludicrous fee of fifteen quid an hour. A gnarly looking individual with a greasy walrus moustache and a Balkan accent. He looked like he hadn't bathed in months.

Barry wasn't caring, so long as he could cook.

The Guff players were due at the pub after the match for their end-of-season bash, and Barry, whilst still not giving a monkey's about the round ball game, wanted everything to be right. Because when he got the chance, there was something he wanted to ask the club's star striker.

Barry and Hans had grown close in the three months since the Austrian arrived on the island, the pair rarely leaving his home above the pub. They'd grown even closer since Barry had taken last Tuesday off and travelled to Yorkshire to confront Hans's ex face to face about the hourly phone calls and letters he'd been bombarding the footballer with. Hans begged him not to go. But Barry was true to his word and didn't kill the man.

He was sure Daryl's arm would work fine once it was out of plaster.

Barry restocked the bar. He shined the old grandfather clock which stood across the open fire. He thought of how nice it would be to get rid of the rambunctious locals for a night. To deal solely with the players and their partners. Tam would be there, obviously, though he'd never given Barry a problem worth fretting about. Then when the party wound down, and Hans and Barry could snatch a moment to themselves, the landlord would tell him how happy the footballer had made him. How he wouldn't only fight for him, but how he'd be willing to lay down his life for him. And how he wanted to spend the rest of his life with him. He'd go to England, Scotland, Europe, Australia, wherever his career would take him. They'd never spoken of it, but Barry knew Hans wouldn't want to stay on the island.

Who in their right mind would?

Barry knew this would mean giving up the pub, giving up everything he had on the Isle of Guff. He was realising that the reason he'd never left the island was because he'd never had a reason.

Love was the reason he'd been waiting for.

He stood proud behind his bar and admired his work. The place sparkled. He might even get his money back if he sold it.

It was three o'clock now. Barry poured himself a celebratory screwdriver. He looked out at the street, the sun suddenly peeking through the dense cloud. There were a few things he'd miss about the island. The fresh air. The slow pace of life. Its free-from-all-pretence locals. That was about it, though.

Then he heard a crash come from the kitchen, followed by a smell of burning.

"*Kurva*!" came a loud curse.

Barry would miss a few things about the island, but he wouldn't miss its food.

The chef rushed out, yelling something Barry couldn't understand. He tossed his leather jacket on, put a cigarette in his mouth, and stormed towards the door. "Shit equipment, shit ingredients, shit everything. I quit this shit."

And with that, he was gone.

Sighing, Barry got on the phone. "Bill … Yeah … Can you come in, mate? … You've worked with a hangover before, you can do it again … Sure. Double time it is."

Eight quid an hour for Bill to do his thing. Cooking fare that, if the health and safety inspector ever bothered to make it across here, would condemn the building and sentence him to death for crimes against humanity.

Perhaps a miracle would happen. Bill would cook something tasty. Guff would stay up and Hans would get offered a contract and stay. If that happened, Barry was going to have to look far and wide for a better, more reliable cook. He couldn't stomach eating this shit any longer.

He angled his head towards the sink as his queasiness got the better of him. He couldn't blame this on the cuisine. This was down to the impact the Guff Rovers number 9 had on him and the uncertain hours ahead.

50

This was the first match Roger had attended without his wife in the twenty-seven years since they met. And though he'd never, ever admit it to her, he was having the time of his life.

He'd got to have two pre-game pints of real ale instead of his usual one. He'd been able to order a pasty from the bakers (the good one) instead of consuming one of the cheese and pickle (admittedly tasty) sandwiches Rowena brought wrapped in foil since Tam had taken over and she'd boycotted spending money at the ground. Roger even bought a program. And the atmosphere was the best it'd ever been since they clinched promotion in 1975. This his wife would've liked to have seen because the situation at the club had been dire since then. Much of this had to do with this being the biggest game in the club's history. A defeat today might send them out of the league. This was high-stakes stuff. But with them playing Carlisle United, a team with nothing to play for, the atmosphere was carnival-like following last week's dramatic win.

Roger couldn't see an empty pocket in the 5,100-capacity stadium, the fans resplendent in brown and pink. He'd lost count of the faces he'd seen from the past. Of people who'd long ago moved off the island and had sailed or flown across for this game. The paper estimated that number to be around the three thousand mark.

Even Roger had to admit that Tam deserved some credit, throwing the gates open and letting under-18s in for free. No one knew for sure why Tam was doing this. If it was in tribute to Jimmy Dolan, to Hillsborough, or if he'd finally listened to the fans and come to his senses about ripping them off. Roger hoped it was the latter, although he'd known Tam long enough to harbour doubts.

Right now, it didn't matter. It felt good to be a Guff fan for once. It felt good to be from the island. As much as he was getting along fine without her, he wished his wife were here to experience it all. However, she was visiting their daughter in London who was expecting any day now. Rowena told Roger it might be the last time they'd see their baby before she became a mother. That he'd miss the birth of his first grandchild. She didn't understand because he could never, ever tell her that this meant just as much to him.

And so, Roger stood up to his wife for the first time in their marriage. She didn't speak to him all week when he told her he wasn't going with her, even if he was arriving just forty-eight hours later.

But despite having the grandest of days, he still missed her.

As the players ran onto the pitch, he saw he wasn't the only one pumped for the match. Dennis sat behind him, wearing a shiny new pink bunnet, which he'd forgotten to cut the £9.99 price tag off. The young squad of fans behind the goal had taken their shirts off and brandished a fresh banner reading 'THERE'S ONLY ONE JIMMY DOLAN'.

The atmosphere was made all the better by the absence of Tam Bam. His ban was up, and yet as the players ran out onto the pitch, he was nowhere to be seen or heard. Instead, young Connor Whelan marshalled the touchline, gesturing and cajoling the players, giving last-minute instructions to his mostly young chargers. And gracefully shaking hands with this opposite number.

In the disabled section where Tam used to hold court (that was putting it mildly) was Clive Rhodes' ex-partner, and a disabled lady in a wheelchair who'd recently started attending games and who Roger didn't know. Wearing a Guff replica shirt, scarf and hat, she was a welcome addition, singing and shouting encouragement to the players.

The most bizarre sight was the contingent of around two dozen fans from the Highlands in full tartan regalia. Wearing new Guff scarves, they proclaimed their love for Ralph McInnes with masks bearing the champion caber tosser's face. Rumour had it that Guff Rovers' highlights were now broadcast in Northern Scotland, Canada and South Africa, so Scots fans could see their man in action. McInnes was consigned to the bench today. He didn't have the fitness to last a full ninety minutes, but he had become a potent weapon for Guff to bring on in the closing period if they were in need of a goal. Which was usually the case.

As the players congregated around the centre-circle for a minute's silence to honour Jimmy Dolan and the Hillsborough victims, Roger wept. Wept at how the disaster put the game into perspective, while underlining how much this crazy, inconsequential pastime meant to him, to everyone here. With no one embodying that more than poor Jimmy Dolan.

As the ref blew the whistle, and the players took their positions, a crescendo of noise went up. No one could have predicted this four months ago. And for that, he had to hand it to Tam.

They kicked off and Guff immediately attacked. Roger pondered how good it was to be a football fan. How unique it was supporting the country's most remote club, the only one off the mainland. If only Tam could share some of his power with the fans, if only he could appoint someone upstairs and in the dugout who actually knew what they were doing. If only ... then this club might stand a real chance of doing something after ninety-nine barren years.

Roger's positivity lasted until the second minute when a speculative long-ball broke Guff's offside-trap and Carlisle's diminutive striker raced through to slot home. Roger and the five thousand home fans sat back down.

This was not in the script.

51

Sheikh Bin-Hassan watched Tam's heart sink once again when the ball hit the back of the net, and the possibility of non-league football hit him like a bullet, with this particular bullet going right through the heart.

The first time that Tam had clutched his heart and fallen back into the chair was moments before, after Tam had outlined his vision for the football club to his newfound half-brother. New pitch, new stand, free entry for all minors so the club could grow the next generation of fans. And purchasing the old toilet paper factory next door and turning it into a training complex.

The sheikh had stung him with a single, well-placed remark. "And how are you going to pay for all this?"

For this, Tam had no answer. The club had bled him dry since he'd stepped in. It wasn't so much the signing of new players or the exorbitant operational costs, though that was a lot too. It was paying off Gary Pullman and all the club's former players. It was the constant flood of bills and invoices, and the uncovering of yet more debts that kept arriving from the chairman. Even now, Gus Pinkle was still pulling a three-grand weekly wage, and racking up endless expenses, despite Tam not having seen him since back in March, and that was only for half a game.

The off-field events depressed Tam as much as the on-field ones. And to top it all off, the visitors had started well. Very well.

With mid-table safety assured for the visitors, Carlisle's fringe players were making the most of the opportunity to be let off the leash, giving the home side all sorts of problems. Guff's skinhead keeper with the beard was called upon to punch yet another effort away that came from close-range.

Tam had appeared so happy before the sheikh's remark. He had opened up the gates of his club (along with his heart) to the fans offering free entry to some and subsidised food and programs to all so they might attract a full gate. And it had been a resounding success.

After the goal, Tam gathered his composure and took his seat. His voice wavered. "I thought that now you're my brother and you're also one of them Arab lot … thought you might want in on it."

"It's true. I'm not just here to see you, though it has been nice," the sheikh lied. "My cousins, the Bin-Alad family, want me to find a club to invest in. One that's situated in the south-west of England." He sat up. "I could give you more than a new stand. I can give you a whole new stadium. State-of-the-art training complex. A hotel too. Even a museum." He gave a sad glance to the trophy cabinet behind which displayed half a dozen pendants, and a cup from a charity game with Wrexham back in 1919 held as a fundraiser for returning servicemen.

The entire collection could have fit in a shoebox.

"I'd like to see Guff Rovers push on and become a global brand,' the sheikh continued. "Tours of the Middle East, blue-chip sponsors. A big kit deal—"

Tam sat up, rejuvenated. "I'll tell you what, sunshine, I doubted at first that we were brothers, but I doubt it no longer. I've been saying all this for years. Years! People think I'm bonkers. But you—*you*—understand."

The sheikh feared he might be about to kiss him and edged back.

"We'll also fund a substantial transfer budget in order to climb the divisions. Say, ten million for new players to start us off."

"Yasssss!" Tam punched the air like Guff had just scored the winner to secure their football league status.

"We'll even get you a new boss," the sheikh said. "I hope you don't think it was presumptuous of me, but we've already sounded out Ron Atkinson, Howard Kendall and Ossie Ardiles."

Tam's face fell. "Why, when you've got me? That lot don't understand our culture."

The sheikh peered out the window at the current Guff Rovers side who were being seriously chewed up out there. The defence was getting torn apart by Carlisle's youth and pace. It was only the goalkeeper and a few last-gasp interceptions by that big scary centre-half that was keeping them in it. "Still, with this investment, who really cares what division we're in next season? A mere blip is what it will be."

Tam grunted. His concentration appeared to momentarily drift from the game, even from the collection of pasties and bottles of Lucozade laid out before them, as he thought about all his fantasies for Guff Rovers coming to fruition.

"I'm not keen on the management plan," he eventually replied. "Though we can talk about that later. Where shall we build the training complex? The smart thing would be to put it on the industrial waste site at the edge of the island. The toilet paper factory next door could be used for the museum and for the hotel which could overlook the stadium. Provided the stadium wasn't too big, of course. What were you thinking? Twenty thousand? I'd plump for something like a mini-San Siro with the potential to add on. There's so much growth potential here. Sure, it'd piss off the neighbours, but it's for the greater good of the island."

"My dear brother." The sheikh laughed. "It wouldn't be happening here."

"Oh, you're thinking about a new site altogether. Probably a good idea given the Taylor inquiry. A lot of clubs will be doing that. The industrial waste site would be perfect for an all-seater stadium. It's only five miles from here. We could build a skyrail there."

"No, no. We'd be moving the club off the island onto the mainland. There's nothing here for anyone." After a second weekend spent on Guff enduring its food, its weather and its culture, the sheikh felt confident making this admission.

Tam sat back down. "You what?"

"Yes, I'm thinking one of the sunnier parts of Cornwall. I wouldn't rule out Devon. Or even across in Somerset, Dorset even. But I can tell you, we are completely dedicated to the south-west region."

"But … but … but the fans won't travel across there."

"You won't have to worry about that. We'll get new fans. In fact, as it'll be a one hundred percent takeover, you don't have to worry about anything at all."

"It's my club!"

"*Was* your club. As the former custodian, we'll obviously sweeten the deal by making you head of catering or something nice and cuddly."

"And what about the other forty-nine percent I don't control?"

"Mr Pinkle has already agreed to sell us his share. All we need now is for you to sign on the dotted line and a new era for the south-west consortium can begin."

"For Guff Rovers, you mean."

"We won't be needing that quaint little name anymore. Like I said, it's a whole new exciting chapter." The sheikh waved his hands. "Think Dorset Thunder. Or the Somerset Supernovas. Something marketable. Something … American."

Tam looked to where Connor Whelan paced up and down the touchline, signalling to his players to switch to a five-man midfield to gain more possession.

"Of course," the sheikh continued. "The young pup you have in the dugout shall have to be moved on."

"Couldn't you give us both some sort of coaching role?"

"We could find you something with the youths, I'm sure."

Tam stared up at the sky. He wasn't blinking. The sheikh wasn't even sure if he was breathing. He looked smaller than he did before, the colour drained from his face. The sheikh worried what the consortium would say about what he'd done to him. He was sure he'd had a stroke.

And then when Carlisle again went on the front-foot, that's when he really started to worry.

52

The Guff players had only grabbed a cup of water and a handful of cut oranges when Tam burst in the room like it was World War III. Ralph McInnes, seated nearest the door, bore the full brunt of it, the impact defying physics and knocking the giant from the bench to the tiles, causing him to land heavily on his backside.

"You bunch of bloody inebriates," Tam shouted. "What kind of performance is that, letting those mainland wankers come here and climb over the top of you and shag you where it hurts? You could play like that all week and you still wouldn't get anywhere nearer the goal. You've gotta get up their arseholes. Get up their fucking arseholes!"

The gaffer didn't stop for breath. Connor tried to interject but Tam was more unrepentant than a Guff gale in January.

"And another thing …"

"Gaffer, gaffer, please—" Connor said.

"Don't interrupt me. You've been worse than this lot put together, acting like a bloody church mouse on the sideline."

"Where were you during injury time?"

"Making my way down here, wasn't I? You know I'm not the most nimble of specimens. No need to rub it in."

"Okay, because—"

"Plus, Mayvis had delivered a fresh batch of pasties for the canteen, and I thought it only right that I sample some of her wares before they went out to the people to avoid any more food poisoning calamities."

"I see, because—"

"And to be kept between these walls, I needed a shite the size of a hay bale, and it proved a little harder to budge than you might imagine."

"We're winning 2–1," Ralph interrupted, rubbing his bruised knee.

Tam spun around, noticing him. "You what?"

"Yes," Connor added. "Paddy hit two. One in the forty-sixth minute, then a solo goal from the restart right before the ref blew for the half."

Tam's face changed from crimson red through anger to scarlet red from embarrassment. And then to luminous red from sheer excitement. He grabbed Paddy Conroy by the ears, planting a big wet kiss on his forehead.

"I knew I did the right thing bringing you here, ya beautiful Irish lush." He planted another smacker right on his lips. "One of the most important moments in Guff history and I'm messing about with the pasties and my bowels." Tam shrugged his shoulders, taking a step back. "Anyway, nothing to see here. Keep it going, lads. Keep-it-going!"

He gave Connor a double thumbs-up and headed for the door. The others couldn't believe that he would leave without making a substitute or two, or changing formation, or making them partake in some sort of humiliating rallying cry or ritual.

Connor was even more surprised. "Gaff. Aren't you going to tell me what to do?"

Tam turned to the players. "Listen to this man, fellas. This man here has it all under control."

Connor could tell by the way the players' shoulders relaxed that if they'd realised a half-time lead would keep Tam Bam off their backs, they might have nabbed one long ago.

53

Tam had felt good ribbing the players like that. He had such flow going that he was almost a little disappointed when he discovered they were 2-1 up. Not for long, of course, but he realised he missed letting off steam. Being a coach wasn't the same as being a fan. You couldn't roar and bawl like that on the touchline near the ears of those pesky officials. The two suspensions he'd already received were a testament to that.

And up here in the director's box, it wasn't the same. Especially since his brother had left for a meeting in London. Some fan-slash-prospective owner he was, not even making it to half-time in Guff's biggest game.

Tam would've stood with the fans, but there wasn't a spare spot in the house. His plan to fill the stadium had come to fruition, so he didn't mind too much. But to him, this wasn't what football was all about. Sat up here by himself with the heating turned up in his ivory tower. He couldn't hear the fans. He couldn't smell the sweat of the players or see the fear in their eyes.

This wasn't football at all.

Not that he'd have admitted it to anyone, but he knew his eyesight wasn't the best, either. He'd been putting off going to Specsavers for years, not wanting to add 'visually impaired' to his long list of ailments, never mind bother to wear specs. He could hardly see the game from up here. No wonder Pinkle didn't have a clue about what the hell was going on out there. His contacts must have been like double glazing.

Tam could just make out the old scoreboard at the opposite end. The one the *actual* blind guy from across the road operated in exchange for free admission. How he knew which numbers were which, Tam didn't know. Why he even bothered about football, Tam wasn't sure either. Maybe it was because he hadn't been able to see for himself just how rank rotten Guff Rovers had been since ... well, since forever.

And Tam could just about make out another thing. The Carlisle United left-winger with the mohawk collecting the ball, sidestepping Ibrahim Deng, then whipping in a cross close to the keeper. It should have been Seth Graham's ball all day. Ninety-nine times out of a hundred it would've been. He hadn't put a foot wrong since stepping up to the first team. But all week he'd seemed distracted at training, since reports of Watford's interest had went public. The ball slithered through his hands like a jellied eel. And it dropped right at the feet of their number 10, who couldn't miss.

2–2 with five minutes to go—now Guff were really in it.

The home side restarted. What Tam lacked in eyesight, he made up with his superior lip-reading ability, and he was close enough to see someone at the back of the stand murmur that Doncaster Rovers were beating Exeter 3–1. Pullman and those Devonshire bastards.

If Guff didn't score, they were done for.

Tam was all nerves, pacing the boardroom. He couldn't go out to the stand. He still couldn't see a spare seat, the fans slumped in them despondently, having lost all their buzz. Even the disabled area was full, comprising of his sister, Zabe and Sam Statham, with a few of his more well-behaved patients. He didn't want to go down to the touchline. Connor needed to be left alone, deserved to be. Him going down there would only put him off and unsettle the troops. He realised that now. He'd only end up getting sent off or something worse, which would lead to the players losing their concentration. This wasn't about him.

But he had to do something.

So, he put his crutch down. He stood up on the boardroom table and got up close to the windows, which looked down onto the ground. He took hold of the rigid window handle. He pulled, and he pulled. The thing was painted over and hadn't been prised opened since the world was in black and white. He pressed his palms against the glass. He felt the pane come away in fits and starts from the crumbling putty. He pushed, then he pushed a little more. He wanted to pop the glass out neatly. Only he underestimated his strength, and it gave way, spinning and falling and landing on the walkway thirty feet below, shattering into a million tiny pieces. The sound even made the players briefly look over.

"Is everyone all right?" Tam shouted below.

"It's landed in my Fanta," replied a young girl.

Mercifully, no one had been underneath when it dropped.

"Terribly sorry. Go to the shop and tell them it was the gaffer who did it. Tell them it was the gaffer and you're to have a new one. A large one as well."

"That was an extra-large one," she told him.

"Don't be greedy."

The other fans nearby were too enthralled in the game to vent too much about the glass, instead giving their hair, coats and scarves a quick shake and returning to proceedings.

Tam would replace the pane first thing. But for now, he could see and hear better, and the air was fresher. He reckoned he could see even better if he stood out on the ledge. He pulled himself up, careful to hold on to the edges of the brick facade so he didn't fall.

He watched as Paddy Conroy gathered a loose ball in the middle of the pitch. In one swift movement, he sold a dummy to two opposition players, then played a peach of a pass through to Hans Schickler. The big Austrian took a touch and glided past the last man and shot for the corner.

The crowd watched. The crowd gasped. The crowd waited.

Somehow, the Carlisle shot-stopper reached out and got a finger to it, deflecting it ever so slightly onto the post, the ball rolling out for a corner.

"Exeter have got a goal back," Tam heard someone below say.

"Yaaaasssss!" Tam punched the air, celebrating. The fans below stayed in their seats, unsure of how to get behind their team. Like they'd somehow forgotten. Tam knew that it was on him to lift them. That this was the true role of the gaffer. He decided to do something he'd never done at a Guff game before. He didn't berate the players, he didn't shout at the ref, he didn't fight with his own fans.

He started chanting.

"Guff! Guff! Guff! Guff!" He chanted louder than he'd ever done. And one by one, like a Mexican wave, it gradually rippled through the stadium. Soon every man, woman and child were on their feet and chanting the same.

Tam had never been to the Maracana, La Bombonera or Anfield. But for a brief second, he imagined that on the big nights there, the atmosphere was something like this.

And by God, it felt good.

This was what being a fan was all about. This was what football was all about. For his whole life he'd rubbed against the grain, telling himself he was kicking against the pricks. That he and he alone was the voice of reason. And if he was honest, it felt horrible and lonely.

Yet here he was, with five thousand of his fellow fans, his fellow Faeries, chanting together. This was what life itself was about. Collectively they could achieve anything. Nothing could go wrong. After forty-seven years, Tam Bam finally got why he had dedicated his life to the game.

Every Guff player was up for the corner, this time even Seth Graham. The ball was swung into the box by Paddy Conroy. And there was The Ox. He outjumped his marker and got his head to the ball. Tam, on the ledge, jumped with him. The forward connected well, sending his header looping majestically towards the top-right-hand corner. The keeper didn't have a chance. Tam landed on the ledge with a thud as the ball struck the underside of the bar and bounced down on the line.

Once, twice.

Then the big Carlisle number 6 with the bent nose got there first, battering the ball up and away into the skies.

"Nooo!" Tam bellowed as he looked at his watch and saw they were in the ninetieth minute. He could barely look as a blue-shirted attacker latched on to the loose ball near the halfway line. He eyed the open goal. He shrugged off Billy Wood, who'd aimed a vicious kick at him. He was caught but kept his feet. The forward took another few paces. Sensing the entire Guff side bearing down on him, he shot from the centre-circle with his injured left foot. The ball swung right, then it swung left, before trickling into the goal.

Guff Rovers 2 Carlisle United 3.

The small pocket of away fans, consisting of four men and a guide dog, cheered.

The home crowd was stunned into silence at the thought of having to score two goals in injury time to preserve their football league status, which they'd maintained for all of their ninety-nine year history. Tam's head was buried in his hands. He thought he heard the man below say the full-time whistle had sounded at Exeter with Doncaster winning 4–2.

Guff Rovers were going down.

Tam Bam let out a banshee wail. The type of sound no one believed man or beast could make. On and on it bellowed, bouncing around the ground. It only stopped when the big man clutched for his heart, feeling it break in two. He wobbled on the ledge. He put his right foot on a spot eaten away by rot. It gave way. Tam fell thirty feet, taking out the girl's fresh Fanta and landing on Dennis in his new bunnet who was returning from the toilet because he'd been sick with nerves.

54

Transcript from BBC Radio Cornwall
Saturday, May 6, 1989
4.54 p.m.

EDDIE REAGAN: And let's go to Faery Meadow where it's the end of the game and the end of Guff's long association with league football. Geoff, are you there?

(*no sound*)

Geoff?

(*we hear sniffles*)

Looks like we're going to have to come back to Geoff.

GEOFF PARKER: Wait, wait, no, no. I'm here.

EDDIE REAGAN: Geoff, we're hearing it's all over for Guff Rovers.

GEOFF PARKER: (*clears his nose*) Yes, it is. They led 2–1 at the break against Carlisle. But two goals from the visitors, one in the last minute, means they're toast.

EDDIE REAGAN: What are the scenes like?

GEOFF PARKER: (*sniffles harder*) Incredible, truth be told. Just like we've come to expect from Guff of late. The gaffer, the coach, the chairman?—I don't even know what he is anymore—Thomas Bamford, fell through the boardroom window, taking out a small group of fans below. Two have been taken to hospital with minor injuries. However, BBC Cornwall understands that Bamford himself suffered a suspected heart attack.

EDDIE REAGAN: High drama, indeed. Our thoughts go out to the man and the club. We will keep our listeners up to speed on all developments.

GEOFF PARKER: (*crying now*) Given all their histrionics, Guff Rovers will be missed.

EDDIE REAGAN: I have to say, I thought you were a Bristol Rovers man, Geoff. You seem to be taking this awfully badly.

GEOFF PARKER: I am, Eddie. I am. And I just want to say, my wife is a cheating cow who I know has been sleeping with my best friend, or should I say former best friend, for the past three months. See you in court, slag. And you can keep the kids, they look like you anyway. I'm off to Crete for a fortnight with that Radio Cornwall weather presenter, like you always feared. Enjoy that one!

EDDIE REAGAN: You are?

GEOFF PARKER: I'm sorry, Eddie, I am.

EDDIE REAGAN: But that's my wife ...

GEOFF PARKER: Your estranged wife.

EDDIE REAGAN: When you come back to the station, you're a dead man!

GEOFF PARKER: We should leave it there.

EDDIE REAGAN: A DEAD MAN!!!

(*GEOFF hangs up*)

EDDIE REAGAN (CONT): Apologies for that, listeners. It's been one long season. Let's go to Andy Chung at Exeter where Doncaster Rovers, unlike Guff Rovers and several relationships, have actually survived today.

55

Doctor Saaj had her first half-cigarette of the day. Lately, on the same shift as Jill, she'd have burnt through half a packet by now. But today, even for a Saturday, had been a busy shift.

"And?" the matron asked, blowing smoke out the window.

"He's just come round," the doctor replied.

"Will he be all right?"

"The specialist will take a look tomorrow. It would've helped if he wasn't twelve-stone overweight."

"He thinks he knows everything. Always has."

Doctor Saaj nodded. In all honesty, she hadn't seen Tam for a while. The football team had finally given him a purpose, so he no longer worried about his multiple minor aches and ailments. She hadn't seen him for anything this serious since his bypass.

The door to the staffroom opened and in walked a man and woman dressed in black suits, both brandishing police badges.

"Excuse me, there's to be strictly no smoking in this building," the woman said in a strong Midlands accent.

Doctor Saaj's stomach dropped, and she quickly threw her stub out the window.

The matron took another puff of hers. "Listen here, Cagney or Lacey. I don't come to your place and tell you what you can and can't do. Now, the minute you have to stitch up the knuckles of wife beaters, or zip-up bags containing chewed-up kids prised from car wrecks, or inform a young family that their daddy isn't coming home, then you can tell me what to do. But until then ..."

"I'm so, so sorry," the lady replied, holding her gaping mouth.

"Until then you've no right to tell me to go out in the cold and have my cigarette."

"Yes, of course. I'm sorry too," her partner mumbled.

"You saints do whatever it is you have to do." The lady smiled.

Whoever they were, the law is the law, and of course they had every right to tell them not to smoke. And after nearly two years of working here, Doctor Saaj had never seen or heard any of the stories the matron mentioned ever happening. The worst thing to occur on the sleepy island was a teenager who lacerated a testicle on a barbed wire fence as he was chased by a kine of cows after getting friendly with one of the local sheep.

"I'm Detective Summers, this is Detective Sinagra," the lady said. "We're here to interview a Thomas Bamford."

"He's had a serious heart murmur," Doctor Saaj informed them. "He's undergone tests. He can't have any more stress." The head nurse nodded to her, motioning that it was in fact fine. "But if you can keep it quick, and if you think that it is necessary …"

She led them out of the staffroom as the matron lit another. "I'm clocking off now, I'll see you in The Wick." She winked. "Goodbye, officers."

As Doctor Saaj led them into Tam's room, she had to laugh at the matron's behaviour. If any of those things she mentioned ever did happen, she would be the first one giving them a body swerve.

They found Tam staring glumly at the ceiling. He hadn't touched his soup. As much as she was against them, she would send out later for a Cornish pasty. Just the one, and just for a mouthful. She knew it would cheer him up.

"There are two detectives here, Tam. They'd like to ask you some questions." She propped up his pillow. He sighed, struggling into its groove. She'd never seen him this quiet, this despondent.

The doctor drifted into the shadows as the two agents came forward.

"Hi, Mr Bamford," Detective Summers said. "We wanted to ask you about a Gus Pinkle."

"Did you have any involvement in his Faery Marine Equity firm?" Detective Sinagra probed.

Tam said nothing.

"You've been named as the primary investor. Seems like you invested over £2M in it over the past four months."

Tam's eyes bulged.

"Do you know where Mr Pinkle is?"

Tam mumbled something inaudible.

"Sorry?" Summers asked.

"He should have been here," Tam said, clearing his throat. "Biggest game in our history. I wouldn't be lying here if he had've been. The club wouldn't be in the state it is if he was."

"You can say that again," Detective Sinagra added. "Gus Pinkle has racked up around ten million in debt. And it's mostly in the club's name. Which means it's in your name to the tune of fifty-one percent."

"If only we'd stayed up," Tam muttered, the figures not registering.

"I think you'll find today's game didn't matter," Sinagra said. "The league would hit you with a significant points deduction, regardless."

Tam looked up. He opened his mouth to shout, scream or wail. Yet nothing came out. He had nothing left to give.

"Could we leave it there, officers?" Doctor Saaj interrupted. "He's had a long day."

"Of course," the man said. "I don't think he can help us anymore for now."

"Thank you, Mr Bamford, and sorry to hear about your illness and your team's loss," Detective Summers added.

Doctor Saaj led them back out to the corridor.

"I'm no doctor," said Detective Singara. "But I reckon the game is killing him."

"You don't know him," the doctor replied. "If it weren't for football, he'd have been dead long ago."

She bade farewell to the pair. Something in her mind bugged her about Tam, so instead of going to the staffroom for another half-cigarette or getting her bag and leaving for The Wick (on time, for once), she returned to his room.

He was still propped up and mumbling. "The bastard ... that bastard. Ninety-nine and out. Never made the centenary."

She straightened his pillows. "Come on, Mr Bamford, it's not worth getting even more stressed out. You've had a big enough ordeal. It's only a game, after all."

Tam fixed his stare upon her. She knew it was the wrong thing to say. Why on earth did she say it?

"I know it's more than a game to you," she backtracked. "But I also know that you're going to sort it out. There's more to you than meets the eye, Mr Bamford. A lot more than this town will admit."

She said things like this all the time to her patients to perk them up. This time she realised she meant it. There was no one so dogged, so determined, so passionate as Tam Bam. If he put his mind to something—like he had with being an invalid—he could be the very best football boss there was.

And as she said these words, a slight, an oh-so-slight smile crept across Tam's dry plump lips.

56

Zabe's daughter yawned and cuddled into her in the back of the cab. It had been so long since they'd shared any time together, let alone went on a fortnight's holiday.

The summer had been a long and glorious one. And now back on the Isle of Guff with the temperature tipping twenty-nine degrees, it looked set to continue for a little while at least.

"How was it, love?" Ralph, the driver, asked. He looked alert and refreshed behind the wheel.

"It was wonderful."

Zabe glanced across at Tam and Janine. Tam was picking his nose. Janine had fallen asleep, a long line of drool extending from her mouth down to her belly button.

It had been difficult persuading Tam to go anywhere, but after a hectic few months following the death of their mother, the football club's relegation and another heart scare, he conceded that both he and Janine could do with a break. Neither had left the country before. Zabe suggested Disneyland. Tam insisted on waiting for Italia '90, or, failing that, visiting Brazil, which he considered the spiritual home of football. It was Janine who had the deciding vote. She was paying for it, as Tam's funds were tied up in football. She opted for Africa and she wanted her carer to come.

The first week, they went to see Zabe's family. Zabe borrowed money for her daughter, Missy, to come. Missy had never met her relatives, and it had been over a decade and a half since Zabe had visited. With her parents gone, Zabe stayed with her brothers and sisters, where they broke bread and lamented all their muddled correspondence and all those lost years. They loved Missy, and the girl met the cousins she didn't know—twenty-three in total—and became close to a boy in the village named Tino.

Janine was made a fuss of, and even Tam took to the village because all they did was play football by day and watch football via satellite all night long in the local cafe. The kids made him a goalie and, no longer wearing that filthy moon boot and having left his crutch at home, even Zabe admitted that he was pretty good.

It was sad to say goodbye, but the next week was just as special as they travelled to Tanzania to go on safari. They got to see elephants, tigers, giraffes and zebras in their natural environment. They went snorkelling, camped under the stars, stayed in nice hotels and ate big, healthy meals.

It was difficult for Tam at first, as there was no chance to eat Cornish pasties, and Lucozade proved tricky to track down (he'd brought a two-week supply with them but consumed the lot within three days). After a few days of moaning, he was good. By the end of the trip, he was even trying items off the menu, which weren't burgers or chips.

"And God willing, we'll do it again another summer," Zabe told Ralph.

"That's the way."

"And how has yours been?" she asked.

"I've had a life-changing summer myself."

"You do look better. How are you feeling?"

"Got the all-clear last week."

"That is wonderful news."

"It sure is. Feel like I've been born again. I'm back behind the wheel and loving every minute of it. I had to be, mind. My brother couldn't be driving cabs for much longer." Ralph peeked in the rearview mirror at Tam, who'd started on the other nostril. "You mob have made him far too busy at the club. Take a look at all this."

He pointed to the old toilet paper factory as they passed. It was flattened, and its rubble was being cleared away by a few of the kids who used to hang around the Jobcentre and The Wick. Others were wearing hi-vis and toiling with shovels and spades, laying cement.

Tam removed the pink handwoven hankie decorated with elephants with their trunks aloft, which he'd purchased on his travels. He deposited the contents of his nose into it.

"Should be ready by mid-autumn, they reckon," Ralph added.

"Hmph," was all Tam said.

"You wait until you see the stadium. Bet you can't wait."

"Oh, I can wait, all right, driver. There's more to life than football, you know."

The driver did a double take in the mirror to make sure he had the right passenger. His wide eyes told Zabe that he never thought he'd ever hear Tam Bam say that. No one on the island would.

Zabe smiled at Janine, who was waking, as Missy gently snored on her shoulder. Spending all that money on the trip had been a small price to pay to get Tam Bam thinking like that.

57

GUFF RISING LIKE A PHOENIX RISING FROM THE ASHES
By Phil Gates
(from the Cornish Post, *August 26, 1989)*

Today the renamed Guff FC are making their first foray into non-league football with a home game against Brislington in the Western League Division One.

Dropping down to the eighth-tier of the English game should be a day of profound sadness for those connected to the club. Especially as their disgraced former chairman, Gus Pinkle, is facing extradition from Jamaica over 157 charges of embezzlement relating to the former Guff Rovers entity. And how former manager and majority owner Thomas Bamford blocked a takeover by the powerful Emirates oil family, the Bin-Alads, which would not only have saved the tiny island club but made them one of the richest concerns on the sporting landscape.

However, today the mood is one of joy rather than sadness.

The new outfit is one-third owned by Bamford, a third by his sister Janine and another third by a consortium led by muesli magnate Roger Greenhill, and the future is looking bright for Guff FC.

The stadium, Faery Meadow, is in the middle of a refurbishment which will make it a six thousand all-seater, and the best outside the football league. And there is a new training complex under construction next door.

On the pitch, things are also looking positive. Connor Whelan turned down job offers from Torquay and Plymouth to pen a three-year deal as manager. The club lost rising stars Seth Graham and CJ Adeyemi to Southampton but managed to retain star striker Hans Schickler, who struck eight goals in eleven matches at the tail-end of last season. He has settled in the area and shares a home with a local publican. Former First Division stars Paddy Conroy and Billy Wood have also been re-signed, with both showing the benefits of a full pre-season.

But the biggest boost seems to have come from Thomas Bamford. Six months ago, he was the most hated man on the island. Now, happy to relinquish his role as gaffer and take a back seat, he's viewed as a beacon of hope in taking the club forward.

Guff FC have offered half-price season tickets for those under twenty-one, and disabled fans will be charged just a pound per game.

Debt-free, with a solid foundation, and possibly the best squad outside the football league, Guff FC is a sure-fire bet to be back in the football league within the next decade.

NB. This is my last article for the Post *as I'm off to commence a new appointment with the British Paralympic Association. Eddie Reagan will take over the reins as the* Post's *Chief Football Writer following his recent departure from the BBC.*

58

The stadium wasn't yet full, far from it, but having the women's team play as a curtain-raiser before the men's match meant the ladies were easily playing in front of the biggest crowd of their lives.

From his old spot in the disabled section, Tam watched as Zabe's daughter darted up and down the left-wing. She'd scored one and laid on another two as Guff soared to a 5–1 lead. Even Tam had to admit that the kid had something. Since the ladies' team had reformed, Zabe said Missy's marks had improved, and she was spending a lot more nights in.

The full-time whistle blew. The girls had lost a late goal but that didn't matter as they shook hands with their older opponents.

"You staying back for the main game?" Zabe asked her daughter as she made her way to the changerooms.

"Of course, Mum. Save my seat."

Tam noticed Zabe beam.

The ladies' game was a slower game, and although he'd never admit it, Tam enjoyed the positive vibe. There were no dirty fouls or tactics. No moaning at the ref. In every way, the girls' game was a lot less bitchy than the men's.

Still, he wouldn't have said no to a yellow card or five. When Missy accidentally clicked that full-back's heels and then jogged back and helped her up, Tam thought he would puke.

He removed another rice cracker from his pocket and bit into it.

"How's the diet going?" Zabe asked.

"I would murder every man, woman and child in this place for a pasty."

"How many crackers have you eaten today?"

"Three packets. But you know what? I haven't had a Rennie in a week."

"That's good news."

"Is it?" He fingered his waistband, which came away from his gut with ease. "I've already had to buy two new pairs of smaller trackies. And I think I need a third. Costing me a fortune, so it is."

"I'm so pleased."

"And they taste bloody rotten."

"You've made some wonderful changes." Janine was in front of them, clapping along to 'Football Crazy' on the tannoy. "Your mother would be very proud." She squeezed Tam's arm, and she could have sworn he had a tear in his eye.

Then the Stone Roses came on, somewhat fittingly singing 'I Am the Resurrection'. Tam drank in the fresh paint smell. He applauded as the players ran out of the tunnel, and a roar went up from the stand, the likes of which he'd never heard in this part of the world. Every space in the ground was near full. Tam peered up to where the boardroom used to be. In its place, construction of a brand-new stand was underway with Jimmy Dolan's name already etched on it in bright-pink lettering.

Tam winked at his sister. She grinned back. How was he to know she liked football? She'd certainly never hinted to him before. He thought all those football posters she had plastering her wall were because she fancied them. Of course, he wasn't over the moon that she was encroaching on his recreation time. Then again, he had to remind himself that if she wasn't here, and if she hadn't put her share of the inheritance into the pot, then there'd be no football team at all to watch.

Tam noticed Roger sitting with someone who looked to be a politician, or at least some sort of businessman. That could be promising, as it might mean more investment. He also saw the priest with that old woman who'd returned from wherever she was. And there was that old codger along from them with the new pink bunnet. They'd never been friends, even after spending a week sharing the same hospital room after Tam fell on him.

The old man gave him a salute and called over. "Surprised to see you still alive, never mind here."

"Don't you worry about me," Tam replied. "My pacemaker has a twenty-five-year battery. I'll be winding you lot up for a while yet."

Tam reached into his pocket, removing a protein shake. He pierced the carton with a straw, sucked, then immediately spat it out as he dry retched. This was going too far.

He felt his inside pocket, removing a pasty instead.

"Tam, what are you doing?" Zabe asked.

"The doctor said that as I don't drink, I'd be allowed one a week. And this will be it. On matchdays. Gotta do something to quell the nerves. It's probably healthier than smoking or taking one of those bloody e-tablets that all the kids are into."

He wolfed into it like it was baked by the gods. He felt like he was wasting away. The new bottoms he was wearing, the new Guff scarf and polo shirt (the lime-green jacket having been binned after the charity shop refused to take it). He needed to cling to some semblance of his old self.

"Come on you, Guff FC!" Tam roared as they won the toss. It inspired the crowd who joined in. The new name was strange on the tongue, but he'd get used to it.

He had to.

The game kicked off. It felt good to be watching the boys in brown-

and-pink check again. Good to be debt-free. Good to have the sun shining for once. Good to have all their troubles sorted. And with the quality of players they had in this league, even the most cynical of onlookers, like Phil Gates, were saying that Guff FC were on the up. And for the first time since he could remember, ever since he was a little boy, Tam Bam really smiled.

Just then, a long clearance caught the Guff backline napping and the Brislington frontman sidestepped new keeper Rory Allen to put the opposition one-up.

The game wasn't even a minute old.

The crowd was silenced. They all looked to Tam Bam, expecting him to leap the hoarding and drag Connor Whelan back to the youth team there and then. To threaten to car bomb the referee. To pay off every Guff FC player on the pitch and buy in another squad before half-time.

But he didn't.

He put his scarf above his head and chanted louder. "Guff! Guff! Guff!"

It was so infectious that the whole ground joined in.

Zabe applauded along. "You did well there, Tam."

"Don't be so sure. If we lose a second before the half, Connor's getting the sack, the players are all going on the transfer list and the referee is getting strung up."

"None of that is happening," Janine murmured.

"Hmph," Tam muttered, knowing she was right and sitting back down.

His mobile phone rang. He moved to the gangway to take it, sidestepping the goth guard.

"This better be good," he said, answering it. "The bloody game's on."

"Is that Thomas Bamford?" the voice replied.

"Might be. Who wants to know?"

"Alex Ferguson."

"Bugger off it is. You're away at the Baseball Ground today."

"Well, if that's your attitude."

"No, no, how are you doing, my good friend? What's life like at one of the world's greatest clubs?"

"I wouldn't know."

"Aren't you humble? We should catch up. Touch base. That sort of thing."

"Had about a million calls and faxes off you. Was about to go to the police. Then I got a bit of a tax bill and thought I'd take you up on your offer."

"You're going to bring Manchester United here for a friendly?"

"Yeah, that's not happening."

"You're going to bring an Alex Ferguson Select over here instead?"

"I could do. If you're legit about the hundred grand."

"It's sat in my secret bank account waiting." Tam Bam almost dropped the phone with excitement. He looked at the fans and yelled, "Alex Ferguson is coming to Guff!"

The fans looked to each other. Normally this sort of remark would have them all laughing. Instead, they offered a sympathetic groan. They genuinely believed that Tam Bam had put these childish fantasies behind him.

"Sit down, you Bam," old Dennis said.

"Give it up, mate," called his grandson.

"Next Tuesday night." Tam stood tall, shouting louder. "As God is my witness, you'll see. You'll all bloody well see."

59

Alex Ferguson put down the receiver and returned to the kitchen. "Problem solved," he told his wife, who continued stirring the pot as she breastfed her newborn. "I called the stalker."

"The one who thinks you're the gaffer of Manchester United?"

"How many stalkers do you think I have?"

"Instead of the Alex Ferguson who's player-manager for Muckleford United in North Devon Division Two Social League, yeah?"

"Got it in one."

She stopped stirring and studied her husband. "I hope you told him the truth."

"I always have done. He never listens. I've never even visited Manchester, never mind Scotland."

She sampled the chicken soup, then added more salt. "What did you tell him?"

"That I'd do it."

"You're taking ten grand of his money?"

"Am I, heck. No, that would be very wrong. I'm taking a hundred grand. He's a millionaire, after all."

"You did tell him that you couldn't get Robson or Hughes, and that Besty retired long ago."

"Loud and clear. He never listens."

"He sounds off his rocker."

"You have no idea. He also offered me a chief scout role on triple my wages."

She dropped the ladle into the pan, the soup splashing up and fortunately missing the tot's thighs. "What did you tell him?"

"I told him I'd get you to pack your bags, pronto. There's also some kit washing, mowing and massaging to do, but we are heading to the Isle of Guff, baby."

She squealed and dropped the spoon, and almost dropped the baby, before falling into her husband's arms. He wouldn't have to haul bricks in all seasons anymore. They could try for another child. They might even make it back to Morecambe for their ten-year anniversary.

Cathy Ferguson had no idea where the Isle of Guff was, but it had to offer something different, something more lively than their council house in the sleepy North Devonshire village of Muckleford.

Didn't it?

THE END

MORE FOOTBALL FICTION FROM POPCORN PRESS

Jarrod Black
Guilty Party

Anna Black
This girl can play!

The End of the
Game

Game

Coming soon
Jarrod Black
Chasing Pack

ABOUT THE AUTHOR

P.J. Laverty is a Scottish-Australian writer specialising in historical football fiction (with a comedic spin).

Under the moniker Paul J Laverty, he is the host of 94.9 Main FM literary book show, The Quiet Carriage, which also airs nationally on the Community Radio Network. He has written two novellas, *Man Overbored* and *Cider Country,* and a short story collection, *In The State of Excitement* (RoadHouseMedia). He also wrote the first biography on Grammy award winners Arcade Fire and another on Beck (Artnik / Schwarzkopf & Schwarzkopf Verlag). He is currently completing a creative writing Ph.D. at Curtin University in Western Australia.

He is a football tragic who will never tire of telling anyone within earshot all about his adventures in Germany during World Cup 2006. He lives in Castlemaine, Victoria, with his wife and two children.

CPSIA information can be obtained
at www.ICGtesting.com
Printed in the USA
LVHW081203281022
731758LV00011B/404